SPECIAL FORCE

A WORLD WAR II COMMANDO NOVEL

DARREN SAPP

Collins & Halsey Publishers / September 2016

ISBN-13: 978-0692767931
ISBN-10: 0692767932

Cover Design: *www.vividcovers.com*

Formatting: Christine Borgford of Perfectly Publishable / *www.perfectlypublishable.com*

Editing: Lauren I. Ruiz of Pure Text / *www.pure-text.net*

ALSO BY DARREN SAPP

Fire on the Flight Deck

The Fisher Boy

*Aaron Bank and the Early Days
of US Army Special Forces*

Discover more at *darrensapp.com*

Dedicated to Aaron Bank,
Father of the Green Berets

"I want a Ph.D. that can win a bar fight."

~ William Donovan
Director of the Office of Strategic Services

ONE

N ICK JORDAN CRAVED the thrill of jumping from an airplane. A midnight jump within miles of an SS Panzer Division would test his thirst for adventure.

Jordan exhaled smoke and stubbed out his Chesterfield as a crewman opened the bomb bay doors of the Stirling bomber that the British had converted for paratroopers. The chilly, November air blew in, causing everyone to turn their heads and shield their faces for a brief moment. The wind made a high-pitched howl but failed to drown out the thumping of the four propellers.

Jordan stood, grasping a knotted safety strap that hung from the overhead of the bomber. The odd, sweet smell of aircraft fuel permeated the compartment. Peeking through the opening of the aircraft's belly, he remembered his first jump, over lush, English fields in the daytime.

A fresh pile of manure had caused his footing to slip, and he tumbled end over end. He opened his eyes to a cow with a mouthful of grass—the beast staring and unimpressed with Jordan's first jump. Subsequent jumps proved more successful as he embraced the skills of a paratrooper.

"What do you say, Nick? Shall we jump into the abyss?" Captain Farrington said to Jordan. The stoic Brit sat calmly as if sipping his afternoon tea.

He stood up next to Jordan and looked through the opening.

Jordan shrugged. "Why not? How else are we going to kill Germans?"

Farrington slapped him on the back. "That's the spirit."

The red light illuminated, signaling the commandos to prepare to jump.

"Alright, chaps, on your feet," Farrington ordered.

The team of five commandos lined up with the captain in the front and Jordan in the rear.

The red light meant that the pilot had spotted the drop site signal—two burning arrows made of logs, laid on the ground, soaked in kerosene, and set on fire. The long arrow was supposed to point toward the direction of the French Resistance camp. If one of the jumpers missed the drop location, they'd have a heading toward safety. The short arrow should point toward the German's location, and the area to be avoided.

Each team member adjusted straps and fidgeted with their gear in anticipation of the jump. One's face whitened and he cupped his hand over his mouth as though he'd vomit at any second. Another made the sign of the cross in front of his chest.

The green light shone brightly, causing each man to focus on the hole at the belly of the bomber.

Farrington turned to the men behind him. "See you on the ground!"

He jumped, followed by each man in a sequence of eight-second intervals.

Jordan inched his way toward the bomb bay opening. He swallowed hard and stepped into the night. The wind hit him like a slap to the face. His body jerked up, violently, as the canopy deployed. The moonlight exposed the four canopies of his commando team floating ahead of him. Normally, they would have avoided jumping when the moon illuminated the sky, but this mission couldn't wait.

He scanned the landscape and spotted the two arrows burning brightly. His training required him to identify and memorize as many landmarks as possible. The short arrow pointed toward hundreds of lights, powered by the city of Caen. Reports stated that the Germans occupied the large town, led by an advance team of the 12th SS Panzer Division. The long arrow pointed toward a hilly area with several huge boulders. The light from the nearly full moon exposed three jagged rocks protruding from a short cliff. He formed a mental map with those rocks as his guide to safety.

A slight breeze offered little opposition to his path toward the drop site. The bomber's engine noise trailed off, and a long, still waterway he knew to be the canal from Caen to the English Channel offered glimmers from the moonlight. Despite the slightly above freezing temperature, the glide toward the ground offered a few minutes of comfort and peace. Although uncertainty lay below, he glided toward it with confidence gained from eighteen months of training and a lifetime of competitive victories.

Zing!

"Whoa!" Jordan whipped his head to the left. He recognized the sound of a bullet zipping past him.

Zing! Zing!

Months of training prepared him for almost anything, but bullets zipping past his body, with him helpless to defend himself, left him with few options.

He noticed several figures—likely Germans—moving toward the drop site. The rest of his team had already landed, but he remained at the mercy of gravity with little control over direction or landing location. Possibilities included trees, hedgerows, bodies of water, and farmhouses. The ground quickly approached as he noticed a small opening between hedgerows.

A checklist ran through his head. Land. Free myself from this parachute. Safety off. Ready to fight.

Crunch!

His body penetrated the top of the hedgerow. Branches slapped and poked every inch of his body. He slid down to the ground, landing on his side. A rough landing, but a welcome condition over floating through the air as target practice for the Germans.

Jordan fought to stand but the brush, intertwined with his gear, held him down. He readied his Thompson machine gun with his right hand and pulled branches away from his body with his left.

"Hey, American. You going to fight the Germans from the bushes?"

Jordan, startled, swung his weapon toward the feminine voice that spoke in French. He looked up to find a woman with a Sten machine gun slung over her shoulder. Her scowl and eye roll deemed her more unimpressed with Jordan's landing than the cow had been with Jordan's first jump.

She motioned with her hand. "Come. We need to hurry."

He rose and freed himself with a swift jerk, ignoring the pain from several scratches and bruises. A branch clung to his musette bag. He jogged to catch up with the woman. "Where we headed?" He offered a demanding tone, attempting to assert his authority.

"Your friends are just up there." She pointed toward the end of another group of hedgerows, her eyes remained fixed ahead.

"How'd you know I'm American? Our team is made up of British and French."

"Because when you landed you cursed like a movie cowboy."

Jordan smirked and extended his hand. "I'm Jordan.

Lieutenant Jordan."

She looked at his hand and then back up without extending her hand. "Colette," she said, matter-of-factly. "It's about time you cowboys decided to get here." Her tough persona seemed at odds with her striking beauty.

"Listen, Colette, I don't think you realize how—"

Rat-ta-tat-tat-tat!

Bits of dirt rose up ahead of them and twigs flew from their branches. The machine gun fire came dangerously close.

"Follow me!" Colette said, darting through an opening in the hedgerow.

He followed her through brush and trees to join Jordan's four commandos and three members of the Maquis—the French Resistance fighters that Colette belonged to.

The commandos and Maquis fired at will as the Germans returned in greater measure. Amidst the chaos, one of the Maquis turned to the entire group and shouted in French. "There are too many Germans. We have to go. Colette, lead the way."

Jordan, fluent in French, translated for two of his team members, who understood minimal French. One by one, the mix of French, English, and Americans followed Colette.

Bark sprayed from the tree next to Jordan as the gunfire landed over his head. He heard shouts in German in the distance and reasoned that the enemy fired from about sixty yards away. He dropped to one knee and unloaded his thirty-round magazine toward that direction, providing covering fire. He had no fear. The event had shocked his demeanor unlike anything he'd ever experienced. He was focused.

Farrington tapped him on the shoulder.

Jordan reloaded, turned, and joined the line of escaping fighters.

His adrenaline ran high after tasting his first combat. Nick

Jordan had turned down a cozy desk job to get into the fight. He had no way of knowing if he'd killed any Germans, but the firefight whetted his appetite—and he loved it. A commando was born.

TWO

" COLONEL, CAPTAIN BRAND is here," the secretary said, waiting for a response by the doorway.

William Donovan stared out of the window and sipped his coffee. "Send him in," he said, without looking at her.

Brand entered with a satchel and stopped in front of the desk at attention.

Donovan turned. "Sit. What do you have for me, Captain?"

"Well, sir, I think we have some fine candidates for clandestine operations. You wanted men who will lie, cheat, and steal their way to victory. 'Gentlemen who conduct ungentlemanly warfare,' I believe is how you put it."

William Donovan wore many labels: millionaire, attorney, and Congressional Medal of Honor recipient for leading an attack during World War I. President Roosevelt appointed him head of the OSS (Office of Strategic Services). Donovan took full control of the office as a means to collect and analyze data and eventually expanded the organization's role to include small-unit military tactics, espionage, raids, guerilla warfare, sabotage, reconnaissance, etc. Donovan's vision for OSS operations was clear—conduct irregular warfare to harass and demoralize the enemy while supporting the conventional Allied forces. The OSS sought people from all walks of life, but they needed to excel in education, daring, and foreign language skills. They needed to be teachable, mature, cultured, and cosmopolitan.

Brand opened a fourth dossier after having finished reading through three others.

"These are close, Brand, but not quite right. I want a unique force. An extraordinary force. A special force. I need very special men for this."

Brand reached to the bottom of his file and opened a new dossier. "I was saving this one, Colonel. Theodore Nicolas Jordan. Born 1918 in East Rutherford, New Jersey. Six foot two. Two hundred four pounds. Graduates from Yale next month. Fluent in French and German."

Donovan sat down at his desk. "Is this former Ambassador Jordan's boy? The ambassador to Germany in the thirties?"

"Yes, sir."

Donovan leaned back in his chair. "Continue."

"IQ 148. History major. Accepted for graduate work at Harvard with intentions to become a professor. However, the war has changed those plans. My sources tell me his father wants him in naval intelligence."

"Sports? Is he an athlete?" Donovan asked.

"Four-year letterman in football and baseball for the Bulldogs. Hit two home runs last week. Likes to box in his spare time."

"Bonesman?"

"Yes, sir. Skull and Bones probably didn't take too long in deciding to tap him."

Donovan smiled. "This is the guy I'm talking about. Any flaws?"

Brand closed the file. "Do you count cocky?"

"Nope. I call it confident. This is the guy for Wolfhound."

Operation Wolfhound was a joint American, British, and

French commando detachment of five-member teams tasked with reconnaissance, sabotage, and combat behind enemy lines. Each operator would need skills far beyond those of the typical soldier. They needed exceptional hand-to-hand combat training, the ability to operate all kinds of weaponry, and street-smart savviness. They'd learn to drive every type of vehicle, survive in primitive conditions, and disregard injury.

Brand stood. "He may be a tough sell. The father has a lot of pull and wants him using his brain rather than brawn. Jordan's a rule follower. I'll need to convince him to disobey his father."

Donovan stood and walked to the window. "Captain, I see several people walking around down there. I'm sure that you could sell half of them life insurance and the other half would feel guilty about not buying it. You guilted me into buying one of your policies before the war. You're a closer, Captain. Close Jordan. I want him."

Brand stood and placed the dossiers in his satchel. "I'll be on the next train to New Haven."

THREE

YALE UNIVERSITY
May 1942

RALPH GAINES HELD up a mug of beer as he put his arm around Nick Jordan. The two stood at the bar of the Old Sport Tavern, a favorite haunt of Yale athletes. Pictures and sports memorabilia dating back sixty years adorned the walls. The barkeep's mutton-chop sideburns, connected to his bushy mustache, gave the place a nineteenth-century appearance.

"Quiet down, you degenerates," Ralphie addressed several men in baseball uniforms. "I want to propose a toast. Once again, my pal Nick here saved our team in the ninth inning. Not with his bat this time. This bloody nose of his came from blocking the plate when that Princeton brute tried to score. 'Out,' the umpire shouted." Ralph motioned with his left thumb to mimic the umpire and then lifted his mug of beer with his right hand. "So, to our catcher and protector of home plate, Nick Jordan!"

Several raised their mugs. "To Nick!" voices shouted in unison.

The baseball players and other bar patrons returned to their conversations.

"Well done, Ralphie. And thanks," Jordan said. A smile curled one side of his mouth.

"I don't get you sometimes, Nick. The way you sacrifice yourself for a game. You're going to get killed one day."

"Whatever it takes, Ralphie. Whatever it takes to win. That's the only way I play it."

Ralph smiled and shook his head. A man in uniform sitting at the end of the bar caught his eye. He looked back at Nick. "Two weeks, Nick. Two weeks and we'll be Yale graduates. You decide yet. Army? Navy?"

Jordan stared into his beer. "Father has me scheduled for some navy officer school. Working in intelligence or something like that."

"Sitting behind a desk? You'll go stir-crazy. No, no. Forget that. B-17 Flying Fortress. That's all you need to tell him. You're going to fly the big boys with me. He'll understand."

Jordan shook his head, slowly. "You don't know my father. Once he makes up his mind, that's it."

Ralph set his mug on the bar. "What about what you want? You're the one that's going to wear the uniform. You're the one with your neck on the line. You have to tell him."

"Yeah. Easy for you to say. He always—"

"Hey, Ralphie. Come tell these guys that story you told me the other day," another ballplayer shouted from a table away from the bar.

Ralph put his hand on Jordan's shoulder. "Just tell him," he said, and walked over to the table.

Jordan looked at himself in the mirror behind the bar, then into his mug. He swirled his beer.

"He's right, you know."

The voice came from the end of the bar. Jordan looked over to find a man, slightly older than him, in an army uniform like so many throughout American cities since the attack on Pearl Harbor. Jordan knew the bars on his shoulders meant he was an officer.

"Right about what?" Jordan said.

"You're the one that's going to wear the uniform. You're the one with your neck on the line, I believe he said." The officer tapped his non-filtered cigarette on his watch and lit it. "We all have our war to fight. Might as well be on our terms, don't you think?"

Jordan turned back toward his beer. "You always listen in on other people's conversations?" He downed the rest of his mug.

"Only the ones I find interesting. And I found that one fascinating."

Jordan looked back over to find the officer smiling.

Screech!

Several chairs dragged across the wood floor as the baseball team headed toward the door.

"Hey, Nick. We're heading out. Papers due and tests to study for. You know the drill," Ralph said.

The officer leaned toward Jordan. "Hey, Teddy. Why don't you stick around?"

Jordan's eyes widened. He disliked the name Theodore but despised the shortened Teddy. His father's hero had been President Theodore Roosevelt and was the driving force behind his father entering public service. He honored the former president by giving his firstborn that name. Only his mother was allowed to call him Teddy. Every time he entered a school or met someone, he offered his middle name. "Nicolas, but you can call me Nick," he'd say. While in the fifth grade, another boy peeked at a roll sheet on the desk and encouraged two other boys to call the young Nick "Teddy Bear." After the melee, Nick gained a bloody lip, but the other three boys fared far worse. One ran away in tears and the other two left their pride on the playground, as Nick beat them all. The incident earned him a sore behind from his father but no boy in that school ever again used the name Teddy in any type of reference toward Nick.

Maintaining his stare on the officer, Jordan said, "You boys go ahead. I'll be along."

The baseball team sauntered out of the Old Sports Tavern, leaving the barkeep, a couple in the corner paying more attention to each other than the stack of books on their table, and an old timer at the other end of the bar. Jordan and the officer remained as well, engaged in a staring contest.

Jordan broke the silence. "I don't know who you are, but I want to know, right now, how you knew to call me Teddy." His face reddened and his grasp on the empty mug tightened.

The man offered a conciliatory posture and lifted an open hand. "Listen. I meant no offense. Let me buy you a beer and explain." He held up his empty martini glass, signaling the bartender. "One more and a beer for my friend." He slid down four spots to sit next to Jordan, opened a silver case, and offered him a cigarette.

Jordan accepted and let the officer light it. "So, who are you?"

"My name is Captain Brand. What I'm about to tell you is confidential. In other words, I'd rather you not share this with your fellow classmen back at the dormitory. I represent Colonel William J. Donovan, head of the OSS. The Office of Strategic Services, that is. He has one question for you. Do you want to kill Nazis?"

"What? I mean . . . yeah. I want to kill Nazis. And Japs. And anybody else that wants to pick a fight with our country."

Brand took a long drag from his smoke. "I thought you might say that. Actually, I know a lot about you, Nick. May I call you Nick?"

Jordan nodded.

"We've done background checks on several candidates we think can fill specific roles in the war effort."

Jordan smiled and leaned in. "Specific roles?"

"You'd wear an army uniform and hold an army rank, but you'll be working for the OSS. We'll send you for infantry training, and you'll learn all the basics. But then your real training will begin. We'll teach you to live off the land. Rig explosives. Jump out of planes. And kill with your bare hands. The specific role is that of commando."

Jordan's beer sat untouched on the bar as he listened intently, hands folded in his lap.

Brand sipped his martini. "You'll work in a small team of five with men from other Allied nations. You're fluent in French and German, and you'll need those skills."

"How'd you know I can speak French and Ger—"

"Like I said, Nick. We've done our homework. I know you were born in 1918 to overachieving parents. I know that your maternal grandmother had emigrated from Lyon, France, and your parents forced you and your two little sisters to speak only in French with her so you'd acquire the language. I know you have a scar on your left calf from trying to jump over a creek on your bicycle when you were eleven years old. Your family moved to Germany the next year for your father's ambassadorship, and you became fluent in German. Upon your return, your father enrolled you at Hollander Prep School in New Jersey. You wanted to attend Princeton after that, but your father insisted on Yale, his alma mater. Shall I keep going?"

Jordan shook his head.

"Oh, and I know that only your mother is allowed to call you Teddy."

Crossing his arms and looking to the side, Jordan opened his mouth but nothing came out. He teetered between anger at the invasion of privacy and amazement that someone cared that much about his upbringing.

Brand nodded. "I know. It's a lot to take in. But think about it. If we can get this kind of detail on you, think of what we can teach you to do."

"I'm interested. But I need some time to think about it." Jordan gulped his beer, which had warmed.

"Sure. Take some time. Meet me here tomorrow at 3:40. Your philosophy class ends at 3:20. That should give you time to walk here."

"So, you have my class schedule."

"Of course I do." Brand smiled.

"One day? You're not even giving me twenty-four hours to think about it, huh?"

"You're a man of action, Nick. You've never thought over a decision for more than twenty-four hours in your life. Why start now?"

Jordan rubbed his chin. "My father's not going to like this. That'll be the real challenge. He fancies me a naval intelligence officer."

The captain lit yet another cigarette, feeding his chain-smoking habit. "You tell him the following. Because it's all true. I mean you can tell him all the commando stuff, but that may not impress him. The Allies will eventually have to invade Europe. Where and when we don't know. Maybe the Russians from the east, us from the south, and the Brits across the English Channel. Partisans in several countries are outmatched and need help. The French Resistance is putting up a brave fight. We need commando teams to go in and evaluate them. Assist them. Teach them. Use your advanced skills to make them more effective. A force multiplier, we call it.

"Hopefully, your father will be supportive. But if he's not, this may be your opportunity to tell him what you want to do for once. Are you going to let him dictate the rest of your life?"

"I'll be here tomorrow. I'll give you my answer. But you seem to be able to read my mind. What decision will I make?"

Brand stood from his barstool and picked up his satchel. "I'll bring the papers for you to sign." He took a few steps and turned. "By the way, Nick, you ever see a wolfhound?"

Jordan cocked his head. "I don't believe so."

"Interesting breed of dog. They used to hunt wolves with them. Never know when you'll need to catch and kill a wolf." Brand grinned and walked out.

FOUR

PARKER JORDAN'S THREE-PIECE suit, free of lint, was of the finest quality. He reached for his pocket watch as Nick Jordan approached the table inside the five-star, New Haven restaurant. His father offered no toleration for tardiness—especially from his children.

"Right on time, son," his father said.

Nick shook his father's hand, kissed his mother on the cheek, and sat between his two younger sisters, Anna, aged sixteen, and Katherine, nineteen, a Rutgers' sophomore.

"I hope this restaurant is acceptable to celebrate your graduation," Nick's mother said.

"It's fine, Mother. I like this place."

"Summa cum laude. Well done, son. Well done. We're very proud." The elder Jordan smiled, beaming with pride. "I can't say I'm thrilled with your chosen field of study. But if the Jordans are going to produce a historian, he might as well graduate with honors from Yale. All that research will serve you well in naval intelligence."

"Actually, Father, I wanted to talk to you about that. I've—"

"May I take your order," the waiter said.

The process of ordering and additional meaningless talk steered Nick from the conversation he needed to have with his father. Anna updated Nick on the latest hometown gossip, and Katherine droned on about her latest boy troubles. After dessert and coffee had been served, Nick made his move.

"Father. Mother. I have something to tell you. As you know, Harvard will hold my graduate spot until after the war. I—"

His father interrupted. "Of course, they will. We're at war. We all have to make sacrifices. I had to put off many personal pursuits during the Great War."

Nick's mother placed her hand on her husband's. "Parker, I believe Teddy is trying to tell us something."

"Oh. Right. What is it, son?"

"Well, as I was saying, with the war, I'll be delaying Harvard. I've been chosen for a unique unit. A special force, they call it, to fight behind enemy lines. Commando work." Nick continued to relay the types of training and responsibilities he'd have as explained by Captain Brand.

"Son, do you realize the strings I've pulled to get you a spot in naval intelligence? It's a highly coveted position. Admiral Bill Prescott is doing me a personal favor. Anyway, you're too smart for all that running around and shooting. You need to use your brains, not your fists."

"I have to agree with your father, Nick. Besides, this special force business sounds far too dangerous." Nick's mother pushed her dessert plate away after only one bite.

Nick's father waved to the waiter for the check. "I know this William Donovan character. Thinks he's in Roosevelt's back pocket. He's not as well liked in Washington as he thinks. Bit of a renegade. You just forget these wild notions. Naval intelligence is where you belong."

"No, sir. I've already made my decision. I leave in two weeks."

Nick's father lowered his head and widened his eyes. "I don't think you've thought this through, son. You've always made hasty decisions. You can get out of this decision. Just tell this Captain Brand you've changed your mind." He stood, counted out cash for the bill, and began to walk away. "I'll get the car."

Nick, his mother, and his two sisters walked toward the door.

Anna grazed Nick's side, "My Teddy, the big war hero."

Her mischievous smile cooled Nick's anger at her for calling him Teddy.

His mother grabbed his arm. "Listen, Teddy. I don't like this commando fighting. Not one bit. But, it's your life to live, and I will support you."

"Thank you, Mother, but I don't think Father understands how serious I am."

"Don't worry about your father. I'll handle that. I always do," she said, with a smile.

"PULL!"

On command, Nick used a clay pigeon thrower to propel the disc high into the air.

Parker Jordan trained his twenty-gauge shotgun into the path of the object, pulled the trigger, and watched the clay pigeon burst into several pieces.

The Jordan family resided in an upscale neighborhood of East Rutherford on six acres. Their estate wasn't a mansion, but Parker's savvy investments gave them a hefty nest egg. Nick's mother belonged to the appropriate social clubs and frequently hosted teas in their home. Nick had spent many a day having a tailor mark his fine wool suit for that perfect look. The Jordans weren't millionaires, but everyone thought they were.

Trap and skeet shooting were one of only a few activities Nick enjoyed with his father, who treated his children as assets. He loved them and would die for them, but he valued what they should become in life rather than who they were. He focused on their career trajectories. He expected his daughters to excel in school so they'd make good catches. Parker was a man of numbers and exactness. Nick's thirst for adventure didn't reconcile with Parker's balance sheet. Parker wanted a son who would follow in his footsteps in business and then become an ambassador, or a senator, or perhaps president of the United States.

Nick used his last two weeks of freedom since graduation to say goodbye to old friends, spend time in the gymnasium, and convince his father that he made the right decision.

"Pull!" Once again, a clay pigeon met its end from the shot of Parker's gun. "You know, Nick, it's not too late for you to reconsider. Admiral Prescott tells me the position in naval intelligence is still open."

"No, sir. You're going to have to let this one go, Father. I'll never be satisfied sitting at a desk with a war on. I need to be in the thick of it. I've attended the schools you wanted me to attend, played the sports you wanted me to play, but it's time I made my own decisions. This decision may not be the best for you or for the Jordan family. It may not even be the best for me. But it's the best way for me to serve my country." Nick readied another clay pigeon.

Parker opened the double-barreled shotgun and rested it over his arms. He turned to Nick. "Your mother worked me over pretty hard. Told me I was too demanding. Too stubborn. And you know what?"

Nick shrugged.

"She's right. As usual. I still don't like your decision, but one thing I know is that you'll be the best commando in America's arsenal. We're Jordans. We don't do anything halfway." Parker locked the barrel and prepared for another clay pigeon. "Just promise me one thing."

"Sure, Father. Anything."

"Come back in one piece."

FIVE

CAMP DELTA
ALDINE, ENGLAND
October 1942

THE OSS PUT Nick Jordan through basic training in the States where he learned the skills of an army infantryman. While many of his fellow soldiers wheezed and upchucked their way through basic, his physical fitness gave him an advantage. Unlike the enlisted men who graduated next to him, Nick attended additional officer training and earned a single gold bar on his shoulders as a second lieutenant. The newly minted officer and gentleman liked what he saw in the mirror. Military life suited him because that all-important characteristic—military bearing—oozed from every pore of his body.

He had steamed across the Atlantic to Europe as a child, but the arrival in Liverpool, England, embodied an entirely different feel. He had inched ever closer to war.

"Well, I wonder where this Mr. Styles is?" Lieutenant Alexander Lowesly stood on the pier at the end of the gangplank next to Jordan.

Jordan looked left and right. "I guess we wait, Alex . . . eh . . . Alexander."

Lowesly looked at his watch. "I don't like waiting. I don't like all this uncertainty."

Their orders had been stamped CLASSIFIED in red letters

and required them to meet "Mr. Styles" upon arrival in Liverpool. From there they'd receive instructions on further training and assignment. The nature of the commando detachment they'd signed up for required extensive training. Jordan and Lowesly trained alongside one another from their first day of basic but neither knew the other was an OSS operative. They discovered this on the day they were pinned as second lieutenants and given their orders. They carried no illusions that they'd be thrust immediately into combat, but they didn't have a guess as to how long their training would last and when that day of battle would come. They didn't even know the location of their next training assignment. The mystery fueled Jordan's sense of adventure.

Lowesly, on the other hand, complained about the secrecy every day on the trip across the Atlantic. His southern drawl stemmed from Georgia roots, but he was a Harvard man through and through. He embraced the Ivy League and all its trimmings. He did things by the book and enjoyed the formality of the military and the rank of officer. He seemed to Jordan a highly capable man. He was shorter and less fit than Jordan, but what he lacked in athleticism, he made up for in intelligence. If anyone called him Alex, he corrected them so they would call him Alexander. An action Nick could appreciate due to his own annoyance at the name Teddy.

A black Packard rolled down the pier, made a U-turn, and stopped next to the two officers. The driver's side rear door opened and an impeccably dressed fellow stepped out. His Savile Row suit and round-framed glasses offered no semblance of a military man. He extended his hand. "Gentlemen. I'm Peter Styles," he said, in a highbrow British accent.

Jordan shook his hand.

"Lieutenant Jordan," Styles said. Jordan cocked his head, realizing that Styles knew who was who. Styles extended his hand toward the other officer. "Lieutenant Lowesly." He reached inside a breast pocket, pulled out a watch, and opened it. "I hope you didn't wait too long. Your ship arrived forty-nine minutes early."

Styles motioned toward the car. "Gentlemen, would you join me?"

As they settled in, the driver quickly placed their bags in the trunk of the extended-length car, which looked more like a limousine. He hopped back in and sped away.

Styles, sitting in the back with Jordan and Lowesly, rubbed his nose with his handkerchief. "Pardon, I have a bit of a cold. This Liverpool weather doesn't suit me. I don't typically make these trips, but happened to have business in town." He reached for a folder and took out his pen. "Let me go over your instructions."

Like Jordan, Lowesly had been sold by Captain Brand on the idea of joining the OSS to serve in a commando detachment whose members would be elite in intellect, physical stamina, and toughness. Styles may have had the intellect, but he possessed no physical prowess.

Jordan cleared his throat. "Say, Mr. Styles. Are you OSS? A commando?" He knew the answer but wanted to see how Styles would respond.

"Oh, heavens no, my dear man. I'm the facilitator if you will." He formed a slight grin.

Lowesly smiled. "Facilitator? You mean a pencil pusher."

Styles's grin disappeared. "No! I'm your boss. I realize you've been kept in the dark, so let me explain. I work for the SOE. The Special Operations Executive. We are very much like your OSS, except our people have been at this game a bit longer. My role is the planning and facilitation of sabotage, espionage, and reconnaissance missions to defeat the Nazis."

"So, you have a lot of experience at this?" Lowesly asked.

Jordan whipped his head back and forth at the intellectual game of tennis.

Styles's grin returned. "I have a Ph.D. in engineering from Oxford. Ever heard of it?"

Lowesly nodded, conceding on the point of the man's intelligence.

Styles continued, "I've planned over thirty operations behind enemy lines since 1939." He opened the folder and looked down. "I plan your training, your team assignment, your missions, and every time you go to the loo. I control your lives. At least until that Hitler chap is laid to rest. Now, as I was saying, let's go over your instructions."

Jordan and Lowesly looked at one another as if wondering what they'd gotten themselves into. Their fate seemed to rest in the hands of this bureaucrat.

Lowesly held up his hands. "All right. We get it. You're in charge. So where we headed?"

Styles pointed to a typed line on a paper in the folder. "I see from your dossier, Lieutenant Lowesly, that you don't like unanswered questions. Neither do I." He closed the folder. "In approximately five hours, twenty minutes, we'll arrive at Camp Delta in the tiny hamlet of Aldine, England, near Ipswich. It's unique for its terrain of forest, hills, and rivers, and its proximity to the sea. A terrain similar to that of occupied, northwestern France."

"So, we're going to be fighting in France," Jordan said.

"I know from your dossier, Lieutenant Jordan, that you lack subtlety. To confirm your statement, yes, you two will join ComDet teams . . . commando detachment teams that is, comprised of five members each. We call it Operation Wolfhound. A mix of British, American, and French operatives. Both officers and enlisted. Your five-man teams will be unlike anything we've ever assembled. You'll be the most well-trained, skilled team the

Nazis have ever faced. You'll engage in every kind of warfare imaginable. You'll jump, swim, run, or ride wherever we need you to go and kill whomever we need you to kill. That is, if you complete the training. Which, by the way, begins now and continues until we send you on your first mission. I'm putting you in ComDet Sixteen, Lieutenant Jordan, and you'll be in ComDet Forty-One, Lieutenant Lowesly."

Jordan grinned on one side of his mouth and nodded.

"Forty-One? You mean there are forty-one or more of these teams? Exactly how many are there?" Lowesly said.

Styles closed his eyes and shook his head. "No, my dear man. We have six teams in the beginning stages and plans for six more. But once the Nazis learn of these teams, we'll leak out those team numbers. We want them to think there are more than forty-one teams. ComDet teams who unleash untold terror and havoc. Who instill fear in everyone from the lowliest Wehrmacht foot soldier to those in the upper echelon of the Nazi regime. We want ComDet teams to be feared."

"OK, Mr. Styles. I'm in," Lowesly said.

Jordan looked at him and back at Styles. "Me too."

Styles looked to his right shoulder and brushed lint from his suit. "As if either of you had a choice. But, I'm glad you're both enthusiastic. First, let's see if you can survive the next few days."

THE PACKARD MOTORED through the English countryside. After a little over five hours in the car, a sign on Jordan's side of the vehicle announced that Aldine lay three kilometers ahead. Leaves on trees had turned into their bright, fall colors. A boy used a long staff to shepherd sheep up a steep hill. A tower windmill peacefully turned. The pastures and farmhouses seemed untouched by the war.

The driver made no stops in the small hamlet but slowed so

that Jordan noticed two elderly men sitting outside a shop and a woman beating a rug. That, and the last-century appearance of the buildings, hardly lent itself to this being the location for a vanguard commando team. Within moments, they reached the edge of town and cruised down a road whose tree branches formed an arch. The driver turned onto a narrow, gravel drive leading toward a farmhouse with several outbuildings and a huge barn that looked on the verge of collapse. Rusted sheet metal patched portions of the roof and mismatched planks of wood shored up the sides. Trees and brush had overgrown at the back end of the structure. A farmer, pitchfork in hand, swung open the barn door, showing an opening wide enough for the Packard to drive through.

Styles gathered his belongings. "Gentlemen, welcome to Camp Delta. Follow me."

Jordan and Lowesly stepped onto the hay-covered floor and followed Styles through a door toward the back of the barn. Wood covered the floor of the next room. Dozens of men and women in uniform busied themselves around tables and at huge maps on the walls. Three operators wore headphones and worked dials on radios. The two commandos had crossed over from what seemed like the nineteenth century into the nerve center of Operation Wolfhound.

The barn, a false façade, cleverly hid a much more elaborate facility with several offices. Through the back window, Jordan noticed the outbuildings under the trees and wondered what was happening in those.

"This way, gentlemen," Styles said, walking past them and into an office.

A sign hung above the doorway with an inscription in both French and English. *Le hasard ne favorise que les esprits préparés.* Chance favors only the prepared mind. Louis Pasteur.

The pungent smell of cigar smoke consumed the room. A beret-wearing officer with a handlebar mustache stood with his arms folded. A tailored jacket contained his wide shoulders.

Styles laid his satchel on his desk and cleared his throat. "Major Tunstall, may I present Lieutenants Lowesly and Jordan."

The two lieutenants, acknowledging Tunstall's rank, popped tall to attention.

"The major comes to us from the British Royal Marines, and he will be your instructor for training," Styles said.

Jordan cleared his throat. "Major. Mr. Styles said our training would begin now and continue until our first mission. How long will that take?"

Tunstall walked toward the two Americans and blew cigar smoke between them. "Your training never ends. You will train twenty-four hours a day, seven days a week. You'll be ready when I say you're ready and not a moment sooner. I know you think you're physically fit? We'll get you in real shape." He turned, stepped four paces, and turned back. "You Americans seem awfully cocksure since entering the war but let's get one thing bloody straight. I've been at this game for quite some time. Killing a Nazi is not as simple as pulling a trigger. It takes careful planning and skill. It takes the right attitude. It takes undaunted courage. Until I'm convinced you have the requisite skills, attitude, and courage, you won't be killing any Nazis. I don't care what the OSS thinks of you. I don't care what Styles here thinks of you. As far as I'm concerned, I don't even know if you can tie your own shoes. If I don't think you can cut it, I'll send you home to your mothers." Tunstall walked to the doorway and turned his head back. "So, wipe that smug look off your faces. We'll see what kind of commandos you'll make. Follow me."

SIX

"EGGS? THE MAJOR wants us to steal eggs?" Jordan asked.

"That's right, Nick. Two dozen eggs before breakfast." Captain Peter Farrington motioned for his five-man commando team to gather around him. He knelt and began drawing on the ground with a stick.

THREE WEEKS HAD passed since Jordan arrived at Camp Delta. From day one, he'd experienced a bevy of physical training. Push-ups, sit-ups, chin-ups, and several mile-long runs over uneven terrain at least once per day, and on occasion—twice per day. The number of repetitions and the standards to complete these tasks increased. One day, the requirement of fifty pushups in two minutes became seventy-five in the same timeframe. The five-mile run in shorts was now required to be done in combat fatigues, in less time, while carrying a twenty-pound log. Every day, the instructors found new ways to ensure the commandos-in-training endured mud, murky water, insects, and burrs.

They learned to climb a tree with one hand tied to their side, run up a wall to gain access to a roof, jump from twelve-foot heights without injury, and hold their breath under water for extended periods. The instructors wanted them to understand they could overcome any obstacle.

Jordan soon realized that he wasn't nearly as physically fit as he needed to be. Still, he was more prepared than most of his fellow commandos and regularly came in first in physical tests. Major Tunstall called this portion of training "phase one."

That first phase included a battery of mental tests. Tunstall would show them ten pictures of random items in quick succession and challenge them hours later to recite the items, in order, and backward. Jordan excelled in this area. As a child, his mother required him to recite, from memory, large passages of Bible verses, poetry, and Shakespeare. His father taught him the system he used for delivering speeches without notes by turning each line into a picture and linking it into a story. It served the young Jordan well and he used those skills for Tunstall's test.

The major presented them with training manuals on military weapons and equipment, which they read and reread. He lectured them on military history and tactics. Every piece of information they consumed was subject to written and verbal tests. The commandos either endured the stress or Tunstall removed them from the training. Thus far, ComDet Sixteen, Jordan's team, had lost no members during phase one.

The commandos began their day at 5:00 AM, although some of their days did not end until 4:00 AM. Sleep deprivation was part of the training.

Once per week, Tunstall gave each team an unusual task to complete. He called them missions, and this latest was one of the most memorable. "I'm teaching you to kidnap, steal, cheat, and kill by the quickest, most ungentlemanly means possible," he often said.

TEAM LEADER CAPTAIN Farrington pointed to the small square he'd drawn in the dirt and relayed the egg mission orders to his team as given to him by Tunstall. "We've been assigned that white farmhouse one point three miles northwest. You've all seen it. It's at the end of that stone wall we go by on some of our jaunts.

The resident, a Miss Sprague, lives alone. She gathers her eggs every morning at 0630, loads them into the basket of her bicycle, and takes them to town to sell. Our mission is to gather those eggs, place them on her porch before she comes out, and return to camp by 0650 with photographic evidence. Miss Sprague cannot know who was ever there." Farrington looked left and right at his team members. "That's the mission, gents. What do you think?"

In addition to Jordan and Farrington, the members of ComDet Sixteen were a French officer, who went only by Jean-Pierre; Sergeant Ian Cummings, a British radio operator; and Corporal Rance Whitfield, who hailed from the hills of Kentucky. Each brought their own expertise to the team.

"Seems easy enough. We go in, grab the eggs, place them, and get out of there," Jordan said.

Whitfield turned to Jordan. "You ever gather eggs, Lieutenant?"

Jordan cocked his head. "No, I guess I haven't."

"Some chickens are mighty particular. They don't take kindly to just anybody sticking their hands under 'em." Whitfield turned to Farrington. "How long has Miss Sprague lived there?"

"Actually, the major told me that she's lived there over forty years. An old maid. Never married."

Whitfield nodded. "People like that live on strict routines and she likely knows her chickens. You see, chickens will make a big ruckus if they don't recognize you. They'll act like there's a fox in the hen house. They know her, though. If we go in there sticking our hands under the hens, they'll make a big ruckus and wake her up. They'll also get to pecking at us."

"Then we'll just have to gather some wigs and dress like the old maid," Cummings said, smiling. The British sergeant had regularly lightened the mood with his quick wit.

This time, no team member returned a smile and then they

looked away from him.

"Let's keep this serious, Sergeant," Farrington said.

Jordan picked up a stick and pointed at Farrington's drawing in the dirt. "Now, wait a minute, Captain. Maybe Cummings is on to something. We can get there and back in plenty of time. We can take the photographs. Our main problem is keeping the hens quiet. If we all go barreling in there, we'll upset the hens. So, only one of us will go in. I don't know how well chickens recognize humans, but our best bet is that, if only one person goes in, they won't know the difference or won't care."

"I agree, Nick." Farrington pointed to Whitfield. "Corporal Whitfield. You're going into the chicken coop and gathering the eggs."

Whitfield's eyes widened. "Me, Captain? Why me?"

"Well, Corporal, you have demonstrated that your expertise with chickens far outweighs anyone else's on this team. But, don't worry, we'll be covering you from all angles. We can do this, men."

"What if there's a dog?" Jordan asked.

"Take some meat," Whitfield answered. "That'll keep it quiet."

Captain Peter Farrington maintained an optimistic attitude with every mission. A graduate of the Royal Military Academy Sandhurst—the British version of West Point—Farrington was a highly capable officer. He'd participated in two reconnaissance missions in Italy a year prior. No shots had been fired. Still, they were real missions with actionable results. His idealism reached over-the-top proportions at times, but no one could fault his patriotic attitude.

"If my father could see me now," Jordan muttered, as the team jogged toward the mission target location.

"What's that, Nick?" Farrington asked.

"My father was against me joining this unit. He wanted me in naval intelligence. I can only imagine what he'd say if he knew I was on a mission to steal eggs."

Farrington held up a finger. "Actually, Nick, I've decided we're not really stealing them. We're relocating them. A very precise operation. We'll use the element of surprise . . . on the chickens that is. We'll be doing this with carefully collected intelligence. We'll do this in utmost secrecy. And finally, we'll return with valuable reconnaissance photographs. While all that seems a bit of a stretch, we're honing some essential skills. We're forcing ourselves to think outside the box. And most importantly, we're learning to work as a team. These missions, as ridiculous as they may seem—particularly this one—have great value."

Jordan nodded. "Point taken, Captain."

WHILE THE LOCALS knew about Camp Delta, they assumed it was a regular training location like the many throughout England, but few knew its true nature. The camp's designers made sure that planes flying overhead saw nothing but a farm with several outbuildings. Miss Sprague probably never imagined her eggs would be used for training.

Corporal Whitfield crouched as he carefully stepped toward the coop at 5:55 AM—the egg basket under his arm and flashlight in his back pocket. He dressed in full combat gear as did the rest of the team.

Dawn had yet to break, but a hint of light gave ComDet Sixteen enough visibility to undertake their mission. The coop leaned to one side, showing its age. The white house with blue trim stood two stories high.

Farrington remained near the chicken coop, offering Whitfield close support. Jordan and Jean-Pierre maintained a position on the far side of the house. Should Miss Sprague come outside too early, they'd create a diversion to draw her away from the coop.

Cummings climbed a tree across from the house but remained hidden behind heavy branches. He held the camera and planned to snap photos of Miss Sprague discovering the eggs on her front porch. From his perch, Cummings watched Whitfield enter the coop and shut the door behind him.

Bawwwwk. Bawk. Bawk. The chickens kept their cackle at a constant but normal level.

Cummings looked to his left and noticed Farrington hiding behind the coop, checking his watch. He had instructed Whitfield to complete the task inside the coop within five minutes—a full thirty minutes before Miss Sprague made her normal trip to the coop. To Cummings's right, Jordan and Jean-Pierre engaged in animated conversation, but out of Cummings's earshot.

Bawwwwwwwwwwwwwk! The chickens unleashed a cacophony of cackles.

A light came on in an upstairs window.

Farrington stood up and cupped his hands, mouthing something to Whitfield in the coop.

The old maid stepped out to her front door wearing a robe. Assorted, twisted cloths intertwined with her hair. "Who's there?" She raised the double-barreled shotgun to a ready position next to her hip and looked toward the coop.

Woof! Woof!

Caw! Caw!

Woof!

Cummings's eyes widened. He smiled and shook his head. From his height, he could see Jordan and Jean-Pierre making a variety of animal and bird sounds.

The old maid whipped her head toward the garden. She walked to it, cautiously, in the opposite direction from the coop.

Jordan and Jean-Pierre used a small hedgerow to conceal their escape as they moved away from the garden. They continued making noise and drawing the woman away from the house and far enough that she lost line-of-sight to the front porch.

Farrington ran to the front of the coop as Whitfield burst out of the door, feathers flying from his uniform. Farrington took the eggs, ran them over to the porch steps, and joined Whitfield on a dead run from behind the coop and into the woods.

Cummings had snapped a picture of Farrington placing the eggs.

"Bloody varmints," Miss Sprague said, as she walked back to the house—her shotgun lowered. She stopped eight feet from the porch. "What in the?" She looked left, then right, and made a few more steps toward the basket. Slowly, she leaned over and looked inside.

An elderly dog, with more wrinkles than the woman, sauntered out from the porch. Its days as a valued guard of the farm had long passed.

Cummings snapped the final picture. He stowed the camera and began climbing down from the tree. The last branch broke, sending him tumbling the last few feet.

"Who's there?" Miss Sprague yelled.

Cummings made a dash into the woods.

Boom!

The shotgun blast sent splinters of bark flying over his head.

Without looking back, he made his way along a creek, and found his four teammates at the rendezvous point—Farrington smiling and the other three laughing. Whitfield had one chicken feather stuck to his shirt.

"I TOLD YOU that the old maid was to not know you were there."

Tunstall paced as Farrington and Jordan stood at attention outside the main Camp Delta building.

Every mission required a debrief. Farrington offered the details and Jordan stood by as second in command.

"Permission to speak, sir," Jordan said.

Tunstall nodded.

"Your instructions, as Captain Farrington relayed them to
our team, was that the woman was not to know we were there.
And she didn't. Not only did she not know our team was there, I
don't believe she knew any people were there."

Tunstall folded his arms. "And why do you think that,
Lieutenant?"

"Cummings, sir." Farrington looked at Jordan and nodded.
"Cummings said the woman complained of 'bloody varmints.'
I'd say our diversion made her believe animals had caused the
ruckus. As for how the eggs were collected and placed on her
front porch, we'll never know what she thought happened.
Perhaps a higher power performed that miracle in her eyes."

Tunstall gnawed on his unlit cigar. "Very well. Dismissed!"

The two junior officers walked away, smiling, having accom-
plished the great chicken mission.

SEVEN

"GENTLEMEN, THIS IS Harry McVee." Tunstall pointed to a pudgy, balding man wearing a black leather jacket. "He comes to us on loan from Her Majesty's Prison Durham. He's the best lock picker and safe cracker in the world. He will be your instructor today."

The commandos sat at school desks in a makeshift classroom.

McVee picked up the pointer and walked toward a drawing on the chalkboard. "Alright, mates, here we have a pin-tumbler lock. Notice the . . ."

"Phase two" of training saw the forty-eight men who had initially arrived reduced to thirty. Those final thirty filled the six ComDet teams. A few either quit the training or were ousted by Tunstall. All five of Jordan's team, ComDet Sixteen, remained as originally formed. The instructional tempo and physical demands remained, but there were no more missions involving chickens and eggs. Every evolution seemed more purposeful in the eyes of the commandos. While phase one lasted for weeks, phase two would last for months.

One cold morning during training, the rain fell hard. The kind that blows directly in one's face. Jordan and his fellow team members looked at one another, exhausted from little sleep in the prior few days. He saw doubt in their eyes. Doubt as to their mission and commitment. Jordan even questioned himself. Had this been peacetime, he would have asked himself why he volunteered for commando training. But the war gave him the motivation to persevere. That, and Jean-Pierre. The Frenchman never offered specifics about his own family, but told them many stories of German atrocities. He also told of the Wehrmacht's skill on the battlefield. The commandos listened when Jean-Pierre spoke. When the rain fell hard. When they were cold, tired, and hungry. It was enough to erase any doubt in their commitment to the mission.

Tunstall pitted one ComDet against another in various competitions, such as bomb-making creativity, land-navigation accuracy, and pistol shooting. While some commando tasks measured individual performance, the vast majority were team efforts. Each team slept together in a hut and ate at their own table. Teams were referred to by their team number. ComDet Sixteen was called "Sixteen." ComDet Twenty-Two was known as "Twenty-Two" and so on. The words "your team" were stressed much more than "you."

Lock-picking was only one of many unique trades they learned. A make-up artist from Hollywood showed them how to produce disguises. A pickpocket earned an early release from prison for teaching the commandos his craft. An acting coach taught them the art of lying and use of body language to prevent giving themselves away. Outdoorsmen taught them how to catch a rabbit, skin it, and cook it. They learned to ride motorcycles, drive large trucks, and perform automobile offensive driving.

Jump training began and continued for several weeks with a focus on technique and safety. Although their expected number of jumps was minimal, they practiced landing in a wide array of terrain, as well as water. The last thing any of them wanted was to begin a mission with a broken leg or near drowning.

In addition, they honed their language skills, speaking only in French on certain days. Those without the language learned to act as if they knew it while picking up key phrases.

They learned to shoot every weapon used by the Allies, the enemy, and the Resistance. An American master sergeant and veteran of the previous war provided intricate details of each weapon's characteristics and capabilities.

"You boys want to be familiar with anything you might pick up and fire in combat. In the Great War, I ran out of ammo while in a German trench. I picked up an MP18 submachine gun from a dead German. Seconds later, a bunch of the enemy came around the corner of the trench, and I mowed them down." He mimicked the action. "Good thing I had intimate knowledge of the MP18."

The master sergeant was one of many colorful characters and experts brought in to train the commandos.

Training lasted up to sixteen hours per day, with a half-day break on Sunday. But even on their break, Tunstall strongly encouraged them to read books such as *The Scarlet Pimpernel* and Sir Arthur Conan Doyle's Sherlock Holmes series. Anything related to deception and deduction. Tunstall's schedule demanded that everything they learned be repeated or reinforced every third day.

Although they began with wooden knives, they quickly moved to real ones, causing the commandos-in-training to collect several minor cuts. One even suffered a stab wound but quickly recovered.

Tunstall twirled a stiletto between his fingers. "I want you to train with the real thing so you become intimately familiar with its weight, feel, and functionality."

The training became, rather than a test of willpower, one of physical survival. It had to be. These men trained for war.

The commandos began calling Tunstall "Old Ten-to-One" behind his back. Early in their training, he introduced them to his ten-to-one concept, which he repeated nearly every day. On the second week of phase two, they began martial arts training. The commandos gathered in an open area behind the Camp Delta barn and formed a circle. Tunstall took that opportunity for the full speech.

"Ten to one, men. Everything you learn must be applied as if you are outmanned ten to one. If your team of five is in a fight, you'll learn to beat fifty men. If you are alone with only your bare hands, you'll learn to defeat ten opponents. That's the way it will be for ComDet. We will be deep behind enemy lines. We will always be surrounded. We will always be outgunned. So get used to it now." Tunstall removed his jacket and beret and laid his unlit cigar on top of the beret.

He walked to the center of the circle. "I need a volunteer."

The men had learned an important tenet of military life: never volunteer.

Tunstall looked over the men, but no hands were raised. "Lowesly. Front and center."

Lowesly, the officer who had trained with Jordan in the states, stepped into the circle.

Tunstall cleared his throat. "Now, before you can defeat ten men, you'll need to learn to defeat one. Like Lowesly here."

Lowesly smirked and folded his arms. His short stature had given him a Napoleonic complex.

"Come at me, Lowesly." Tunstall stood still, hands at his side.

Lowesly looked left, right, and then lunged at Tunstall—arms extended.

The major sidestepped to the left and ran his right arm around Lowesly's right arm. Tunstall locked his hands and with a swift jerk took Lowesly to the ground.

Several commandos winced as Lowesly moaned.

Tunstall folded his arms. "Now, men, do you want to be the

one standing or be like Lowesly down there?"

Two commandos reached down and helped Lowesly to his feet.

Phase two continued through the winter of 1942 and into 1943. By spring, the commandos realized that phase two had no set end date. There would be no graduation. There would only be that first, real mission.

ComDet Sixteen regularly won team competitions due to Farrington's leadership, Jean-Pierre's wisdom, Cummings's practicality, and Whitfield's knack for explosives. Their strongest member, and ace in the hole, was Nick Jordan. No other commando could touch his athleticism. Jordan could beat any other commando in a contest of running, throwing, or jumping.

Major Tunstall made hand-to-hand combat a daily element of their education. Every morning they formed "the circle." One man would square off with another in the middle of the circle as others watched and cheered. Sometimes one sparred against three or more. However, a man never faced a member of his own ComDet team.

Jordan had boxed throughout his high school and college years and enjoyed his time in the circle more than any other commando. Although punches were pulled and throws were light, the men trained hard. Black eyes, bloody noses, and bruises marked most of the men.

Peter Styles used a beautiful, spring morning to watch the day's martial arts session. Jordan had already bested two challengers, one-on-one, from ComDet Twenty-Two and stepped back out of the circle to catch his breath.

"Alright, Twenty-Two, let's see if the remaining three members of your team can handle Mr. Jordan at the same time," Tunstall said, lighting his cigar and nodding to Jordan.

Styles walked over to the three members of Twenty-Two as they formulated a plan to take on Jordan. He put his hand on one of the men's backs and whispered in his ear. The man nodded.

Jordan walked to the center of the circle, opening and closing his fists.

"You can whoop 'em, Lieutenant," Whitfield said.

The three men approached and formed a triangle of attack around Jordan.

The man to his left opened with a haymaker punch. Jordan glided the punch past his own head and landed a solid blow to the man's side, causing him to double over. Another moved toward Jordan. Pushing the first opponent away, Jordan spun around and delivered a side kick to the man's stomach.

"Bravo, Nick!" Farrington yelled.

The third man crouched. Jordan approached him but he sidestepped and bought time for his partners to recover. Jordan backed up in the circle so the men couldn't form another triangle around him.

The first man Jordan had struck held his side. "Alright, Teddy, let's see you try that again."

Jordan's brow furrowed and his face reddened. He took a long, fast-paced stride forward and dropped the man with a punch to the solar plexus. Another of the men quickly jabbed Jordan in the face, sending him reeling back, but he maintained his footing. The two remaining opponents lunged at Jordan, who locked the arm of the one closest, and landed a roundhouse kick to the head of the other, quickly dispatching him. He turned to the man whose arm was locked and blasted his nose with a palm.

Two of the opponents lay conscious but barely moving. The one who called him Teddy crawled away with a hand holding his chest.

Jordan's team surrounded him and patted him on the back,

but Jordan rebuffed them and walked away. He knew he'd gone too far with his strikes. His temper had gotten the best of him.

Tunstall walked over and stood next to Styles. "Mr. Styles, I hardly think you need to antagonize Lieutenant Jordan to perform."

Styles rubbed his chin. "Let's just say I was experimenting with Mr. Jordan. You saw that he flew into a rage at being called Teddy. It's not becoming of an officer or a special forces commando."

"Rubbish! Jordan might be our best man. His instincts are uncanny. He has no fears. His team loves him. He has a photographic memory and he's the best pistol shooter in camp. Hell, Styles, he shoots better than I do."

"He has faults that we should evaluate now," Styles said.

Tunstall turned, squaring off to Styles. "I don't particularly care if he has a fault or two. Everyone does. I don't mind if my commandos fly into a rage on occasion. I might fly into a rage myself. Especially when someone conducts psychological experiments on my commandos. Now if you'll excuse me, Styles, we've got real training to do." Tunstall popped his cigar into his mouth and headed for the circle.

EIGHT

CAMP DELTA
September 1943

COMDET SIXTEEN GATHERED in the Camp Delta class-room. After nearly one year together, they shared cama-raderie unlike any of them had experienced before. They could finish each other's sentences and read one another's facial expressions with pinpoint accuracy. They had, in essence, become a small family.

"Just our team in class today? What's the big secret, Captain?" Rance Whitfield asked.

Farrington held up his hands. "I couldn't tell you, Rance. The major said 'Report to the classroom with your whole team.'"

Peter Styles and Major Tunstall entered the room. All five commandos popped tall—their uniforms crisply ironed and boots shining. Farrington insisted they maintain the highest military standards of any combat team.

Tunstall swatted with his hand. "Take your seats, gentlemen." He sat on the desk and lit a cigar.

Styles flipped the chalkboard to reveal a map on the other side. "Although Major Tunstall is fond of saying that your training never ends, your team is moving on to phase three—Operation Wolfhound. Ultimately, we see Wolfhound's mission as eliminating Nazis. And if we get the chance, we'll kill old Herr Wolf himself—Hitler.

"The Germans know that the Allies will eventually invade France. However, their long lines of defense make it obvious they don't know where. They probably think it will be the Pas-de-Calais since it offers the shortest distance between England and France." Styles used the pointer and touched Calais on the map. "The exact invasion location is classified and will be revealed in due time. For now, we must assess German strengths and defense locations. We must know their level of communication and supplies. We must know their command of roads and bridges. How much do they know about the invasion? We'll give you quite a list of information to collect."

Styles looked back at the map and stabbed the city of Caen. "Gentlemen, your mission is to assess the Germans' occupation of Caen."

"So Normandy is a possible invasion location?" Farrington said.

Styles smiled. "As I said earlier, Captain, we don't know, but that would certainly seem plausible."

Tunstall stood and revealed another map showing details of Caen and its surrounding areas. Styles handed him the pointer. "You'll drop here, and be met by a local group of Maquis. They'll be your host for the three days you'll be in the country. I want—"

"Only three days?" Farrington interrupted. "Pardon me, Major, but that doesn't seem like nearly enough time to establish ourselves and collect that level of information."

Tunstall puffed on his cigar. "We don't want you to establish yourselves. For now, we don't want you leaving a footprint. The Maquis will give you much of the information. You'll need to determine its validity as well as conduct several scout missions near Caen to verify. We need your trained eyes to see for yourself and your assessment of our Maquis friends. Are they willing and able to handle this invasion?

"As I was saying, I want you in and out as cleanly as possible. Observe and assess. The less contact with the enemy, the better. There will be time for that later."

"And if we come in . . . let's say . . . contact with the enemy?" Jordan asked.

"Eliminate them!" Tunstall answered. "But first, any information they're willing to share would be most helpful."

Jordan grinned slightly and nodded.

Styles cleared his throat. "Remember, Lieutenant Jordan, this is not a kill mission. This is a carefully planned reconnaissance mission. Several weeks in the making."

"We all know that, Mr. Styles. But please do keep in mind that your engineering approach doesn't always allow for variables experienced in combat." Tunstall popped his cigar in his mouth and folded his arms.

"How should we leave?" team member Jean-Pierre asked, in a heavy French accent.

Jean-Pierre wore no rank on his uniform. In the hierarchy of the commando team, he stood between officer and enlisted. None of the other team members knew his last name or whether Jean-Pierre was even his real name. As with many French soldiers, he likely hid his full name for fear of reprisal against his family. At thirty-four, Jean-Pierre was the oldest team member, although his salt-and-pepper hair made him look even older. A veteran of the Battle of France in 1940, he'd experienced more combat than any other team member. The other commandos had deep respect for his patriotism for France and often sought his wisdom. When asked of his family, he'd only answer, "I have no family." The team learned not to press him on this.

"Good question, Jean-Pierre." Tunstall referred to yet another map with even more detail. "You'll notice this small strip. It's a road leading to a power plant that was under construction before the war. The project was abandoned and the road is rarely used. However, it's long, straight, and flat, like a runway. A small transport aircraft will land at your appointed retrieval time. We've chosen the best pilots for this. You'll have only seconds to board. They'll likely attract attention, but our hope is that by the time the Germans find where they landed, you'll be long gone."

"And if they should be shot down?" Jean-Pierre asked.

Farrington raised a finger. "Yes, Major, what about that or what if we're late to the rendezvous point?"

Tunstall paced as he often did during lectures. "We've been experimenting with different routes for these planes and feel that this path will get them in and out without incident. And as for you, don't be late. If you are, you'll have to find your own way home. Any more questions, gentlemen?"

THE BRIEFING HAD lasted two hours, but the training for the mission lasted two weeks. They rehearsed every detail of the mission, from their infiltration and meet-up with the Maquis to their exfiltration. Other ComDet teams served as Maquis or Germans for mock scenarios. As with all other training, Tunstall constantly tested each team member for knowledge of mission details, equipment readiness, and situational responses.

"Jordan! Three of your team members are killed and Whitfield there is mortally wounded. What do you do?" Tunstall's questions were always relevant and highly stressful. He wanted them on the edge but thinking clearly. Ready for anything. Ready for change. Ready for combat.

Jordan would jump into this mission ready for immediate combat. He'd carry an M1911 .45 pistol with four extra magazines, a Thompson machine gun with three thirty-round and two twenty-round magazines, and a stiletto fighting knife. Miniature binoculars hung from a lanyard around his neck. K-rations, toiletries, French francs, and a first-aid kit filled his musette bag. A flashlight, a compass, a canteen, and four grenades were tucked in several special pockets inside his jacket or strapped to his belt. Rather than a helmet, he wore a wool watch cap and blackened his face with shoe polish. The other team members carried a variation of these items depending on their role within the team.

If the need arose to ditch the extra weight, the musette bag, and its contents, could go. The binoculars and canteen could be tossed aside. But the weapons and ammunition would remain on his person.

A neighboring, operational dairy farm concealed a workshop where all manner of gadgets were created and manufactured for the commandos. Items the typical foot soldier lacked, such as a pack of cigarettes that could cause a smoke diversion, a specialized lock-picking set, and a small blade able to be hidden in the soles of their boots. The commandos trained for every contingency and would rely on help from the tools of spycraft.

"Commandos must think on their feet and look for weapons of opportunity," Tunstall would often say.

"This ordinary fountain pen, when properly applied, can disable a man in a second. Everything must be thought of as a weapon." He grabbed the nearest man and thrust at the trainee's neck with the pen. "Just like that. Be aware of your surroundings and the weapons at your disposal."

Tunstall's method of keeping the men on edge, forcing them to think critically, maintaining their elite physical fitness, and instilling confidence gave the commandos a supreme advantage.

COMDET SIXTEEN MADE one night jump in full gear on each of the two nights leading to the missions. Tunstall called them dress rehearsals. He ordered them to pack and rest on the day of their midnight departure.

Farrington sat at the table in their hut crafting a letter.

Jordan sat down next to him and sipped his coffee. "Writing the wife and kids?"

"Every week, Nick. Keeps them from worrying."

Other than Farrington, only Whitfield was married but he had no children.

"How old are your kids again?"

Farrington leaned back and smiled. He picked up the small-framed photograph of his wife and children. "Charlie is five and Alice is three." He handed the picture to Jordan.

"I bet they miss their father. Hopefully, we'll get this war over with after a mission or two and get you home."

"I'm afraid it will take a little more effort than that, Nick. Unfortunately for my wife, she married a soldier. Separation was inevitable. Who knows? Perhaps I'll have had enough of war and want to settle into some office job. As an accountant or something."

"I guess little Charlie will be ready for you to kick the soccer ball around with him when you get home," Jordan said.

Farrington's eyes widened. "Soccer, Nick? We call it football, as you kick the ball with your foot as opposed to that bloody American style."

"No, no, no, Captain. We call it 'real' football. A man's game." Jordan folded his arms.

"Bloody Americans. So arrogant."

Whitfield, Cummings, and Jean-Pierre burst through the door. They appeared to have been having their own friendly argument.

"I guarantee you, Old Ten-to-One ain't killed no thirty Krauts," Whitfield insisted.

Jean-Pierre shook his head.

Cummings appealed to Farrington and Jordan. "What do

you think? We know Major Tunstall fought in the Great War. He must've killed many. I say thirty and no less."

Farrington held up his hand. "Gentlemen, I'm afraid that as hard as we've worked to discover the mystery that is Old Ten-to-One . . . Major Tunstall, that is, we have to rest in the fact that we may never know."

Whitfield and Cummings argued at least once per day over the most trivial matters. It was never antagonistic, and they'd bonded as the only two enlisted members of ComDet Sixteen.

Cummings typically won most arguments with his quick wit. He could fix anything and used that skill to rig up an array of practical jokes. Many a commando walked into a room or lay in their cot to find some contraption snapping at them and pouring out a pint of flour. He'd spent his growing up years tinkering in his grandfather's blacksmith shop. While his main role on the team was radio operator, his ability to rig explosives from the most rudimentary elements gave great value to ComDet Sixteen. Farrington allowed the mild pranks to break the monotony.

While Whitfield lacked the above-average intelligence of his fellow team members, he made up for that with homespun wisdom. Any time the team needed that extra edge while on an outdoors mission, Whitfield provided the solution based on years of camping. His father would take him and his brothers into the woods with nothing more than a pocket knife with the charge to "live off the land." He could start fires with stones, sticks, or some random item from his musette bag. He trapped fish in the river and scooped them up with his bare hands. While other ComDet teams came back from their several-days-long wilderness missions starving, ComDet Sixteen came back with bellies full of rabbit or some other animal.

While Jordan remained the best pistol shot on the team, Whitfield excelled with the long rifle. As the team packed for their midnight jump, Whitfield cleaned his M1903 Springfield sniper rifle with telescopic sight.

Farrington gathered his team in Camp Delta's operation center one hour before departure. "Now that we've each triple-checked our gear and supplies, I want another member of the team to check your gear. Let's leave no stone unturned."

The team began digging through one another's musette bags, checking weapons.

"Thanks, Captain," Jordan said. "From all of us."

Farrington cocked his head. "Thanks? For what?"

"For being our leader. You've done an outstanding job and we're ready." Jordan extended his hand.

Each commando followed suit, shaking Farrington's hand.

"It's my pleasure, gents. Now let's make a clean jump. You know your jobs. We have Styles's checklist memorized. We're well trained. Be alert. In three days, we'll be back here toasting a successful mission."

The members of ComDet Sixteen had each completed eight jumps with three of those occurring at night. The jump near Caen would be their first under gunfire.

NINE

AJOR REINHOLD WERTZ took a long drag from his partially smoked cigarette. The red ember glowed in the dark room where one of Caen's prominent councilmen sat tied to a chair.

Wertz leaned over and blew smoke in the man's face. "I think you're lying to me." He spoke in perfect French. "I think you have been supplying these terrorists living in the forest. These Maquis will be hunted down and killed like the dogs they are. I'll ask again. Are you giving supplies to these dogs? Money? Information?"

"No, Major. I don't know what you're talking about. I don't know any Maquis." Sweat poured down the councilman's face. His right eye was swollen shut from repeated blows by one of Wertz's henchmen—an SS sergeant with rolled-up sleeves and calloused knuckles.

Wertz paced. "I will find out what you know. Either you tell me or one of the three others in the next room will tell me. You can imagine that things will go much better for the first one that tells me the truth." Wertz smiled and lowered his deep, raspy voice. "Spare yourself all this pain."

"I told you. I don't know what you're talking about."

The Germans had taken over City Hall during their occupation. Wertz used the mayor's second-floor office for his work.

The councilman glanced at a Monet painting that hung on the wall depicting a peaceful pathway toward the sea as if wishing he could escape to that path.

Wertz approached the man while inhaling deeply from his cigarette and producing a bright red ember. He grabbed the back of the man's head by the hair and pushed the cigarette inside the councilman's ear.

"Ahhhhhh!" The councilman's body tensed and rose in the chair.

"We've used both ears so we'll have to get a little more creative." Wertz returned the cigarette to his mouth for another drag. He lifted his foot onto a stool and rested his arms on his thigh. A shimmer of light from the window reflected off his perfectly shined boots. "Now, Councilman, let's try again." Wertz rubbed the side of his neck with the back of his fingers over blister scars from a poisonous gas attack during the First World War.

Volunteering at a mere sixteen years old, Major Wertz saw his loyalty to the Fatherland refined during trench warfare. His heroism earned him the Iron Cross. After the war, he returned to private life, earning a psychology degree from the Humboldt University of Berlin. A speech by Adolf Hitler swayed him toward Nazism. He later joined the newly formed SS in 1934 serving in intelligence. His superiors commended him for finding and eliminating SS members with questionable, potentially Jewish, ancestry.

Wertz had studied mentalism and body language during his university days. Others thought he could read minds, but Wertz read body language and verbal cues. To him, it was science. SS members feared a meeting with Wertz. When the Germans invaded Poland in 1939, several Polish officers suffered and died during Wertz's interrogations.

The 12th SS Panzer Division had sent Wertz along with one company of 200 men to Caen two months prior to assess the city's occupation. The regular German army exacted brutality on a daily basis. They stole, pillaged, and disrespected Caen's citizens. They rounded up every Jewish inhabitant and loaded them on railcars for work camps in Germany. They forced many of the able-bodied French into menial service. The local baker provided fresh bread for German troops before anyone else. Mechanics had to give German autos first priority. The occupiers regularly propositioned women for inappropriate acts, leaving their husbands or fathers defending their honor at the tip of a German gun barrel.

Under Wertz's leadership, the 12th Panzer Division took those oppressive acts to a horrific level. So much so, that a Wehrmacht colonel, who outranked Wertz, confronted Wertz about the SS's terroristic tactics. He was told to conform to the SS ways or find himself in a Wertz punishment room. The colonel relented, well aware of Wertz's reputation.

The Maquis had successfully operated with help from Caen for years. With the expected cross-channel invasion, the Germans needed complete control of the city, and that included finding and eliminating the bands of Maquis operating in that area. They needed a strong hand to reclaim the city's occupation. Hitler had allowed the SS to operate freely for years for one main reason: their tactics worked. Wertz was that strong hand.

The Caen councilman served as Wertz's latest challenge. Once he established that his subject was lying, he applied various methods to expedite the confession and gather the information he needed. A burning cigarette to the ear was one method that required little exertion. Nails inserted into the fingertips provided another. Many times Wertz laid out the instruments of torture and picked them up one at a time. The victims' body language told him which one they feared most. Many times, merely waving that instrument in front of their face was enough to extract the information.

Seconds before the third cigarette burn, the councilman opened his mouth. "No, no! Wait! I'll tell you! I'll tell you everything."

Wertz leaned back. "Of course, you will, Councilman."

TEN

ORDAN AND COMDET Sixteen's first combat jump succeeded with zero casualties. Aside from the brief firefight, everything occurred according to plan. Other than Jean-Pierre, none of them had ever set foot in France.

They followed Colette and the rest of the Maquis greeting committee for forty-five minutes before reaching their camp.

The meandering route had included a mix of woods and rocky terrain, much of it uphill. Jordan attempted to memorize landmarks, but the darkness made it difficult. The farther they trekked, the darker it became. As they walked through heavy brush, bodies disappeared through an opening the width of a doorway.

Colette turned. "Put your hand on the shoulder of the one in front of you."

Jordan placed his hand on Colette's shoulder, and Corporal Lance Whitfield placed his hand on Jordan's shoulder.

At thirty-one paces, Jordan sensed a dampness in the air. At fifty-six paces, he noticed a shimmer of light. Jordan stopped his pace count as they entered a large room with a fire burning in the center. Several faces looked up at the commandos.

Rather than entering a room, they had entered a cave.

Mother Nature had provided a uniquely designed hideout for the Maquis within a brush-covered hill. Water trickled down one wall. The occupants had sprinkled hay across the floor. Furniture found in any French home filled the space, giving it a somewhat livable appearance.

A man stood with a plate of food in one hand. At his height, he slightly inched over the six-foot-three Farrington. "Welcome to our little abode." The unshaven Maquisard extended his hand to each commando. "I am Valère. I hope Colette gave you a proper welcome."

Farrington nodded to Colette and looked back at Valère. "Actually, the Germans welcomed us with gunfire. Thankfully, your friends escorted us out of the situation."

"Please, have a seat. Are you hungry?" Valère asked.

Farrington shook his head. "We're quite well. Thank you, though. I expected your group to be asleep. Everyone seems wide awake for 3:00 AM."

Valère laughed. "I guess you could say we work the night shift. We cannot do much during the day, so that's when we sleep."

Farrington's brow furrowed.

"I know what you're thinking. How will you conduct your reconnaissance at night when you cannot see? Don't worry. We can get you close at dawn. We have a series of safe houses for our movements. We vary our paths each time to keep the Germans guessing. However, we have encountered a problem in the last few weeks."

All the commandos looked up.

"Problem?" Jordan asked.

Valère nodded. "The Germans have moved in troops from an SS Panzer Division. They've been interrogating the locals for information. Especially about us."

"Interrogating?" Colette scoffed. "You mean torturing. Terrorizing. They're murdering people every day!"

Valère swallowed the last bite from his plate. "You must forgive Colette. She is very direct. But it's true. The SS are brutal. They're led by a Major Wertz. We've heard horrific stories. Stories of him drowning people. Beatings. Breaking fingers. It's almost unthinkable."

"We've got to take them out. Kill them all. That's why you're here, right?" Colette asked.

"Not exactly," Farrington said.

"You see, Valère." Colette pointed at him. "I told you. The Allies are taking too long. We cannot stand by and watch our countrymen be executed by the Nazis. You've said it yourself many times. We need to do more. We need to destroy their supplies. Attack their sentries. Offensive actions you call them."

"Calm yourself, Colette." He closed his eyes and slowly nodded. "In due course."

Valère had become the leader of the Caen Maquis group through persuasive speech. He'd worked as a journalist for Jean Prene, an influential resistance leader who the Germans had captured two years before. Prene produced a series of pamphlets in support of the Resistance while bashing Vichy France, which he considered a puppet regime of the Germans. He denounced those in the unoccupied zone that sought political solutions and encouraged those in the occupied zone to take up arms. "France will be liberated by blood, not hot air" was one of his famous sayings.

After Prene's capture, Valère failed to keep the pamphlet in operation once a series of raids by the Germans had resulted in the discovery of their presses. He took to the woods and formed a small band of fighters willing to participate in guerilla warfare. He wooed the fighters with speeches that typically began with

"Jean Prene once said—"

Two other Maquis groups, as well as many stragglers, joined Valère's group, bringing their total to thirty-four. Most of them had the same story. They faced deportation to Germany for forced labor or they were swayed by the teachings of Jean Prene or Valère.

While several women aided the fighters, few lived with them in the cave. Those who did helped the fighters with supplies and intelligence. Colette, however, was a fighter, and one as capable as any man. She agreed with Valère's talks but didn't need any persuasion.

She and her brother François had watched as their Jewish father was dragged from their home and murdered. A German soldier, looking no older than a teenager, shot him at point-blank range with his rifle. The Germans executed their mother at the same time in the same manner for marrying a Jew. The two siblings escaped by hiding in their barn loft and watched helplessly as the Germans set their house on fire but spared the barn. Members of Valère's Maquis discovered them with nothing but the clothes on their backs.

While Colette's brother François was willing to fight with the Maquis, he maintained a numbness and a calm spirit. Colette thirsted for revenge. She wanted nothing less than to kill Germans. Valère continually had to calm her down.

Valère's interest in her was compounded by her striking features. Men turned their heads when she approached. Her long brunette hair, when pulled back into a ponytail, exposed high cheekbones and big brown eyes. She stood a little over five feet but had the strength to handle a Sten gun without much effort. Most men were rendered speechless by her mere presence, and those who dared speak to her were typically put in their place by her sharp tongue. Colette was a woman to be reckoned with.

Jordan, usually a steely-eyed commando, caught himself distracted by Colette a second time since entering the cave.

He broke his stare at Colette and looked to Farrington. "Captain. Looks like we've got some SS to spy on."

THE MAQUIS LED ComDet Sixteen down rocky terrain toward Caen. The breaking dawn provided just enough light to prevent poor foot placement and a tumble down the hill.

François jogged up the path next to his sister. "So, Colette, what do you think of our new heroes . . . these commandos?"

She shrugged. "I don't see what's so special about them. We can fight as well as them. You heard their leader, Farrington. They're not even here to fight. Just spy. We need to eliminate the Germans."

"Ha, ha. Always ready to fight. You need to relax more. Here we are on this leisurely, morning stroll and you are thinking of killing Germans."

Colette rolled her eyes.

François looked over his shoulder and then leaned close to Colette. "I noticed one of them kept staring at you. I think he likes you." He grinned.

She shook her head. "Do you think we're in school? Have you forgotten we are fighters? You need to think more about avenging our parents and less about trivial matters."

"Ah, Colette. Always so serious."

"Maybe you should be more serious. You are too reckless, like Valère. You don't think. You just act."

François repositioned the strap of his Sten gun around his shoulder. "Not me, Colette. I have too much life to live to be serious all the time."

Valère, leading the pack of Maquis and commandos, held

up his hand and dropped to one knee. Everyone behind him followed suit.

With Caen visible in the distance, Valère pointed to a farmhouse four hundred yards away at the end of the line of trees. "Look. Germans," he said to Farrington, who knelt next to him.

Jordan, crouching, approached and joined them. He pulled out his binoculars, mimicking Farrington. "I count twelve, Captain. That and six locals."

"That farm is the Poiriers' place. It's one of our safe houses," Valère said. "They are probably just harassing them. Asking questions."

Farrington took another look through his binoculars. "Those are SS."

"We can go around them. But we better take a closer look to see if any German soldiers are lingering around. They might have a reserve squad nearby," Valère said.

The remaining three commandos and three Maquis joined them.

"Jordan and I are going to take a closer look at that farmhouse. This will be a good chance for a close-up view of an SS unit," Farrington said.

Valère put his hand on François's shoulder. "François will go with you. He can lead you to the Caen rendezvous point. I will take the rest with me and go on ahead. Don't spend much time. It's probably nothing."

Farrington nodded. "OK. Whitfield, you take a position at the end of that hedgerow in case we need you. We'll meet you back here."

Valère, Colette, and another Maquisard started walking away. Jean-Pierre and Cummings of ComDet Sixteen joined them.

Using the cover of a tree line, Farrington, Jordan, and

François moved within sixty yards of the farmhouse and lay on the ground.

The family of six stood next to the barn. Mr. and Mrs. Poirier along with their son and three daughters. They could overhear an officer yelling at them. "You've been harboring the Resistance. Your councilman told us. By order of Major Wertz, you must be executed as an example to other traitors."

The Poirier girls screamed and hugged their mother. The Poirier son charged the officer and met the butt of a German rifle, which knocked him to the ground. He staggered back to his family.

"Please, please don't do this. Kill me, but please spare my family," Mr. Poirier pleaded.

François pushed himself up. "We've got to do something."

Farrington pushed him back down. "Quiet! We're greatly outnumbered. Besides, there may be other units in the area. We have a mission to complete."

"Maybe we can do something, Captain," Jordan said. "We'll surprise them and take out half of them immediately. Whitfield will see what's happening and pick a few off."

Farrington shook his head. "It could jeopardize our entire mission if we're discovered. We need to fall back and join the others."

The Germans pushed the family against the barn and eight soldiers lined up in a firing line.

"They are going to be killed!" Francois said.

Jordan pointed toward the barn. "It's not even ten-to-one. It's three-to-one. We can—"

"I said 'no,' Nick. We don't know if there are other units nearby. There may be more in the house. We cannot even see what's on the other side of the house."

Jordan nodded. "Yes, sir."

The execution squad lifted their rifles.

Mrs. Poirier shielded her daughters as her son stood defiant-ly with arms folded.

François stood up and ran toward the farmhouse.

"Damn him!" Farrington said.

Within seconds the Germans noticed François on a dead run toward the barn. The Germans swung their rifles toward him and began firing. Dirt flew up near his feet. François raised his Sten gun and fired at them. One German, hit in the shoulder, yelped and fell down. The Poirier girls screamed as their father pushed them into the barn.

The German on the end of the firing line fell straight back, suffering a bullet in the forehead from Whitfield's Springfield rifle.

Jordan leaned up, looking at Farrington for direction.

Farrington shook his head, stood, and took off toward the farmhouse, Jordan on his heels.

François reached an outbuilding, which protected him from further fire.

Farrington and Jordan unloaded the magazines of their Thompson machine guns. Three more Germans fell, one from Whitfield's rifle and two from Jordan's fire. They reached the outbuilding and slammed against the wall next to François.

"What's the plan?" François asked.

Farrington looked at him, incredulously. "There's no bloody plan, you fool."

Jordan leaned around the outbuilding and fired only to be met with more firepower from the Germans. "We can't stay here," he said.

Crack! Whitfield fired again.

"Keep firing from there, Nick. We're going to work our way around. We'll try to pick them off at the ends and work toward the center. It's our only chance. Follow me, François."

"Halt!"

They had moved three steps before encountering six German rifles—the Germans who were inside. Eight more Germans came out of the other end of the house toward Jordan. The two commandos and one Maquisard lowered their weapons.

THE GERMANS LOADED Farrington, Jordan, and François into the back of a truck—hands tied behind their backs. Jordan looked back to see the Poirier family once again lined up in front of the barn. As the truck drove away, several shots rang out.

Jordan's face reddened. *Bastards!*

ELEVEN

JORDAN'S HEAD ACHED from repeated punches, though he was more concerned about potentially broken ribs than the taste of blood in his mouth. He looked over at François. Jordan had assumed the kid couldn't handle the rough treatment of Major Wertz and his thugs, but François proved himself much tougher than his carefree demeanor suggested. François's spitting in one of the guard's faces earned him a pistol butt to the side of his head that sent him tumbling to the floor in his chair. As the guards picked him up, he looked at a painting on the wall and smiled.

Farrington sat stoically.

"We know the Allies are coming, but I want to know exactly when and where. You will be providing me this information," Wertz said as he looked out the window. "I'm quite confident you will."

Farrington smiled, awkwardly due to a swollen lip. "I doubt it, Major."

Wertz turned his head toward Farrington. "You doubt it? Of course, we know the Allies will invade."

Farrington slowly shook his head. "No. I mean that I doubt any of us will tell you this information. Even if we knew it, we wouldn't be giving you any of it."

Jordan smiled and nodded at Farrington's defiance. Wertz had already had a round of one-on-one interrogations with each of them. Bringing the three prisoners into the same room must have meant the other interrogation failed. The three all sat in wooden chairs, hands tied behind their backs as well as to the chairs. They formed a triangle with Wertz in the middle going back and forth among them. Two guards remained in the room, seemingly exhausted from the work of handling and beating prisoners. They both carried sidearms.

Jordan thought he had contributed to their predicament. His second-guessing of Farrington might have encouraged François to take off and help the Poirier family. How could this highly trained commando team have been captured so easily? Inexperience was the real answer. Compassion another. Neither excused the team from putting themselves in that position, and Jordan had no intention of wallowing in self-doubt. He surveyed his options.

Wertz pulled a handkerchief from his pocket and wiped his brow. Despite the chilly November day, the stove heater warmed the room and a window with curtains drawn back brought in the afternoon sun. Jordan noticed a worker across the street perched on the top step of a ladder. Two doors led into the room. One to the hallway and one that he presumed led to another office. Wertz had gone in and out of the door a few times. Jordan's bindings were tied tightly to the chair, but he managed to loosen them around his wrists.

Wertz paced, seeming to consider his next move. The three captured men had given him nothing.

"Go get my instruments," Wertz said to one of the guards.

The guard rolled in a cart, parked it in the middle of the room, and pulled back a towel that covered the top. The brute use for the hammer and pliers was evident, but the smaller elements had a more mysterious, surgical nature.

WHITFIELD HAD MANAGED to evade capture. In the confusion at the Poirier family farm, the Germans failed to spot Whitfield before he had picked off three of their firing squad. A few Germans chased him in the woods but gave up after a quarter of a mile.

Whitfield had referenced his cloth map and made his way to the rendezvous point to meet up with Valère and his two fellow commandos: Sergeant Ian Cummings and the French officer Jean-Pierre.

Whitfield updated them on the events at the farm.

Valère turned from the group and threw up his hands. "That fool! I knew he would cause trouble." He turned back. "You see, Colette. You see the problem he's caused."

Colette shook her head, void of answers for her brother's behavior.

No one doubted François's bravery for trying to save the Poirier family, but the consensus among the fighters was that some battles were better left for another day. François had put the commandos in a dangerous position, jeopardized their mission, and threatened to cause the Allies to distrust the Maquis.

Jean-Pierre put his hand on Valère's shoulder. "Do you know where they might have taken them?"

Valère nodded. "City Hall. High-value prisoners are taken there for interrogation by Major Wertz."

Colette stepped toward them. "Yes. They will be there. We must rescue them. We must go now."

"What do you suggest, Colette? We just run in there shooting like François?" Valère swiped his hand at her in a dismissive tone.

"Perhaps we run in there without shooting," Jean-Pierre said.

"What do you have in mind?" Valère asked.

Jean-Pierre looked at Whitfield and smiled. "Looks like we need a diversion so we can snatch some chickens."

Valère, Colette, and the other Maquisard looked at one another confused by the chicken remark.

"Valère, can one of your men get into town and confirm their location?" Jean-Pierre asked.

"Yes, no problem. The shop across from the mayor's office is a friend's. We can climb up a ladder pretending to be fixing the roof and see right into the interrogation room. That Major Wertz is very cavalier. He wants everyone to know that he's torturing people."

Valère further explained the intelligence they had collected over the past few weeks. The SS, in their arrogance, left City Hall lightly guarded. They assumed the small bands of Maquis would never try to sabotage or infiltrate them.

Valère and Jean-Pierre planned to set off a bomb in the center of town and fire shots in the air hoping to draw the small unit at City Hall toward the scene.

Whitfield rubbed his hands together and then slapped Cummings on the back. "Well, Cummings, looks like you can use your skills for something other than pranks with flour."

Cummings replied with a smirk.

WERTZ PICKED UP each of his torture instruments, one at a time, and waved them in front of the three prisoners.

In his chair, François, exhausted from the day of beatings, let his head hang.

The commandos fared better. They'd experienced Major Tunstall's POW briefings and his cardinal rules. The first, and most important, involved constant escape planning. That thought process forced prisoners to work together and depend on one another. In addition, they'd keep their minds sharp and focused on when they'd be free. The second was to hold out as long as possible. Make the enemy exhaust themselves to get the slightest bit of information. The third rule was more of a suggestion: hold onto whatever faith you have. "I believe in the Almighty and will hold on to that until my dying day," he'd say.

Wertz moved behind Farrington. Then he looked at Jordan. "What do you think, Lieutenant? Will your captain here tell me what I want to know?"

Farrington looked at Jordan and very slightly shook his head.

"I think the answer to that question is 'no,' Major," Jordan grinned.

"You know what, Lieutenant? I think you are correct." Wertz grinned back.

Wertz took two steps away, unsnapped his holster, pulled out his Luger pistol, and fired at Farrington's head.

The captain's blood and gray matter sprayed Jordan's face. Farrington slumped in his chair with a large hole on the left side of his head.

"Nooo!" François screamed, his eyes widened.

Jordan turned his head, away from Wertz, hiding his grimace.

The seminal moment in Jordan's life had just occurred. This was no struggle on the gridiron. He was a long way from Yale. This was life and death. Farrington's blood covered Jordan's clothing. His right ear was ringing. His decision to become a commando had never been more serious than this. A normal person might descend into shock. Curl up into a fetal position. Beg for their life. But Nick Jordan was no ordinary person.

His next action was not the result of denial or a lack of

remorse. It was one of survival and the perseverance to finish the mission.

He turned his head back toward Wertz. "Well, Major, I guess you better shoot me because I'm not telling you anything either."

Wertz smiled. "Why, yes, I believe you. I do believe you are willing to die rather than give me this simple information. But, are you willing for him to die?" Wertz pointed his Luger at François.

Jordan didn't look at François and maintained a cold stare at Wertz.

François shook his head vigorously. He shuffled his feet, moving himself and the chair several inches. One of the German guards braced his body against the chair and stopped the movement.

Positioning himself next to François, Wertz rested the Luger's barrel at François's head.

François squeezed his eyes shut.

Wertz looked at Jordan. "Your thoughts, Lieutenant. Is it worth this French pig's life?"

Jordan's face showed no emotion and he gave no reply.

Wertz lowered the Luger and fired into François's thigh.

"Ahhh!" François screamed. His body's reaction caused the chair to lift, and he fell to the side. Blood oozed from the wound.

Wertz, maniacal, lifted his hands in the air. "We're having fun now, eh, Lieutenant?"

Boom!

The noise caused everyone in the room to turn their heads toward the window. Wertz and the guards rushed to get a better look. Jordan extended his neck and saw a ball of smoke behind the buildings across the street.

"You stay here and watch them," Wertz said to one of the guards. He pointed at the other. "Come with me." They darted out of the room.

Jordan, one guard, and the wounded François remained.

The boom's distraction had given Jordan the opportunity to pull his right hand free of his bindings. His left hand remained tied to the chair.

"Ahhh." François's groaning continued. Blood covered his pants and the floor under his thigh.

Jordan engaged the guard in German. "Why don't you help him? Wrap his wound or something."

"Shut your mouth! No talking!" The guard turned back to the window and looked at the commotion.

"He's going to die!" Jordan said.

The guard turned back toward Jordan. "Why do I care what happens to this French pig?"

"Don't you see? If the major wanted him dead, he'd have shot him in the head. He knows he has valuable information. If he dies, you'll be the one in trouble with the major."

"Shut up," the guard said. "You're trying to trick me."

Jordan shook his head. "No, no. Please. I'm just trying to help. You know the major needs him alive."

The guard looked at François. He threw his hands in the air in frustration and grabbed the towel that had covered the torture tray. He knelt and began wrapping it around François's thigh.

Jordan jumped up, lifting the wooden chair over his left shoulder. He grasped one of the chair legs with his right hand and brought it down on the German guard. The chair broke apart, leaving pieces attached to Jordan. He picked up one loose chair leg.

The guard attempted to get on his feet but Jordan stomped down on his neck and delivered multiple blows. Blood splattered on the ceiling and walls as Jordan whaled away with three blows beyond what was necessary.

Jordan stopped and stood over the unconscious guard. He breathed heavily—eyes widened. His arms hung at his side.

François looked up. "Help me."

Jordan grabbed a knife from the instrument tray, cut himself loose of the chair pieces, and then freed François's hands. He picked up the towel and finished wrapping the wound.

"We've got to get out of this building and then we'll fix you up. OK?"

François nodded.

Jordan took the guard's sidearm and stuffed it into the back of his pants. He reached down and pulled François to his feet.

François put his arm around him, his wounded leg doing little more than dragging behind as they exited the room.

Jordan paused at the doorway and looked back at Farrington, almost unrecognizable. He regretted having no time for mourning.

The Germans had made the mistake of bringing the prisoners into the building without blindfolds. Jordan knew exactly where he was and where he needed to exit. Where they'd go after that was less certain.

As they moved down the hallway, a secretary coming from another office bumped into them.

"Ahhh!" she screamed and ran back into her office, slamming the door shut.

Jordan and François found the stairwell at the end of the building. François had trouble on the first two steps. Jordan lifted him over his left shoulder to carry him and pulled the Luger from his pants—gun at the ready.

At the bottom of the stairwell, two SS troops ran by them to the doorway and quickly turned back, astonished at the sight of an American commando with a man on his back. One of them lifted his rifle only to be met by two bullets in the chest from

Jordan's Luger. The other German received one bullet in the forehead.

Several people ran down the street as other gunshots echoed, masking the shots Jordan fired. He brought François back to his feet and propped him up against the wall. Jordan leaned out of the doorway and looked left and right. "We can't go that way."

They moved toward the building's rear and Jordan opened the door to the back alley.

A man and woman burst into the building.

Jordan put his Luger to the woman's forehead.

"François! What happened?" Colette reached for him.

Jordan dropped his head and lowered the Luger to his side. He looked back up. "He's been shot. He's lost a lot of blood."

Colette touched her brother's head. "François, what happened?"

Valère had entered the building with Colette. "Come, we must move quickly. Where's your captain?"

Jordan shook his head. "He won't be coming with us."

Valère looked him up and down. "You don't look so good."

Valère positioned François between himself and Colette. "Come, Lieutenant. We have a truck to get us out of town."

The three Maquis and Jordan meandered through alleys to be met by a short, older man with a long white mustache.

He pulled back the tarp covering the truck bed. "Quickly, in here."

After loading François, Jordan and the others crawled under the tarp held up by several boxes. Already sitting beneath it were Jean-Pierre, Cummings, and Whitfield.

"Geez, Lieutenant, you look like hell," Whitfield said.

Wertz's interrogation had left a cut over Jordan's right eye and several bruises. He thought he might have some broken ribs. The strain of the day's activities showed on his face. "I feel like hell. But François is worse."

Jean-Pierre had already begun looking at the wound under the light of Cummings's flashlight. The collapsing tarp gave them good cover with which to make their way out of town but made battlefield dressing difficult.

François's eyes rolled back, and he passed out.

"François! Wake up!" Colette shouted.

Valère grabbed a frantic Colette. "Calm down. You must be quiet."

As the truck pulled out, Cummings looked to the back of the truck. "What about the captain? Where is he?"

"He's gone," Jordan said. He dropped his head. "That Nazi bastard shot him, point-blank."

"Who?" Jean-Pierre asked. "What bastard?"

Jordan looked up. "Wertz. Major Wertz. And I'm going to kill him."

TWELVE

HAMLET OF MOLIERE
NEAR CAEN, FRANCE

COLETTE HELD FRANÇOIS'S hand as blood drenched the white sheets. Jean-Pierre's tourniquet failed to hold off the nicked blood vessel of the femoral artery. Sulfa powder and field dressings tied around the leg did little to save François. He needed a surgeon.

The shot of morphine eased his agony. He continued to perspire. His respiration decreased as his pulse quickened.

François looked over to his sister. "I'm sorry. Tell Mama and Papa I'm sorry." He turned and stared at the ceiling. "Where are they, Colette?"

"Who, François?"

"Mama and Papa."

Colette sobbed, empty of a response to his delirious ramblings.

The bed François lay in belonged to Mr. and Mrs. Frère. Their dairy farm was nine miles east of Caen next to the hamlet of Molière. Aside from weeds growing around the wreckage of a British bomber, the unassuming village seemed untouched by the twentieth century. Horses and wagons parked in front of stone buildings. No children played in the streets. Men and women with graying hair went about their daily activities. Most of the men, like Mr. Frère, had served France in the previous war. Everything moved a little slower in Molière. As such, the Germans never bothered the residents, assuming them uninvolved in the war.

In reality, the men and women of Molière had harbored and supplied the Maquis for years. Some of the men occasionally joined them on their missions, offering their experience as veterans of long-ago battlegrounds such as Lorraine and Verdun. Those farmers with pitchforks were actually shrewd participants in the Resistance.

Mr. Frère dragged large branches behind his team of horses to cover the tire tracks where the truck carrying the commandos had left the gravel road and headed toward concealment in the barn. Tall trees that his grandfather planted in the previous century lined the farm.

Mrs. Frère sat at François's bedside cooling his forehead with a damp towel and shook her head at his grave wounds. "Rest easy, son. Just try to rest."

François grunted and his back rose off the bed. His face turned white as his body lowered. His eyes rolled back and then closed. His head turned slightly to the right toward Colette. No more movement. No life.

"Noooo!" Colette collapsed onto his chest, sobbing.

Mrs. Frère cupped her hands over her mouth and shook her head. She placed a hand on Colette's shoulder. "I'm so sorry, child."

MR. FRÈRE WALKED into the barn where the four commandos and other Maquis rested, eating cheese and bread. "I'm afraid our friend, François, is no more."

Valère threw his food down. "It's his own fault. His recklessness."

"No. It's only one person's fault. The same person who's at fault for Farrington's death—Major Wertz." Jordan stood, agitated, one hand holding his ribs, sore from the repeated blows by Wertz's thugs. His unshaven face and drooping eyelids showed his exhaustion and sleep deprivation.

Jean-Pierre stood, placing his hands on Jordan's shoulders. "Sit down, Lieutenant. Nothing we can do today. This isn't exactly how we planned to gain the information we needed, but I'd say we've learned some valuable intelligence. We should rest here tonight and then make way for our link-up with the plane in the morning."

Jordan nodded. "I know, Jean-Pierre. I know we can't go in guns blazing. But he's terrorized these people. We need to do something to rid France of these Nazis. To kill those like Wertz. The Allies can't wait forever to invade."

"Please, Lieutenant. Please, sit." Mr. Frère pointed to the box Jordan had been sitting on.

Jordan sipped water from his cup and chewed on a piece of hard bread.

"There are many ways to resist the German horde. Many ways to fight them." Mr. Frère sat on another box near Jordan as the men in the barn all looked his way. "We've been at this game a few years. Our resistance is strong because we've picked our battles. Some of them big and some of them small. Our little village focuses on the small ones. When the German soldiers stop in our village and demand bread, the baker asks if they've heard the rumor that Hitler is a homosexual. This upsets them. While they're distracted, his wife pours sugar into their gas tank. These things seem like nothing, but we hope they weaken morale among the Germans."

Mr. Frère picked up a piece of straw and chewed.

"Our main efforts are in supporting the Maquis. We make

sure Valère gets the most accurate information about the Germans' activities. We provide food and other provisions as we can. While in town, I managed to steal four boxes of vegetables while the German guards were distracted by a pretty young lady who helps me with this sort of thing. Our greatest work lies in communications. My neighbor, Mr. Montague, is a good black-smith. But his radio skills are excellent. He hides his equipment in a false wall in his shop. So you see, we don't do much, but we do what we can."

"Mr. Frère is too humble," Valère said. "The truth is, we couldn't do half of what we do without their support. And we've learned a lot from these soldiers of long ago."

Mr. Frère gave Valère a thankful nod.

"Mr. Frère, thank you for helping us." Jordan looked at the other commandos. "We better get a few hours' sleep. As soon as it's dark, we'll head toward our exfiltration spot."

Bang!

The barn door swung open. Colette rushed in. "Where is he?" She pointed at Jordan. "You did this. You stupid Allies killed my brother. He'd still be alive if you hadn't dropped from the sky."

She raised a hand to slap Jordan but Valère caught her arm. "Stop this, Colette. It's not his fault."

She lowered her head into Valère's chest and sobbed.

Jordan stood and made a step toward Colette, seeking reconciliation.

Jean-Pierre placed his hand on Jordan's arm and shook his head. "Leave it."

THE MEMBERS OF ComDet Sixteen, now numbered at four with the loss of Farrington, concealed themselves behind a hedgerow.

As dawn approached, they heard nothing but the sound of trees swaying in the breeze.

The road leading to the abandoned power plant remained still and silent. Their ride home would soon land. Although the act of boarding a plane seemed simple, Major Tunstall drilled them on every contingency.

"We cannot prepare you for everything that will go wrong, and I assure you something will go wrong, but we can prepare you for as many things as possible," he said.

They had practiced the extraction seventeen times. In some instances, there'd be no problems, but in others, they trained as if Farrington and Jordan were injured and had to be carried. Sometimes they experienced gunfire or simulated mortars. The plane might stop or keep the wheels rolling. Tunstall might walk up and say, "The pilot's dead. Now, what do you do?"

Most likely, no Germans would be in the immediate area, and they'd be picked up without incident. Their mission had already endured several contingencies.

Whitfield broke the silence. "Almost home, boys."

Jean-Pierre looked left and right. "Yes, it should be here any minute."

An open-top vehicle and a following truck rambled down the road that intersected with the makeshift runway. Gravel and dust left a trail.

"Shhh!" Jordan motioned down with his arms. "Everyone quiet. Let's hope they get far enough away before they hear the plane."

All four commandos knelt as the two-vehicle convoy rolled past them. An officer in the front car looked toward the power plant construction and held up his arm. The car and truck skidded to a stop. The officer stepped out and peered through binoculars. After a few seconds, he stepped back into the vehicle and raised his hand to signal the driver to proceed.

The whirring of an aircraft gave him pause. The plane appeared in the distance; the German officer trained his binoculars on it.

"Everyone out!"

Twelve German soldiers jumped from the back of the truck and assembled. Two of them set up a machine gun on a bipod.

"We've only got a minute," Jordan whispered. "Whitfield. In forty-five seconds, take out that officer and then work down the line. Jean-Pierre, you shoot anyone who gets on the machine gun. Cummings, you're with me. We're getting close enough to lob grenades. We have no choice. We take them all out, or they'll take out that plane when it lands."

Jordan and Cummings ran down the hedgerow toward the enemy. The Germans made enough noise in their preparations to mask the noise of the commandos.

Whitfield laid his rifle on a log and relaxed his breathing.

Jean-Pierre pushed his Thompson machine gun through the brush and looked through a small opening.

The plane made a slight turn in the air and lined up to the road that would serve as a landing strip.

At forty-five seconds, the bullet from Whitfield's rifle passed through the German officer's head. His knees buckled and he dropped straight to the ground. His fellow soldiers looked at him, frozen in shock, except for the two who turned toward the gunfire.

Two grenades flew through the air and landed in the middle of the group, followed seconds later by two more. The detonation caused the Germans to break apart—leaving three dead. Five more immediately met their fate from the commandos. Within seconds, the remaining Germans lay dead or dying.

Cummings ran over and offered a *coup de grâce* to those still breathing.

The team searched the dead for papers or anything of significance.

Jordan approached the opposite side of the parked vehicles and swept for any remaining threat. Finding none, he inspected the contents of the car and removed a small leather pouch.

The plane landed and turned 180 degrees at the edge of the road. A door dropped down and the commandos hopped on board as the wheels continued to slowly roll. Within moments, ComDet Sixteen was airborne.

THIRTEEN

CAMP DELTA
ALDINE, ENGLAND
November 1943

COMDET SIXTEEN FARED well after three days of walking, running, fighting, and little sleep—and, in Nick Jordan's case, enduring a torture session. Their extensive training had served them well. The doctor told Jordan that his bruised ribs would heal in a few weeks. Food and sleep helped restore his body's other needs.

However, the loss of Farrington left a gaping hole in their team. In a few weeks, his family would receive a letter from Major Tunstall outlining his bravery and sacrifice for his country. Jordan wanted to write the letter and tell his wife how Farrington honored his country. To tell his children that their father died with honor and valor. That he vowed to meet them one day and share how bravely their father had acted.

He told Tunstall of his plans.

"You can't make those kinds of promises, Jordan. You don't know that you'll survive to carry out that pledge. I know it sounds heartless, but they'll receive my standard letter. That's the way it has to be." Tunstall said.

Putting his feelings for Farrington's family aside, Jordan ran through the mission in his head several times as he analyzed his mistakes and took full responsibility for his part in Farrington's death. His debrief to Tunstall and Styles outlined an operation that for the most part succeeded, but also had its flaws.

"Well, I guess the Jerrys have been introduced to our ComDet teams," Major Tunstall said.

Styles scoffed. "Yes, but did that introduction give them more information than we wanted them to have?"

"I don't think so," Jordan said. "I'm sure they know we weren't regular army. They probably know we were highly trained. But we never gave them any indication about our numbers or our mission. Based on Wertz's interrogation, I believe he was more worried about the Allied invasion."

Styles folded his arms. "And what did he want to know about that?"

"They know it's coming, but they don't know when and where," Jordan said. "I don't suppose you sirs know that?"

"In a moment, Jordan," Tunstall said.

"Well, he beat the hell out of us for that information and was about to introduce us to some more medieval forms of information extraction. I guess he got impatient. That's when he shot Farrington."

Tunstall lightly banged his fist on the desk. "Regrettable. Highly regrettable, but that confirms our other intelligence. The Jerrys have no idea where we'll invade. They'll probably continue to beef up forces in cities like Caen and across the coast of the English Channel."

"Tell us about the Resistance," Styles said.

Jordan rearranged himself in his chair, grimacing and touching his side. "They're vital to our success. They know the terrain and are highly motivated. They're a wealth of information about the Krauts' movements. Their operations are sporadic. Hit-and-run missions. They disrupt and aggravate the Krauts in many ingenious ways. Blow their stores and disrupt rail traffic.

But they're also undisciplined. Hence, the incident that got us captured. We—"

Tunstall interrupted. "Yes, that was unfortunate. You and Farrington should have left the young Frenchman to his decision. However, we have to look at the positive. It put you inside an SS unit and you gained actionable intelligence. It wasn't exactly how we'd draw it up on paper, but that's war. From what I read in the after-action report, your firefight at the airstrip was textbook. You can focus on that if you like. That little pouch of papers you collected shows German defenses along the coast. It's already been sent to the supreme commander's headquarters."

"Back to our French friends," Styles said. "How do you feel about our ComDet teams working with them?"

"We need to go in early and train them. Give them that tactical discipline. Valère isn't exactly a military leader, but we can work with them. We can learn a lot from each other. They may lack unit discipline and have a haphazard chain of command. But they know every nook and cranny around Caen." Jordan pointed at the large map of Caen on the wall.

"That's the spirit, Lieutenant." Styles stood up and flipped a chalkboard around. "Operation Overlord" was written across the top with several dates and action items. Next to "May 1944" was the word "Normandy." "As you can see, the plan for the long-awaited invasion is well underway. You can imagine how badly they'll want to hold Caen."

Jordan mouthed the word "Normandy."

Tunstall approached the board. "Caen's vital roadways make that city one we'll need and one the Jerrys will fight to the death to keep. Our invasion forces will land by sea, preceded by paratroopers and glider forces. Your mission will be to distract and pull the Jerrys away from Caen. In essence, ComDet Sixteen will serve as a diversion and delaying force. You'll use the Maquis as a force multiplier and conduct quick-strike missions to keep them wondering from where the next attack will come. Thousands of paratroopers will drop further inland. Like you, they'll keep the Jerrys from throwing all they have at the beach. That'll give those chaps the chance to get on shore and establish the beachhead."

"I don't even want to think about this not working," Jordan said.

"It'll work. It must. It might even end the war by Christmas."

Jordan nodded. "I like the sound of that."

"Your fellow ComDet teams will be doing the same all over France. Unlike your last mission, this will carry more of the intent of Operation Wolfhound. You'll have freedom to eliminate any Nazis that threaten your mission. It's not like you'll have facilities for prisoners anyway."

"No prisoners, eh?" Jordan asked.

Styles leaned in. "We're not saying this to be ruthless, Jordan. We're talking in practicalities. You have a seek-and-kill mission. Hopefully, any enemy you fight will be dead before they have the chance to surrender."

Tunstall cleared his throat. "I'm not going to lie to you, Nick, there's no plan for exfiltration. Until your team is relieved by the invasion force, you'll be on your own. You up for the task?"

"Absolutely, Major. When do we leave?"

"Early April. Right now Operation Fortitude is in effect to deceive the Jerrys on when and where the invasion will take place. We're forcing them to consider invasions from nearly every point other than the East. This includes an invasion via Scandinavia. Other leaked invasion points are the Pas-de-Calais in Northern France, the coast of Belgium, and from the southeast through the Balkans. In addition, we have false intelligence reports, artificial radio traffic, and fake troop movements."

Tunstall tapped the board with a pointer. "Since the

Pas-de-Calais is the most obvious choice for an invasion point, we have the greatest amount of deception there. The Jerrys consider General George Patton the most capable field commander in the Allied arsenal and he has movements to areas of England where he is supposedly marshaling an invading force. The Allies have even constructed a false army of rubber tanks and dummy paratroopers and are conducting pre-invasion bombing and running commando raids to keep the Jerrys' attention there.

"Obviously, your team carries a great risk of capture. Your team will endure interrogation, torture, God knows what. But, you'll each have to resist until you absolutely reach your breaking point. Then, under extreme duress, you'll each reveal the invasion plans for the Pas-de-Calais. That's the answer they'll beat the hell out of you to get. Not Normandy. It cannot even enter you mind. Is that understood?"

Jordan nodded. "Absolutely."

"We'll nail down your departure date as we get closer. Until then, your team will prepare. Since you'll be dressing, eating, and living with the Maquis, you'll train as such. We have a railroad expert coming in that will show you how to best disable rail traffic. And I think your team needs more work with explosives. Lots in store for you. That's all for now."

Jordan stood and headed for the door.

Styles whispered to Tunstall.

"Ah, yes. Hold up, Jordan." Tunstall walked over to Jordan while reaching into his pocket. "These are captain's bars, courtesy of your American command. Congratulations!"

"Thank you, Major . . . I guess," Jordan said with an ambivalent grin. Although a high achiever, he'd always eschewed the trophy. The victory he enjoyed for victory's sake. But he didn't brag. He certainly didn't need medals on his chest or increased rank on his collar. He never had aspirations to be a general. He wanted to do his duty and know that he'd served with honor.

Tunstall put his hand on Jordan's shoulder. "I think you've beat yourself up sufficiently about the mission. Use it to train. To learn. But no more feelings of sorrow. No time for that." Tunstall turned to walk away but looked back. "And, eh, Captain. I've also assigned Lieutenant Dick Moody to your team. He'll serve as your number two in command."

Jordan folded his arms. "Moody? Don't get me wrong, Major. I like Moody and he's a solid commando. But what about Jean-Pierre?"

Tunstall shook his head. "I think we both know Jean-Pierre's not up to the task. Oh, he's got the experience, but he's not much for issuing orders. Moody will do just fine."

DICK MOODY SAVED his first life in 1940 as a Santa Monica lifeguard. He'd grown up near the beach and spent his childhood summers swimming in the Pacific Ocean. His mother would tell friends that he was "part fish." He quickly grew a reputation as a ladies' man at not only the beach but at UCLA as well. Blond locks topped his Adonis-like physique shaped by years of sit-ups, pushups, and pull-ups. He was tailor-made for Hollywood, only a short drive away.

The war interrupted his social career, as he volunteered for army officer training. While he outperformed his peers physically and mentally, a certain Captain Brand had paid him a visit and asked if he'd be interested in elite forces. Moody said "yes" within seconds.

He arrived at Camp Delta four months after Jordan. His original ComDet team had lost two members in training accidents: one from a failed parachute and one from the mishandling of explosives. Tunstall had since used their remaining members to fill other teams. Moody's placement took some time, as the groupings of ComDet teams were a delicate balance.

His French was passable, but he carried a heavy American accent. He complained of the French language's inefficiencies, such as assigning nouns with a masculine or feminine gender. However, once he learned that his female classmates enjoyed his using the language, he studied it with gusto. During commando training, he excelled in marksmanship and won his fair share of hand-to-hand contests in the circle. Unlike Jordan, and in particular Farrington, Moody didn't believe in repetitive training. He wanted to train at something one time and move on. He felt combat carried too many variables. Those too fixed in their ways were hindered from handling battlefield adjustments naturally. This was all theory for him since he'd never experienced combat.

Moody stepped into the ComDet Sixteen shack to the silent stares of Jordan, Jean-Pierre, Cummings, and Whitfield. Each ComDet team was notoriously tight-knit and their shack was off-limits to outsiders. They all knew Moody, but he wasn't family.

Jordan stood and extended his hand. "Welcome aboard, Dick. You can bunk over there."

Moody placed his gear on Farrington's bunk.

The remaining commandos walked over and offered a handshake. Cummings and Whitfield each offered a "sir" with a head nod.

Although ComDet teams operated on proper relations and order between officer and enlisted, an experienced commando held unofficial superiority over someone with less time in. Moody was an officer but the most junior commando. There'd be a time of initiation before he'd earn the respect of the others. He was a commando, but his full-fledged membership in ComDet Sixteen had yet to be solidified.

NEAR CAEN, FRANCE

Major Wertz knelt and picked up the .45 bullet casing, rolling it between his fingers. "Any survivors?"

"No, Major." The German soldier looked around helplessly at the dead bodies near the abandoned power plant. "Those French pigs. They've slaughtered our brothers."

The French countryside stood seemingly still and peaceful except for the immediate area around Wertz. In front of him, a dead soldier's wide-open eyes stared back. Blood soaked into the dirt next to the body. One of Wertz's men covered his mouth and nose from the stench. Drag marks followed one of the dead into a pit as if he'd attempted to crawl away from the scene.

Wertz stood. "This is not the work of the Maquis. It's those Allied troops. The same ones we had in custody. They were very well trained. Willing to die, even under torture."

"Major!" Lieutenant Bader, a junior officer serving under Wertz, waved from the road leading to the power plant. "Look." He pointed at tracks on the ground. "I recognize this. These are from an aircraft."

German troops searched the nearby hedgerows and found numerous bullet casings from a Thompson machine gun.

Two German soldiers whispered.

"What are you two saying?" Wertz barked.

"That they're here. The Allies have invaded," one of them said.

"No." Wertz looked in the distance toward the direction of the English Channel. "When the Allies invade, it will be hell. This is nothing. This is the work of a few annoying flies. They are nothing. But they didn't do this alone. They had help from the Maquis."

Soldiers began loading dead bodies onto the truck.

"Bader!" Wertz yelled. He rubbed the scars on his neck. "Count the dead. Then go into that village up the road and execute twice that many French pigs."

Bader cocked his head. "You think the Maquis are there?"

"Doesn't matter." Wertz shrugged. "I really don't care if they helped the Allies or not. We need to make an example. You murder our German brothers, and two French pigs will die for each one of ours."

"But, Major. Shouldn't we question them and try to understand what happened?"

Wertz grabbed the lieutenant's lapel and spoke in a slow, robotic tone. "I don't need to question them. I don't care what they think. I just want them dead."

THE GERMANS SPARED Mr. and Mrs. Frère for no other reason than they had already dragged enough Molière citizens from their homes to satisfy Wertz's order. The Frères's neighbors of twenty-two years were shot in front of their home. They'd already given two boys to France and now the entire family was gone—vanished in the wake of the German occupation.

Once the soldiers had walked along the bodies and fired shots into the heads of those still moving, several of them lit cigarettes as if they were on a break from factory work. A lanky man with gray hair lay atop his wife as if he had attempted to protect her. Pockmarks littered the stone wall where the victims had been lined up for execution.

A door slammed in the distance. Faces peeked out of the windows but no one dared venture outside.

"Perhaps I should get my Lebel," Mr. Frère said, stepping out of the closet they'd gone in for cover. Two years prior, the Germans moved house to house confiscating weapons. The Lebel rifle he had carried in the previous war had remained carefully hidden in a part of the outhouse where the Germans chose to avoid searching.

Mrs. Frère poked her head out of the closet. "And what would you have done?"

"I would first shoot that one," he said, pointing at the German officer who had ordered the executions.

"And then what?"

He pointed at a German soldier slinging his rifle over his shoulder. "And then, I'd shoot that one. And the next. And the—"

"And then you would be killed, and me, and our other neighbors who are still alive. When does it end?"

Mr. Frère walked away from the window and back toward the closet. "It ends when the Germans are all dead or run back to Germany with their tails between their legs. And some of us may need to die for that to happen. Why not me?"

Tears welled up in her eyes. "Why not you? Because you're all I have. Ever since our daughter met that Jewish boy and moved away. You've heard about the work camps. They might have taken both of them away. And our grandchild."

An engine roared to life.

Lieutenant Bader ordered his soldiers to mount their vehicles. He stood in his car and turned toward seemingly empty buildings, though cries could be heard from within their walls. "You French pigs listen to me. Tell your friends that hide in the woods like cowards that this is what happens when you do not obey orders. Tell them this is what happens when they help the Allies. Next time, it will be you that pays the price." He turned, sat in his seat, and waved his arm forward. "Drive."

Mr. Frère turned back toward the window. "I don't know about our daughter or grandchild. I do know one thing. We must fight. We must fight in any way we can. And that is exactly what I intend to do."

FOURTEEN

A MIDDLE-AGED WOMAN, named Marie, operated a local eatery called Le Café de Patrice. Rumor had it that her lover, Patrice, left for war in 1915 and never returned. She had never married. Marie always seemed tired but offered a smile to every patron in her establishment. The café sat on a corner of a busy street, opened at the same time every morning, and closed at the same time every evening. The same pudgy businessman in a three-piece suit sat in the same corner drinking the same cappuccino that he did every day. The same dairyman dropped off fresh milk every morning. Even in war, certain routines continued.

The café seated up to thirty at its nine tables with two more tables on the front walkway. Since the war began, she rarely had a full crowd. Cracks adorned the walls, but Marie kept the place clean. She lived alone in the flat over the café. It was her life.

She despised serving German soldiers but had no choice. Sometimes they paid; sometimes they didn't. She fantasized about slapping them or poisoning them but restrained herself, realizing that it would do no good. She hated Major Wertz—a frequent patron. His Nazi fervor was bad enough, but his smugness and disgusting advances offended her even more. She'd smile at him, turn, and then roll her eyes.

The beautiful young woman sitting near the pudgy businessman would certainly draw Wertz's attention. Her bright, red lipstick left smudges on her coffee cup. She sat with her crossed legs in view of others and her dress pulled just above the knee.

Marie shook her head. *What is she thinking, dressed like that? She is asking for trouble.*

Colette sat in the corner of Le Café de Patrice, sipping coffee, for the fourth day in a row. As opposed to her normal Maquis attire of long pants, Sten, and ponytail, she wore a floral dress, hair down, and gently applied makeup, along with striking red lipstick. She read from Alexandre Dumas's *The Count of Monte Cristo*—a tale of betrayal and revenge.

Six months had passed since her brother François had died, and vengeance had consumed her ever since, intensifying her thirst for righting the Germans' wrongs, which had existed since she witnessed the murder of her parents for the crime of being Jewish. She envisioned a specific plot for revenge, and she wanted the man who killed François—Major Wertz.

Her sources informed her that Wertz frequented this café. Rumors suggested the proprietor, an attractive woman in her mid-thirties, engaged in flirtations with the major in exchange for protection from other Germans taking advantage of her.

Colette planned to engage in similar flirtations so that she could take advantage of the major. Her plan involved getting him alone, in a vulnerable position, and thrusting a stiletto into his heart. She hid the blade in a sheath strapped to the inside of her thigh.

Valère had considered her plot far from foolproof and had argued against it on numerous occasions. Their latest argument replayed in her mind.

"I forbid you to do this," Valère had said.

Colette folded her arms. "Why? What are you afraid of?"

"That he'll figure out your little plan and arrest you. That we'll have to come and rescue you."

"Ha," she scoffed. "I'm the little girl that needs to be rescued by the big strong man."

"That's not what I mean. I—"

"I know what you mean! I don't want to be rescued. I don't care if I die. As long as I kill him first."

Valère shook his fist at her. "Don't you think he'll have guards? You think you can just waltz into his office and have a glass of wine?"

"Oh, I can get him alone." She twirled the ends of her hair.

Valère had never seen her flaunt her beauty, and his shock showed on his face. His feelings for Colette often conflicted with the mission at hand to harass the Germans. Any other Maquis who wanted to go on a suicide mission to kill Major Wertz would likely go with his blessing, but the thought of losing Colette scared him.

"Listen to me, Colette. You are not doing this. You are not going. I don't want to hear of this again. Besides, the Allied ComDet team will be back here in a few days, and we don't need any distractions." Valère walked away from the corner of the cave where they had been arguing, leaving Colette with her back turned as she stared at the wall.

Two days after that argument, she had left at 4:00 in the morning and arrived at the café twenty minutes after it opened. That first day, Major Wertz had not walked through the door, so she stayed nearby in the loft of an elderly couple who harbored the Maquis.

The second and third day had gone the same, but she remained determined.

On the fourth day, the bell rung on the café door, and two

German officers, Major Wertz and Lieutenant Bader, walked in and sat near the window.

The pudgy businessman peeked over his newspaper.

Wertz nodded at him, and he nodded back.

Marie approached their table.

"Ah, mademoiselle." Wertz smiled wide. He removed his peaked cap and laid it on the table. "Such a beautiful morning. The lieutenant and I decided that we must take a walk and visit your wonderful café."

Marie politely nodded. "Of course. What can I get you?"

"Baguette and jam! Your famous baguettes for both of us. And espresso. We must have espresso." His over-the-top eagerness caught the attention of the other patrons.

The pudgy businessman banged his cappuccino down loudly on the saucer and spilled it.

"Ah. What have I done?"

It was the signal Colette waited for. The pudgy businessman, who worked for the Resistance, could recognize Wertz. The action and phrase confirmed to Colette that her target sat only feet from her. The "major" insignia on his collar distinguished him from the other officer.

Colette shivered. She reached for the blade's sheath and felt it, ensuring it remained in place. Her confidence withered. She looked at the door. She could still leave. She could just walk out of there. She lowered her head to her book but read nothing.

Marie returned to Wertz's table with their order.

He watched Marie walk away and looked back at Bader, smiling. "You know why I like this city, Lieutenant?"

"No, Major. Why?" They spoke loudly enough for most of the café to hear.

"No . . . Jews," he said, offering an approving, okay hand gesture.

Colette lifted her head slightly and tuned deeper into their conversation.

Wertz sipped his espresso. "What a pleasure it is to stroll through the streets of this lovely city knowing all the vermin have been removed." He looked outside. "Extinguished one might say. It must have been like walking in a sewer before the Jews were removed. Like filthy rats scurrying about."

Colette peeked over her book at the other patrons. No one responded although they likely heard. What could one do?

A chair screeched on the wooden floor as an elderly couple made their way to the door.

"Well, Major, I suppose the Jews are good for something, or else we wouldn't be sending them to work camps," Bader said.

Wertz leaned back in his chair and folded his arms. "There's a flaw in your reasoning, Bader. Let's suppose the Jew were equal to . . . let's say an ox. One could put a yoke on a team of oxen, farm the land, and produce a bountiful crop. That would be useful. If we considered them equal to a chicken, then we'd have food. But the Jew is like the sewer rat. They serve no useful purpose. They only annoy and spread disease. They are mindless. If they aren't controlled, they're a threat to the human race. Like the Black Plague."

Bader held up a finger. "Ah, but the work camps. Some of them must be doing something."

One side of Wertz's mouth curled up. "Do you think we need the vermin to work? We only use the work camps to keep the vermin calm as they're led to the showers." He whispered the last part of the sentence. "The workers will eventually follow. And one glorious day, no Jew will be left on earth. And that is God's plan. For the German race to rule the earth and clear it of vermin. We are God's agents for cleansing. It's difficult work. The English are too stoic to do it. The French are too weak. And the Americans?" He scoffed. "They are too stupid. No. We are the superior race that will bring about a new earth. The Americans, French, and British are like children, and we are the adults. The children may exist and we may even care for them, but they need a parent. We are the only ones that can do this. Yes, God's agents to parent the weak and eliminate the vermin."

Colette stared past her book. Frozen. Her mouth slightly agape. She feared him no less but was now more resolute to carry out vengeance. He had to die.

She reached for a cigarette and feigned looking for a lighter.

Wertz threw back his last swallow of espresso.

She stood and approached the two German officers. "Pardon. Do you have a light?"

Bader reached into his pocket but Wertz was quicker. "Of course, mademoiselle."

She leaned toward him, slowly. Her red lips embraced the cigarette.

Wertz held up the lighter and cupped it with his other hand.

"Merci," she said. Turning, she took her time returning to her seat.

Wertz leaned his head to one side, his eyes following her. "I've not seen you here before. What brings you to this quaint café?"

Colette blew smoke into the air. "I'm from Noville. In the forest. I came to visit my uncle and aunt for a few days."

"Really. Perhaps I know them. What is their name?"

Colette hadn't planned for that. What if he wanted to see them? She couldn't reveal the couple that housed her the last few days. She had to give a convincing answer. She looked directly at him. "I doubt it. They don't get out much. They're the Debrays."

Wertz nodded. "The Debrays. Well, I'll have to pay them

a visit and ask them why they've been hiding such a beautiful niece."

She grinned and nodded politely. "Thank you."

"Tell me something. Caen is such a beautiful city. Do you know much about it?" he said.

"Of course. I've been here many times."

"Well then. We always have a nice stroll back to our head-quarters at City Hall. Perhaps you could join me and tell me some interesting things about the city."

Colette opened her palms. "Why not. I have no plans. It's on my way." She stubbed out her cigarette and left 120 francs on the table.

Wertz and Bader rose, leaving no money. Bader exited and Wertz held the door. "After you," he said, smiling at Colette.

Standing on the sidewalk, Wertz adjusted his cap. "Lieutenant, you go on ahead and make sure things are in order."

Bader cocked his head.

Wertz lowered his head and stared at Bader.

Bader leaned his head back. "Ah, yes, sir." Then he turned and briskly walked away.

Wertz held out his arm. "Shall we."

Colette stared at his outstretched elbow and reluctantly clutched it. She glanced into the café.

The pudgy businessman nodded very slightly.

Marie, who had begun clearing the German officers' table, looked toward Colette and shook her head.

As they began walking toward City Hall, Colette ran through her plan. Everything had worked perfectly so far. She only had to get him alone. In his office perhaps. His bedroom. Even an alley.

Colette talked about some of the shops and the age of the buildings. She pointed to a theater her father had taken her to as a little girl.

"What does your father do in Noville?" Wertz said.

"He's dea . . . eh . . . I mean, he doesn't work. He's older."

Colette quickly pointed to another building to cover up her stumble.

Wertz rubbed his chin. "Did you hear my discussion in the café with the lieutenant?"

"Uh . . . no," she lied.

Wertz repeated his theory comparing Jews to rats.

Colette, cringing on the inside, nodded.

"Well, what is your opinion? Do you agree with me?"

"I don't have an opinion on the Jews. I'm not a Jew. I don't really know any. So, I don't really think about it."

"Interesting," Wertz said. "However, even if you do not know a rat, you must be aware that they are lurking everywhere. They might even be right under your nose. And we don't want any sewer rats running around, now do we?" His expression became stoic.

Colette breathed in deeply. Her eyes widened, but she gave no response.

"Well, here we are." Wertz pointed to the front door of City Hall. "Please, you must come in and see our headquarters. It's quite impressive, and we have some wonderful art."

Colette looked up to a second-floor window. The same room where Wertz had tortured and shot her brother François. "Sure."

As they headed up the stairs, Colette felt the leather sheath holding her stiletto knife rub against her inner thigh.

They entered Wertz's office. He laid his cap on the desk and sat against the desk's edge. He pointed to a painting on the wall. "Notice how the sunshine through the window highlights the water?"

Colette folded her arms and feigned interest.

"I like this painting. After the war, I'll hang it in my office in Berlin." Wertz cocked his head. "On second thought, it might look better in the family room of our new beach house at Lion-sur-Mer. I have just the place picked out. Fortunately, it's remained free of damage from Allied bombing. A nice peaked roof and plenty of windows to view the sea. The current inhabitants, I predict, will no longer have use of the dwelling. It will make a nice summer home for my family."

"So you like art?" Colette asked.

"I do. In fact, the Führer is building one of the largest art collections in the world. It will be greater than any museum. An entire city of art, statues, and monuments. It will be the envy of the entire world. However, nothing wrong with keeping a few choice pieces for myself. Spoils of war, they call it."

She brushed her hair back and nodded. "What is that? That small brown part in the corner."

"Ah!" Wertz walked toward the painting.

Colette pulled her dress up enough to unsheath the stiletto. She charged him and drove the blade toward his torso.

Wertz turned, catching her arm with one hand and clutching her throat with the other.

She struggled to break free, but he easily overpowered her.

He squeezed her wrist until the knife dropped to the floor.

Wertz pulled her face within inches of his.

She noticed the mustard gas scars on his neck.

He whispered, "Do you have any idea how much smarter I am than you?"

FIFTEEN

"AGAIN? C'MON, NICK. We've run this one a hundred times. We've got it down," Lieutenant Dick Moody said to Captain Nick Jordan.

Jordan nodded. "Yes, we've done it a hundred times and I wish we had time for a hundred more. When we jump tomorrow, I want us to have considered every possible thing that can go wrong. To run through every scenario."

The rest of ComDet Sixteen stood by ready to run another drill. Six months had passed since they had successfully returned from their inaugural mission to assess German strengths in and near Caen, France. While Moody rolled his eyes, the others were combat veterans and knew what it was like for a mission to go wrong. For the unthinkable to happen. While Jordan now led the team in place of the deceased Farrington, Moody was second in command, but only had potential. Like the others, he had the skills, but he didn't have their experience and their trial by fire.

Although initially apprehensive, the team was won over by Moody and his sociable personality. They knew he was "one of them." The type that would take a bullet for anyone on the team. His confidence reassured them.

Jean-Pierre, the older and wiser Frenchman, maintained his role as big brother to everyone on the team. He'd seen combat ever since Germany set foot in France. The Germans had rolled over his hometown near Paris in less than a day. A fellow Frenchman in another unit, named Dreux, liked to say that "Humiliation sits on Paris like a huge toad." The stakes were nothing less than restoring his homeland.

Sergeant Ian Cummings brought the British perspective to the team. He didn't have the proper upbringing of a Farrington or Tunstall. He was rougher around the edges. During the Battle of Britain, he'd seen his parents' flat demolished by German bombers. Rather than finish his engineering studies and join the RAF as an officer, he chose to get into the fight. ComDet Sixteen entrusted him with maintaining their communications equipment and rigging all manner of explosives.

Corporal Rance Whitfield served as the team's sniper. A Kentuckian with hillbilly know-how, he had more practical knowledge than anyone on the team. Should they need to start a firefight, he'd fire the first shot.

Jordan ordered the team to jump with the fifty-round drum on their Thompson machine guns. His last jump had left him open to German gunfire, and fortunately, the Maquis of the French Resistance had provided covering fire, but he wanted the ComDet team to jump in closer file and provide that covering fire if needed. Once on the ground, they could switch to a more mobility-friendly, thirty-round or twenty-round straight magazine.

Unlike their previous mission, which lasted only a few days, this mission had no specific timeframe. The long-awaited invasion of Normandy, originally scheduled for May, had been pushed to early June for logistical reasons. They would operate in and around Caen until ordered out by Tunstall.

ComDet Sixteen planned to dress, eat, fight, and live as Maquis serving in a somewhat advisory role. Although Valère's

Maquis had many successful missions to boast, Jordan was tasked with harnessing their power for an even greater effort in disrupting the Germans' hold of Caen and, hopefully, hastening their eventual retreat or preventing reinforcements from joining them. Once the Allies secured a lodgment in Normandy, ComDet Sixteen and the French Resistance would no longer be fighting near Caen alone.

Despite Moody's objections, Jordan ordered the team to run through their jump scenario three more times that evening, "killing off" all but Moody and Cummings in one situation to see how Moody would handle it. Moody compensated his disdain for over-training with his ability to think on his feet.

Jordan agreed with Tunstall's method of mixing in elements of all their training as often as possible. He didn't want any commando going too long without picking a lock, rigging an explosive, or creating a disguise. Everything had to be second nature and nothing was more important than shooting.

Jordan drilled them on focused groupings with their Thompson machine guns. "Don't waste a single bullet," he'd say. Whether shoulder-fired or fired from the side, bullets needed a plan and purpose, be it to kill, maim, or provide covering fire. They set up elaborate scenarios with targets where some were meant to be the good guys and some the bad. Tunstall called it selective shooting. He wanted them to arrive at a scene, indoors or outdoors, and immediately assess who needed elimination.

They carried their 1911 handguns everywhere and learned to fire them from every body position, including right handed or left handed. They might stop in the middle of a six-mile run, practice shooting for eight minutes, and then resume the run. Jordan demanded that his team have the ability to group rounds on a chest shot by conventional aim or instinctive firing—all from multiple distances. Jordan, who expected no less of himself, participated in every challenge, typically leading in accuracy and speed. No member of ComDet Sixteen had any doubts as to who led them, his capabilities, and his willingness to partake in every job in the unit.

The day of the mission departure, the team rested, checked their gear, and rechecked their gear.

Jordan gathered everyone together in their hut. He'd considered a motivational talk as Farrington had done, but it wasn't his style. He opted for simplicity.

"Any questions?" He looked left and right.

Cummings shook his head. The other three stared blankly.

Jordan nodded. "Final equipment check at 2210. Try and get some sleep."

Each man returned to his bunk, but no one slept.

Jordan sat on his bunk next to Moody's. "Seriously, Dick. You got any questions?"

Dick, lying in his bunk reading, closed the book and looked over at Jordan. "Seriously, Nick. You got questions about me?"

Jordan leaned in and whispered. "I just want to make sure you're ready. I might get killed tonight. Will you be ready to lead this team?"

Moody sat up in his bunk and extended his hand. "I'm ready. No question."

Jordan shook his hand and nodded.

CITY HALL (SS HEADQUARTERS)
CAEN, FRANCE

COLETTE PACED IN the darkened room she'd been locked in. The only light came from a small round window far above her reach. Wertz had left bruises on her wrist and neck and allowed his guards to throw her to the floor, but she was otherwise un-harmed. He said nothing to her beyond that one sentence re-garding his intelligence and gave no hint as to her fate. She had lost track of time but guessed that she had been in the empty room for nearly thirty hours. She had slept a few hours on and off and used a bucket in the corner for a toilet. A guard had twice given her a cup of water and bread but remained silent to her questions. He'd simply closed the door and turned the lock.

Valère's warning ran through her mind. "He will figure out your little plan and arrest you. We will have to come and rescue you." How stupid of me, she thought. Valère was right. Her pas-sion had gotten the better of her.

She leaned against the wall and slowly slid down to the floor, sobbing. She felt the inside of her thigh. The strapped sheath re-mained but Wertz had kept her dagger. Remnants of failure.

The lock slowly turned, and the door opened one foot. Wertz poked his head in and smiled. "Mademoiselle! I hope you find the accommodations to your liking."

Was this a joke? Was he insane?

She rubbed her eyes and looked to the side.

He showed an exaggerated frown. "Tsk, tsk. You're upset."

He pushed the door fully open and motioned for a guard, who brought in a chair and table. Another delivered a saucer and cup of tea. The guards exited, leaving the door askew.

"You mustn't be upset. You're so young and naïve. Many people your age make these kinds of mistakes." Wertz sat and took a sip.

Colette looked up and defiantly folded her arms.

He leaned toward her and rested his forearms on his thighs. "You know, I was suspicious the moment I walked into the café. Some things were not quite right. I notice little things about peo-ple and the environment. Call it a hobby of mine. For example, that fat, French pig reading the newspaper usually arrives several minutes later than I do. But he was already there. And you, such a beautiful young lady sitting alone. I'd never seen you before, and yet, there you were. But you weren't just sitting. You were reading, but you never turned a page. You seemed distracted. I also noticed you kept reaching between your legs and touching something. I wasn't sure what it was but now know it was the sheath that held your dagger."

Colette looked at the door. Could she escape? Just run out? No. Not a chance. She looked back at Wertz.

The Nazi lit a cigarette. "The door is open. Look at it again. That is your way home. But not just yet. We have a few more things to discuss. Like your connections to the Resistance. That fat, French pig collaborates with them. We know about him, but we let him go on as if we don't. He is weak. We will turn him eventually. When he spilled the cappuccino, I noticed your demeanor changed. It was a signal, wasn't it?"

She stared at him. No emotion. I'm not a weakling, she thought. I'm not giving him the satisfaction of seeing me fall apart.

He wagged his finger at her. "Yes, of course, it was. Let's see, what else? Oh, I know, when I was comparing Jews to rats, your blood boiled. You tensed up. I could feel your anger. I must say, you are very passionate. And when I asked you for your uncle and aunt's name, you said Debray. You know, I've read *The Count of Monte Cristo* and distinctly remember a character named Debray. I believe he leaked government secrets for his lover. I'll bet you were on that page or had just read about that. The name was right there in your head, wasn't it? It's human nature. When you need to make something up, you use what's on your mind." Wertz opened his palms. "How am I doing so far?"

She said nothing and turned to look up at the small attic window. The light that came in through the open door revealed a layer of dust. It was hardly a cold prison cell but an uninviting room nonetheless.

Wertz inhaled deeply. "I think I'm doing pretty well, no? Let's see, what else? Ah! When we left, the fat, French pig nodded at you. Yes . . . I saw that. When I asked about your father, you hesitated and looked to the side searching for an answer. Another lie. When we entered this building, you breathed deeply and your teeth even chattered ever so slightly. You also touched your thigh again to feel for the sheath." He leaned back in the chair and crossed his legs. "I find it very curious that you never gave me your name. I purposely did not ask. I think it's because you assumed I'd be dead soon. Why give someone your name that you're about to kill, right? And you already knew my name, didn't you? You had done your homework."

She turned her head and peered at him with a fake smile. "Colette. Wonderful to meet you."

"Ah, Colette speaks. And what a beautiful name." He stood and walked across the room, looking toward the tiny window. "You know, a French pig in here several months back whispered the name Colette to an American prisoner. I shot that pig in the leg. You wouldn't know him, would you?"

She looked to the side, staring at the wall, her mouth agape.

"Do you know what the biggest thing that gave you away was, Colette?"

She stood and brushed herself off. "No, but I'm sure you'll tell me."

Wertz turned, his smile and smugness gone. He walked slowly toward her and whispered as he had done when she tried to stab him. "Why would a beautiful young French woman go on a stroll with a much older German officer with these scars?" He rubbed his neck with the back of his fingers.

Colette reared back and slapped him.

He turned back from the slap. "So much passion." He clenched his fists. A grin slowly appeared. He reared back and punched her face. Not a reckless backhand but a deliberate, close-fisted punch to her nose.

The blow knocked her down and her head whipped back, hitting the floor. Her eyes watered. She cupped her nose with her hand and looked at him in shock.

Wertz approached and knelt. "That's how I deal with liars. And now you know that I can tell when you're lying. I'll give you some time to think about that. When I return, I'll be asking more questions. But I will not allow you to remain silent. I want to know all about your friends that cower in the woods. I want to know about those Allies you're helping, especially the American that murdered my guards and ran off with that little, French pig. And I want you to tell me when and where the Allies will invade." Wertz stood and walked to the door.

Colette wiped the blood trickling from her nose. Her eyes watered and the room blurred. She reached back and felt a bump forming on her head.

"I know what you're thinking. That you are tough and can take any pain I inflict. But, trust me, you can't. Your pain will be a different kind as I allow every German soldier in Caen to come visit you. You think about that until I return." He slammed the door, and the lock turned.

SIXTEEN

S HORTLY AFTER MIDNIGHT, Jordan floated down from the sky free of German gunfire—a much more pleasant jump than the one six months earlier. A fortunate occurrence since each team member floated down with seventy pounds of extra gear that they would stash all around Caen. They landed with an abundance of weapons, ammunition, and explosives, but they'd rely on the Maquis for food, water, and shelter.

The Maquis greeted the five ComDet Sixteen members and escorted them to their camp inside the ingeniously hidden cave.

They entered one by one to see an agitated Valère pacing. Another shook his head. Two of the older ladies that did domestic work for the group sobbed.

"I knew this would happen," Valère said. He noticed the Allied commando team. "Jordan! I'm glad your team made it safely. I'm afraid we have some trouble. Colette ran off yesterday morning on this foolish scheme to kill that German officer."

"Who's Colette?" Moody asked.

"She's one of the Maquis. Tough as they come," Jordan said. He looked back to Valère. "Where is she?"

Valère walked over to the map of Caen that hung on the cave wall. "City Hall, we think. The same place they held you. She was last seen leaving a café with Wertz."

Jordan lowered his brow. "You mean he kidnapped her?"

Valère shook his head. "No. She had this plan to trick him and get him alone, then stab him with a knife. Vengeance for François. I urged her not to go. Begged her. She couldn't be reasoned with. I've been so angry with her. But I suppose she's not the first person to do something stupid out of revenge."

"Alright. What are we doing to get her back?" Jordan asked.

Moody walked up and grabbed Jordan's arm. "Nick. Is this really the thing we should get involved in? We just got here."

Jordan gathered his team in a corner. "Our mission is to lead this group. Look at them. You can see how distracted they are by this. As far as I see it, we need to get her back. Right the ship so they can focus. Besides, she's one of their best fighters."

Jean-Pierre nodded. "I don't think we have much of a choice."

"We're in, Valère. Let's get her back," Jordan said.

Valère smiled. "Thank you. I do have an idea. One of Wertz's junior officers is Lieutenant Bader. The same one that led the Molière massacre. He likes to visit a young lady on the outskirts of town every Wednesday afternoon. We'll call her a . . . collaborator. She scratches his back, if you know what I mean, and he provides her protection, food, goods, etc. Anyway, he always goes alone, except for one driver that stays in the car. Bader will know where Colette is being held. If we're correct, that she's being held in City Hall, we still need to know where in the building. It's a big place."

"And today just happens to be Wednesday." Jordan turned to his team and smiled.

Valère put his hand on the shoulder of a fellow Maquisard. "Gentlemen, this is Henri. He knows the neighborhood very well. He joined us a couple of months ago and has been a great asset. He can help."

Henri stepped forward quickly and offered a wave. He towered over the others. His disheveled clothing hung on his lanky frame. He lacked the self-assuredness of the other French and quickly looked to Jordan's side rather than directly in his eyes—much like a whipped puppy.

Jordan nodded at Henri and looked back at his team. "Boys, what do you say to a little snatch and grab?"

"Just like snatching eggs," Whitfield said.

THE COLLABORATOR'S FLAT lay in the back of an apartment building on a busy street that led into the industrial section of town. Several shops catered to commuters that drove, rode, or walked daily to and from their business or manufacturing jobs. Valère had warned them that anything out of the ordinary might raise suspicions. Someone, like the collaborator, the driver, a neighbor, or a shopkeeper, might alert the Germans. Bader typically arrived at the flat shortly after 5:00 PM and returned to the car forty minutes later.

Jordan and Valère weighed their options. Captured Germans or those with knowledge of their whereabouts created a liability. The Maquis had no facility for prisoners, and killing innocents presented more complications. If they snatched Bader in the flat, the collaborator would know. If they kidnapped him from the car, the driver would know. They decided on a tactic somewhere in between.

On cue, Bader and his driver arrived at 5:08 PM. Bader quickly hopped from the car and entered the apartment building. The driver turned off the ignition and lit a cigarette. He leaned back and tilted his cap up.

ComDet Sixteen dressed as local French. Jordan wore a double-breasted suit and carried a briefcase, blending in with numerous other men walking up and down the street. He made one slow pass by the car, surveying the area. Cummings and Whitfield had dressed the same and stood around the corner.

The team benefited from a Caen tailor that swore allegiance to the Resistance. He gladly prepared clothing and disguises for the commandos and stored their military uniforms in a false wall of his shop. Although many of their missions involved local dress, from coveralls to leather jackets, their military attire presented a professional fighting unit when needed. Many of the Maquis dressed as military in beret and tactical belt, but the commandos avoided the look, focused on blending in.

Jean-Pierre, Moody, and Henri stood by a parked boxed truck three spots forward of Bader's car. Henri carried a clipboard and inspected items in the truck while the other two climbed onto the bumper and acted as if the truck had a mechanical problem.

"This Colette must be very important to go through all this," Moody whispered.

Jean-Pierre smiled. "Well, let's just say Valère might have feelings for her that go beyond what he feels for the other Maquis."

Moody offered a slow nod. "Oh. Now I get it."

Jean-Pierre peeked around the hood at Bader's driver and pulled back. "Lieutenant, Colette has likely earned the affection of many, including our own captain."

"Oh, great," Moody said. "Jordan has a thing for this girl."

"Maybe not. But, I think he feels as if he owes her after her brother François's death at the hand of Wertz. Jordan did nothing wrong, but Colette blamed him. Our captain might not have a weakness for the opposite sex, but he does have a desire to reconcile things. He may see this as an opportunity to fix that little mishap. I do agree, though, this group cares deeply for Colette. She's like everyone's sister. It's important we get her back, for no other reason, so that one person from her family survives this war."

Jordan approached at 5:45. "Should be any minute. Ready?"

Jean-Pierre and Moody nodded.

Moody tapped the engine two times with a hammer.

Henri jumped out of the back, climbed into the driver's seat, and started the truck.

An elderly couple crossed from the sidewalk to the street in front of Bader's car, stopping near the rear. They pointed in different directions and argued.

Cummings and Whitfield walked down the street and headed into the doorway of the collaborator's flat. After one minute, Bader rambled down the stairs. They blocked his path.

"Pardon me, Officer. We hear the Allies could be bombing our city soon. What do we do? Where will we go? Will you help us?" Cummings asked.

Bader shook his head. "You shouldn't listen to silly rumors." He tried to pass but Whitfield blocked him. "You must know something."

"No . . . I . . . don't! Now get out of my way."

At the same time as they held Bader in the building, the elderly man that had been arguing fell to the ground, clutching his chest.

The driver turned toward the commotion.

The wife reached for him. "Please, help us!"

The driver jumped out of the car and knelt by the man. Six other pedestrians approached and surrounded the old man on the ground.

Whitfield stepped aside in the building and let Bader pass. Cummings followed closely behind Whitfield.

Jordan walked along the passenger side of Bader's car.

When Bader stopped three feet from the car to look at the

commotion, Jordan released a blackjack from his sleeve. He struck Bader on the neck with the small leather club—stunning him. Whitfield threw a hood over his head. Cummings, Jean-Pierre, and Moody surrounded them, and the group quickly moved Bader to the back of the truck. Moody yanked the canvas down, covering the back end of the vehicle and concealing them.

One bystander turned toward the truck just in time to see the canvas fall but then turned his focus back to the old man on the ground.

Henri stepped on the accelerator with the five members of ComDet Sixteen and their passenger, Bader, in the back. Bader's wrestling and cries were met with swift punches to the head. Whitfield held his hand over Bader's mouth, muffling him.

As the truck turned the corner, the old man opened his eyes wide, looked at his wife, and said, "I feel much better now, dear. Another one of my false alarms. This old heart of mine must have a few more days left in it." He held up his hands, hinting for help up.

The driver shook his head and helped the old man to his feet. The other bystanders dispersed.

"Thank you, son," the old man said to the driver."

"Of course."

The driver returned to the car and lit another cigarette. He looked at his watch and up toward the building. He leaned backed, tipped his cap, and took a long drag from his smoke.

BADER'S HEAD MOVED slightly as he moaned. His fingertips tapped the arms of the wooden chairs where his hands were tightly secured. He jerked and convulsed in the chair, but his bindings allowed little movement. "Help! Help me!"

Jordan stepped toward him and lifted off the hood. Chunks of Bader's previous meal littered the inside of the hood and his jacket. "Guten tag, Lieutenant Bader. Actually, I guess it's evening now."

Bader had a small contusion above his right eye, and his upper lip showed some swelling.

"Who are you? Where am I?" Bader looked around. Sweat poured down his face. Hay covered the floor, and the smell of manure permeated the air. Evening light barely shone through separated boards. The popping sounds of large rain drops began. Several men stared back at him.

Cummings smiled at Bader.

"You. You were the one going on about the Allies bombing Caen. Who are you?" Bader asked Cummings.

Jordan placed a chair near Bader. "Who we are is not important. What is important is who you are. And, even more, what you know."

"I'll have you shot!" Bader tried to get up but the chair was nailed to the dirt floor.

The door opened and Mr. Frère walked in. "How is our guest?"

"We're just now getting acquainted," Jordan said.

Bader's eyes widened. "Who are you? What are you doing with these men?"

Mr. Frère walked up to Bader and folded his arms. "I'm sorry I didn't greet you in front of your mistress's flat, but I was busy having a heart attack in the street. Funny thing is that I feel much better now." Mr. Frère grinned.

"Fortunately for you, this can go very quickly. Unless you're stubborn that is." Jordan patted him on the knee. "We know who you are, Bader. We know you work for Wertz. We know—"

"You!" Bader cocked his head. "You are that American we captured. I remember you."

Jordan punched Bader's mid-section.

Bader coughed, spewed, and lowered his head.

"Don't speak until I tell you," Jordan said. "We know you have a friend of ours locked up in your headquarters at City Hall—a young lady. She was last seen leaving Le Café de Patrice with your major, and we're quite confident she's being held in your headquarters. I want to know exactly which room she's in."

"I don't know what you're—"

Jordan's fist blasted Bader's nose. His head whipped back against the chair. Blood oozed from his nostrils.

Jordan sat in his chair. "We're not going to waste any time with you. You're going to tell me exactly which room she is in. Where all the guards are stationed. Everything. Then, we're going to leave you in this chair while we go get her. If she's not exactly where you say, I'm going to come back and shoot you in the head." Jordan used his index finger to poke Bader's forehead.

Bader shook his head. "No, no. I won't. You can beat me. I won't. I serve the Führer. I will not betray him. I will not betray the Fatherland."

"Mr. Frère. Do you have those big sewing needles I asked for?" Jordan held out his hand toward Mr. Frère but kept his stare on Bader.

Mr. Frère placed them in Jordan's hand. "Compliments of Mrs. Frère."

Jordan held a three-inch needle in front of Bader's face. "You're probably wondering why your hands are bound so tightly to the arms of this chair with your fingers extended. It's amazing how many nerve endings are in your fingertips. I'm going to insert this needle into your finger. And then . . . Uh . . . Mr. Frère, how many needles did you give me?"

"Exactly ten, sir," Mr. Frère said.

Jordan continued, "OK, I'm going to insert a needle in each of your fingertips. If that doesn't work, then we'll get real creative."

Jordan placed his hand on top of Bader's and held the needle at his left ring fingertip.

Bader jerked.

Whitfield put his arm under Bader's chin and held him tight.

Jordan slowly inserted the needle.

"Ahhhhh!" Bader convulsed and breathed heavily. "Ahh!"

Jordan shook his head. "You know, I did that way too fast. Don't worry, Bader. I will go very slowly this time." He aimed another needle at Bader's left middle finger.

"Wa . . . wa . . . wait! OK. She's in our headquarters, but I don't know which room."

Jordan pulled the needle in his hand away but thumped the needle sticking out of Bader's ring finger.

Bader rose in the chair. "Ahhhh!"

Jordan returned the next needle and held it at Bader's left middle finger.

Whitfield secured his grip around Bader.

"Nooooo!" Bader screamed. "Storage! The storage room! She's in that room!"

"Where's the room?" Jordan said.

Bader exhaled. "The north end of the fourth floor. There's a door that says 'storage.' But it's locked, and Major Wertz keeps the key. The guards have to get it from him."

Jordan leaned back and held the needle away from Bader's hand. "Well, isn't that specific? We appreciate you sharing with us so freely." Jordan leaned back in and held the needle in front of his face. "Now, I want to know how many soldiers are in that place, where they work, and what time they brush their teeth. Do you understand?"

Bader vigorously nodded as urine filled the wooden seat.

AFTER COMDET SIXTEEN and the Maquis left Molière, Mr. Frère, along with two others, escorted a hooded Lieutenant Bader to the outskirts of town.

Bader stumbled as they walked along a rocky path. "Where . . . where are you taking me?"

"In due time, Lieutenant. For now, you should remain silent," Mr. Frère said, clutching Bader's arm.

Aside from a mooing cow and their footfalls, the long walk offered Bader nothing. The screech of an iron gate broke the silence.

Bader felt tree bark against his wrists as his hands were bound to a tree.

Mr. Frère removed his hood.

"Wha . . . where am I?" Bader noticed several gravestones and crosses. Some upright, some leaning. He made out the years 1892 to 1943 on one to his immediate left. Many of the graves were humped with grass sparsely covering them.

Mr. Frère marched several steps past Bader, turned, and lined his Lebel rifle at his side. "Sir! You have been found guilty of crimes against the French people. Many of these graves belong to those you ordered massacred six months ago. Many of them were simple farmers and shopkeepers doing their best to live their lives with a war going on around them. Some of their sons lost their lives defending our land against your country's illegal invasion. You callously arrived one day with your troops and took their lives without merit."

Bader shook his head, furiously. "No! No! I was only following orders. It was Major Wertz. He ordered this. He is the one—"

"Silence! You'll notice my two friends have no shovels. You

will not be digging your own grave. We would not dishonor the memory of these fine people by having your dishonorable remains invade this space. You will spend the night, tied to that tree, looking at these graves and thinking about your actions. Think about the mothers, fathers, grandparents, and siblings whose lives you took. At dawn, we will take you in the woods where you'll be shot by my trusty Lebel rifle. It killed many Germans in the last war, and I'm sure it will do the job just fine tomorrow. We'll strip off your clothes, burn them, and leave your body for the animals. That is the death and burial you deserve.

"Gentlemen." Mr. Frère nodded for his two companions to follow him.

"Wait!" Bader pulled at his bindings. "No. Don't leave me. I have more information. I can help you. That American said I would be shot if I lied. I told the truth about where the girl is."

Bader's pleadings fell on deaf ears. His whimpers echoed in the village throughout the night.

SEVENTEEN

SS HEADQUARTERS
CAEN, FRANCE
May 1944

"GEEZ, NICK. I didn't realize you had it in you. You really worked fast on that Nazi," Moody said to Jordan as they stood in an alley, three blocks from Wertz's headquarters.

"Truth be told, I hated it. No human should have to do that to another. But I'd have gone all the way if needed."

"It's Operation Wolfhound, Dick. It's our job. You can't feel guilty about that."

"I have no problem putting a bullet through his brain. I don't mean that I would enjoy it, but I have no reservations about doing my duty. No guilt. Wolfhound is about elimination, though, not torture. I would never do that if there was another way."

"Confirmed," Jean-Pierre said, as he walked up with Maquisard Henri.

That confirmation gave Jordan the assurance he needed. Bader had divulged that the SS headquarters' guards changed shifts at 6:00 AM. However, breakfast was not available until 6:00 AM, so those coming on to their shift missed that morning meal. Apparently, Wertz didn't care that he inconvenienced his men. All those coming off duty would gather at one end of the building for breakfast, and half of the new guards would sneak off for food as well. In their cockiness, the SS guards felt they had too many guards on duty.

Wertz had doubled the guards after Jordan's escape and gave orders that no matter what happened near the headquarters or in the streets, the guards were to stay in place. Although the SS headquarters held little strategic value to the Resistance, Wertz felt that holding Caen's City Hall presented a great psychological advantage. Jordan knew a diversion would likely not produce the desired effect. With a basic reference of the building's layout from his previous stay, he planned to go in alone. In addition, a friend of the Resistance had worked as a carpenter seven years earlier on a remodel of City Hall. This, along with Bader's information, gave Jordan the confidence that Colette's rescue would be successful.

Valère, Moody, Jean-Pierre, and anyone else with a voice had disagreed. They raised their objections during the night that although Jordan might overcome several of the guards, reaching the attic where Colette was held, and bringing her out with both of them unscathed, seemed unlikely.

Jordan ran through the ideal scenario several times in his head. There wasn't enough time to run drills with his team. He considered options should variables occur, but focused on what the intelligence told him. Variables would be dealt with as they happened. This was the "ten to one" scenario Major Tunstall had trained him for. The belief that Colette might be enduring torture eliminated any delays.

Two ComDet members and two Maquis covered one potential exit while a similar group covered the other. If Jordan and Colette emerged with guards chasing them, the support teams would return fire.

Jordan dressed in business attire. Should a German stop and ask for his papers, his would show him as Marcel Marchand from Lyon. He negotiated contracts for manufacturers favoring Germans. Since Jordan learned his French from his grandmother, his accent matched the Lyon cover story, and as a contract negotiator, he'd have more latitude for travel than a typical French citizen. In addition to Wertz's SS, Wehrmacht soldiers might be on any street in Caen at any time. Any German in uniform could stop any citizen and arrest them. Although careful to avoid a commotion, Jordan would silently kill any soldier that attempted to constrain him.

One year before, a ComDet team, operating north of Paris, was overheard arguing about the 1943 World Series, in English, by a Wehrmacht soldier who happened to understand some English. The soldier notified his lieutenant, who reacted quickly. This forced the two commandos to flee from their position. One escaped but the Germans killed the other. Major Tunstall reacted by strengthening each member's cover story, and his own staff tested them relentlessly. In certain scenarios, they'd spend forty-eight hours in their cover while eating dinner, drilling, or under duress in extreme conditions. The team members were also required to know each other's cover stories. Those with weaker skills in French or German typically used an Italian or Portuguese cover with the hope that their German questioner didn't speak the language.

Jordan left the alley and strolled toward the SS headquarters at 6:10 AM. Although few businessmen typically milled about at that hour, it wasn't unusual for someone to be headed to their office at the break of dawn. He dropped a coin with a vendor and picked up a newspaper one block from SS headquarters. Nick Jordan was a long way from Yale.

MOODY AND JEAN-PIERRE hid behind crates in the alley where

Jordan and Colette would most likely exit. Two Maquis hid in an empty building with boarded-up windows. They trained their weapons on the garage exit. According to their briefing, Jordan would be in and out in six minutes.

"I'm still thinking this seems like a lot of trouble and risk for one person," Moody said. He shook his head. "I certainly hope the captain doesn't have feelings for her."

"Perhaps not. He's never said as much, and maybe I should not have brought it up. But, I am French after all. I can tell when there is a romantic tension. And based on my observations, I see that between the captain and Colette. Fortunately, our leader has a one-track mind when it comes to the mission at hand. He has emotions like anyone else. However, I think he'd be doing this regardless of who he was rescuing.

"It's war. Rescuing Colette may be about her, or it may be an attempt to make up for the loss of her brother. But, as was said before, this group of Maquis is very fond of her and wants her rescued. From a moral standpoint, it's worth it."

"Would you do it?" Moody asked.

"Do what?"

"Rescue Colette."

"Absolutely, but not for just anyone. That poor girl has seen her parents and brother murdered. Her home burned to the ground. But for this mission, our captain is the best man for the job. He's the only man for the job. Who else do you know that could sneak into SS headquarters, overcome dozens of guards, rescue a woman, and get out? It's a suicide mission, by calculation of most.

"But he has a certain tenacity. I noticed this the first time I faced him in the circle at Camp Delta. I faced him along with two others. He went through us like he was swatting away flies. A mere annoyance. Nothing fazes him. He fears no man. He is the perfect one to rescue the proverbial damsel in distress."

Bader's driver never reported Bader missing, assuming he'd get in trouble. He considered knocking on the door of Bader's mistress, but he didn't know which flat was hers. Darkness had begun to fall and he was in danger of missing the evening muster—an offense for which Wertz exacted a severe punishment. Weighing trouble with Wertz or Bader, he chose to leave Bader to his mistress and drove back. He checked in for muster and went to bed.

One of Wertz's personal guards woke him at 5:42 AM. "The major wants you. Now!"

Bader's driver rubbed his eyes, quickly dressed, and headed to Wertz's office.

When pressed for answers by Wertz, the driver lasted thirty-eight seconds before divulging Bader's frequent trips to his mistress and his failure to return from the apartment building.

"That idiot!" Wertz shouted. He paced to his desk and back.

The driver stood at attention, his face wrinkled from sleep.

Wertz approached and kneed his groin.

"Umph!" The driver dropped to his knees.

Wertz knelt down to reach the driver's ear. "Next time, perhaps you'll consider immediately reporting the disappearance of an SS officer. Get out of here."

The driver, doubling over, waddled out of the office.

Wertz motioned for his guard to step in. "Ready my car and a squad of troops. And bring that idiot." He pointed to the driver struggling down the hall. "We're going to find the other idiot, Bader."

Jordan approached the garage entrance at the side of the City Hall building. The commotion of morning deliveries would provide the distraction necessary for him to go in unnoticed.

He stopped at the corner and propped his shoe up while a teenage boy applied polish for a shoe shine. This young friend of the Resistance strategically set up his operation at the corner to give Jordan a full view of the garage opening.

Three guards stood outside while a fourth lifted the bar blocking the entrance. A convertible pulled out with a truck close behind. Wertz sat stoically in the right rear seat.

Jordan recognized him and lowered his head behind his newspaper. As they turned the corner, he looked back toward the garage entrance.

All four guards gathered—engaged in a discussion. Three broke away and headed into the garage as the fourth waved goodbye. One SS soldier stood between Jordan and his entrance to SS headquarters.

Jordan gave the shoe shiner a coin, his newspaper, and a wink. He crossed the street and stayed close to the wall of the entrance.

Walking by the entrance, he smiled at the lone guard. "Bonjour."

The pale, clean-shaven guard nodded in return. His crisp, gray uniform had two S-shaped lightning bolts on a black collar. His trousers were tucked into shined boots, and his pristine helmet concealed the color of his hair. An MP40 machine gun hung at his side by a shoulder strap. He followed Jordan for two seconds with his eyes and then looked back in the opposite direction.

Jordan glanced into the opening and noticed an empty garage. He turned and walked directly in.

The guard did a double-take, perhaps in shock that this man would so brazenly enter the building.

"Halt!"

Jordan turned back and continued a slow walk. "I have an appointment. This way is quicker."

The guard pulled his machine gun up to a firing position. "Halt! You cannot come in here."

Jordan turned to face the guard but kept walking backward.

The guard followed further into the garage and out of view from pedestrians on the street.

"Easy. Easy," Jordan said. He reached into his jacket slowly. "I have papers. I'll show you."

The guard kept his weapon trained on Jordan. "Show me."

With his arm extended a foot out, Jordan offered a folded sheet.

The guard took two steps closer and reached cautiously for the papers with his left hand while keeping his right index finger on the trigger. He lowered his head.

Jordan grabbed the barrel and pushed it to the side.

The guard looked up from the paper; his eyes widened. He began to lift his left hand to regain control of his weapon.

Jordan's open hand struck the guard's throat with great force.

The guard dropped flat to his stomach on the floor, losing his helmet. His MP40 slid next to Jordan's feet.

Picking up the weapon, Jordan looked left and right.

The guard, clutching his throat and coughing, looked up at Jordan, who brought the MP40's butt down on the guard's forehead, rendering him unconscious.

He dragged the guard behind boxes and felt his pulse. The guard was alive, and Jordan considered whether or not he might wake soon and alert other Germans. He pulled his stiletto from a sheath strapped to his calf.

I'll have Colette out of here before he wakes up, he thought. No reason to kill this guy.

Using the guard's uniform would offer a good disguise, but the force that guarded headquarters was small enough that the guards likely all knew each other.

He maintained the clutch on his knife and headed for the

door marked SERVICE, directly in front of him. He quietly entered, hoping to use the service stairs without encountering any more Germans. His pistol was holstered on the small of his back.

Jordan worked his way up each flight of stairs, two steps at a time. He moved slowly, hugging the corners. Halfway up the third story, he heard voices in German heading toward him. He backed down and took cover between the wall and an open door leading to the second floor.

The footfalls grew louder. He estimated seven or eight soldiers descended the stairs. His hope for a quiet entry was replaced with his .45 pistol in his hand.

"He's an idiot," one of the German soldiers said.

"I agree," another said. "He might even be insane."

Several others muttered on mundane issues. One by one they passed by the door.

As the footsteps and voices died down, Jordan emerged from behind the door, holstered his pistol, and resumed his journey up the stairs.

"I forgot something. I'll be down in a bit," Jordan heard from below.

It was too late for him to return to the cover of the second-floor door. He also heard voices above him. He took two steps up and two back down and came face-to-face with a German soldier on the landing. Jordan cupped the knife behind his back.

"Who are you?" he said in German, startled.

Jordan maintained his French. "Pardon?"

Wertz didn't allow civilians beyond the first-floor entrance without an escort.

"How did you get up here?" The German noticed his hand behind his back and looked up. He reached for his sidearm.

Jordan brought the stiletto from behind his back and drove it into the side of the German's neck. He pushed it in a half-inch from the hilt and gave it a one-quarter turn. Blood squirted out in three different directions.

The German never pulled his weapon from the holster. He fell back, dead.

Voices above continued.

With nowhere to stow the dead body, Jordan left it where it lay and headed up the stairs. He passed the opening to the third floor but those talking remained far enough down the hallway that they could not see him.

Someone would soon find the dead body. Jordan had to work fast. He moved up the final flight of stairs to the fourth floor, quickly but quietly. Peeking around the doorframe, he realized the accuracy of Bader's information. A long hallway one way, with not a soul in sight, and a short hallway the other. At the end, a bored guard paced in front of a door with the words STORAGE.

Jordan waited for the guard to turn away from him and stepped into the doorway. "Come here. Major Wertz wants you," he said in German and quickly stepped back into the stairwell.

The guard cocked his head and walked through the doorway.

Jordan, from behind, grabbed the man's forehead, turned the head, and drove the blade through the back and into the kidney. The guard dropped to his knees. Jordan kicked the man's back as the knife slid out, causing him to spurt blood on Jordan's trousers to match the blood already on his jacket and white shirt. He no longer had the appearance of a typical French businessman.

He moved into the hallway and jiggled the storage room door knob. It was locked as expected. He knocked. "Colette!" he whispered. "Colette!"

He heard shuffling. "Who is it?" she whispered.

"It's Jordan. Nick Jordan. I'm getting you out of here. You OK?"

"Nick! Thank God."

Jordan pulled a small leather pouch from his jacket pocket. He knelt in front of the door and rolled out the pouch, revealing his lock-picking set. Using a tension tool, he discovered that it was a two-lever warded lock. He slowly slid in his skeleton key and manipulated the levers.

"C'mon. Hurry," Colette said.

Jordan squinted at the lock and turned it slightly. "Almost got it." He gently moved the skeleton key left and right and felt the bolt give way. He turned the knob and opened the door.

Colette stood near the door, expressionless. Defeated.

Jordan stood. Other than her bruised nose, she appeared unharmed. Her confidence had left her. This was not the Colette he met six months earlier.

She collapsed in his arms, tears streaming down her face. "Thank you! Thank you!" A much different reception than during their last meeting.

He pushed her back at arm's length. He cocked his head, slightly.

Her bruised nose had dried blood in the nostrils. Her makeup ran down her face. Her hair, normally pulled back in a neat ponytail, hung from her head in a mangled mess. Her blouse was partially untucked and she wore no shoes. She seemed, to Jordan, a woman who had aged a few years.

Her lip quivered.

"We've got to go," he said.

She nodded and wiped her eyes.

They headed down the stairs, Colette picking up the dead SS guard's MP40.

Down one flight, Jordan stepped over the dead SS guard he had stabbed without looking at him. Colette paused and looked into his eyes, still open.

Jordan grabbed her elbow. "We've got to keep moving. A

little further and we'll be in the garage."

As they passed the entrance to the second floor, a guard, startled, lunged at Colette and grabbed her hair.

Jordan drove a powerful side kick into the German's ribs.

He doubled over, releasing Colette.

She swung the butt of the MP40 and pistol-whipped the guard. As he fell, she aimed to fire.

Jordan pushed her machine gun down. "No. It will make too much noise." He pulled out his knife.

The German's eyes widened. "Help! Help!"

Jordan fisted the knife and punched the guard, knocking him unconscious.

Using the machine gun as a club, Colette whaled away at the guard—rendering his face a bloody mess.

"Bastard!" she screamed. The quivering and helpless Colette suddenly transformed into the fierce Maquisard fighter she had been before her capture.

Jordan dragged her back. "That's enough!" He didn't wait for her to respond and pulled her toward the steps.

"Something happened to Katz!" they heard from above.

Multiple footsteps sounded in the hallway below. "You four go up."

Jordan and Colette stepped into the second-floor hallway. To the right, two SS officers stared back in shock. One reached for his sidearm. To the left, voices and shuffling feet approached. Jordan heard the distinct sound of an MP40 charging handle slide back and forth.

Ten to one. Old Ten-to-One Tunstall would probably love this, Jordan thought.

EIGHTEEN

RING. RING.

A young boy rolled passed the Nazi headquarters on his bicycle, taking no special notice of it. He swerved his bike to avoid one of the many puddles from the previous evening's rain. From the outside, the headquarters showed no signs of unusual activity. The sun had yet to break through morning clouds, offering a gloomy morning in Caen. The only other sounds were those typical of the morning bustle.

A heavy-set woman swept the walk in front of her shop across from the garage where Jordan had entered—and would presumably exit—any minute.

When the Germans first occupied Caen's City Hall, local citizens would walk by and shake their heads. Some covered their mouths in disbelief and a few wept. The Nazis possessed not only the building but the power and authority it represented as well. Most of the officials and staff were forced to leave. Only a few essential personnel remained to keep vital city functions operational. The Germans kept whatever they wanted and discarded the rest out of the windows.

Madame Roux had served the city of Caen in various roles since 1907 and refused to leave her office. She had served no less than six mayors, training the last three on the ways of city government. She had no husband but, rather, was married to the job. Many wondered why she didn't run for mayor herself. When the Germans came, she barricaded herself in her office. When they burst through her door, she threw books at them.

Her exit was through a back door bloodied and bruised. Since then, she walked by the front of the building every morning, spat on the sidewalk, and delivered a few choice words to whatever German guard had the displeasure of receiving her greeting. They simply referred to her as the crazy lady. She walked up that morning but found no guard to receive her insults. She spat, regardless, and moved on.

Moody and Jean-Pierre hadn't seen the guard in front rush inside. They covered the rear alley entrance with two Maquis. Cummings and two Maquis hid in Resistance-friendly shops with a view of the garage exit. Whitfield perched in a corner window adjacent to City Hall with a view of both exits. His sniper rifle would pick off anyone chasing Jordan and Colette.

"How long has it been?" Moody said to Jean-Pierre.

"Just over five minutes," he responded.

Moody rose. "I'm going in."

Jean-Pierre shook his head. "No. With all due respect, we must stick to the plan."

Although Moody outranked Jean-Pierre, the Frenchman remained the most seasoned combat veteran on the team. When he offered advice, they listened.

Moody lowered. "I don't like this. I know Jordan said six minutes, but that was a guess."

"I must admit; I thought we'd hear some commotion by now. Perhaps the captain has managed to get to Colette unnoticed," Jean-Pierre said.

Moody raised his eyebrows. "Or he got caught." He looked at the Maquis members nearby and held up his index finger, signaling one minute. One more minute to allow Jordan a clean extraction, or they would all go in.

No less than ten Nazis closed in on Jordan and Colette from four different directions. Several guards blocked their exit leading down to the garage where Jordan had entered. The door to the left, which led to the rear entrance, presented an equally daunting challenge. His stealthy entrance had provided a relatively easy path to Colette. As the call went out among the Nazi guards that an intruder lurked about, that exit path became increasingly more hazardous. Drowsy guards emerged from their sleeping quarters. Dining guards pushed their plates away. Every German in a uniform reached for a weapon. All were converging toward Jordan and Colette.

Jordan flashed backed to one of Major "Ten-to-One" Tunstall's training principles. "When completely surrounded, limit your attackers' path to you, which might mean backing yourself into a corner."

Conceptually, that principle seemed counterintuitive. However, fighting from the middle of the pack meant defending against multiple and simultaneous attackers. If a defender can move into a corner, he has eliminated seventy-five percent of the attacking locations. He might only have to defend himself against one or possibly two attackers.

Jordan trained his 1911 sidearm at the two SS officers directly before him and fired four rounds. Two landed in the chest of one and two in the other. As the officers fell, more ran up behind them. Some darting in and out of offices down the long hallway.

Colette raised her MP40 to fire at three guards rushing toward her and Jordan from the other end of the hallway. Her shots hit one, causing him to reel in pain. The others ducked into offices.

Several shots zinged past the couple, punching holes in the wall above them. The guards coming from below fired from down the stairs.

A bear of a man with a clipboard opened a door next to

Jordan. Startled at first, he pulled his arm back to punch. Jordan whipped around and delivered a reverse side kick in the man's chest, sending him back, arms flailing, and crashing into a desk.

Jordan had options: multiple attackers from each direction or one big German in an office. He chose the big man.

He grabbed Colette's shoulder and pulled her into the office while she held down the trigger of the MP40 and rained fire down the stairs.

"What are we doing?" she asked.

"Keep shooting!"

Colette dropped to one knee and fired from the side at nothing in particular. She squinted at the firepower as spent brass casings flew out against the wall.

Jordan turned and took a step toward the window.

The big German he had kicked jumped up and tackled him. His 1911 slid across the floor to the corner of the room.

Colette's MP40 ceased firing as the magazine emptied. "I'm out. What do I do?"

Jordan lifted his head from under the German. "Close the door!"

She slammed it shut and slid a chair under the doorknob.

The German brought down a hammer fist on Jordan's head with a terrific scream.

Jordan moved his head to the side and the fist crashed into the wood floor.

Colette noticed the gun in the corner and charged toward it, but the German grabbed her hair, pulled her back, and pushed her into the wall.

Jordan brought his knee up into the German's groin, delivering an open-hand strike to the neck.

The German leaned back, one hand on his groin, and one on his neck.

Jordan lunged toward the pistol. His fingertips brushed it just as the German grabbed his ankle and yanked him back. The pistol slid further away behind a box. With his free foot, Jordan drove his heel into the big man's nose.

Colette tried for the gun again but eased back as gunfire erupted through the closed door. She covered her ears and crouched against the wall.

The German wiped the blood from his nostrils and upper lip, ignoring the gunfire.

Jordan cudgeled the man with a telephone seven times on the side of his head with great force and quick succession.

Colette regained her composure, scurried across the floor, and reached the 1911. She turned to fire as Jordan brought a typewriter crashing down on the German's head. The big man tumbled over, eyes closed. He fought no more.

More shots came through the door until someone shouted in the hallway. "Stop firing!"

The doorknob shook.

Jordan pointed. "Shoot at the door in bursts! Here." He tossed her a full magazine for the 1911.

Colette rolled up to one knee and fired four rounds at the door. The slide stopped in the open position after the last round fired. She dropped the empty magazine and loaded the full one.

Jordan opened the window at the back of the office and stuck his head out. He turned back. "Keep shooting."

He threw one knee over the ledge and held out his hand toward Colette. "C'mon. We're leaving."

She turned her head from the door. "What?"

"We're jumping."

She fired two more rounds. "What? Are you crazy?"

"Trust me, Colette."

The office door crashed partially open with a cacophony of

shouts from German guards. An arm pushed through the splintered wood.

Though she shook her head, she grabbed his hand. They leaped from the second-story window and made a safe landing eighteen feet below.

Colette opened her eyes to see Jean-Pierre helping her out of the pile of trash that broke their fall.

Jordan worked his way out of the heap and moved a few paces with a slight limp as a burst of gunfire skipped off the pavement next to him. He looked up to see a German firing from the window they had just escaped from.

Moody approached with his Thompson and sprayed the window, sending the German back in.

Germans approached from the side of the building. Two Maquis fired at them from behind crates in the alley.

Jordan, Colette, Moody, and Jean-Pierre ran the opposite way of the SS on the street.

Three more Germans came around the other end, surprising the group. As one raised his MP40 to fire, his face opened up. The bullet from Whitfield's sniper rifle killed him instantly. Moody quickly dispatched the other two.

Several guards attempting a garage exit were turned back by Cummings's squad of Maquis fighters.

Moody pulled a whistle from inside his jacket and blew.

The signal caused the Maquis and ComDet members to decrease their fire and run down the alley for exfiltration. In groups of two, they would stop, drop to one knee, and deliver covering fire, allowing the other pairings to move farther down the alley.

Whitfield slung his rifle and shimmied down a pole attached to the building.

After the Allied group had moved two blocks, the Germans gave up their chase.

Rather than pile into one slow-moving and easy-to-spot truck, the Allies split up between three cars. Each took a different route out of town.

Jordan sat in the passenger seat of one car, Valère at the wheel. Colette, Moody, and another Maquisard were in the back.

"Well, that was interesting," Jordan joked.

Valère looked over at him. "You're bleeding."

Blood soaked the top of Jordan's left shoulder.

"I think a bullet nicked me. I'll be fine." He placed his hand over the wound.

"You're charmed," Moody said. "Luckiest guy I know."

Colette, Jordan, and Valère smiled.

"Thank you," Colette said, looking at Jordan.

However, Valère, driving, responded, "You're most welcome, my dear."

The Maquisard in the backseat doubled over onto Colette's lap. Blood soaked his side from a wound unnoticed by the group and perhaps, due to shock, unnoticed by him.

Colette touched him and pulled her blood-stained hand away. Moody placed two fingers on his neck and felt his pulse. "I'm afraid he's gone."

Colette stroked his hair as a tear rolled down her cheek.

Jordan's smile subsided, and he stared out the window.

BLANKETS COVERED SEVEN dead Nazis on the garage floor of the SS headquarters. Wertz paced in front of the others in ranks.

"I leave for ninety minutes and this happens." He pointed toward the dead bodies. He walked up to a junior officer standing in front of the ranks. "Tell me how one man does this to a supposed elite group of troops."

The junior officer clicked his heels. "Sir, we—"

"Silence!" Wertz screamed. He paced again, rubbing the scars on his neck with the back of his fingers. "Let's see how this day has gone so far. I found out that idiot Bader was fraternizing with some French tramp and has somehow deserted or been captured. Does his driver report him missing? No. He cowardly drives back here and goes to bed. We attempt to locate him and all we manage to do is execute one French tramp." He looked at the junior officer. "Do I have this correct so far?"

The junior officer nodded and wiped sweat from the side of his face.

Wertz pointed at the dead bodies again. "And this. Some American waltzes into our headquarters. He tiptoes up the stairs." Wertz mimicked the tiptoeing. "He manages to cut through several guards with little to no resistance. He easily unlocks the door to release that girl. Several guards with fine German-made weapons are unable to bring him and the girl down. He even managed to kill this fat pig." Wertz kicked the side of the big dead German Jordan had hit with the typewriter. "Then they fly out of the window like a crow." Wertz flapped his arms, mimicking a bird. "They join a couple of their little French friends and scurry off. And not one of them lies dead in the street. You didn't manage to kill a single one, yet seven of ours lie here dead." Wertz paced again and looked toward the street through the garage entrance. "It's almost as if one of you were working with them."

The majority of the SS troops knew to stand tall at attention without expression or reaction. They knew he'd sense the slightest movement on their part. Some of them thought he could read their minds.

One reached up to adjust the bandage around his head. He had confronted Jordan in the garage and received the throat strike and gun butt to the head.

Wertz caught the movement out of the corner of his eye and pointed toward him. "You. Come here."

The young soldier stepped out from the second row and stood next to the dead bodies.

"Look at them," Wertz said. "This is many people's fault. But I cannot help but wonder why you survived this episode. Everyone else who confronted that American is dead. But you survived. Can you explain this?"

The young SS soldier adjusted his bandage again, his blond hair sticking out. "I don't know, sir. I tried to stop him. He had papers. I was trying to check them and he attacked me. I—"

Wertz held up his left hand. "I think I understand." The SS commander quickly pulled his Luger sidearm and shot the young soldier in the head. His body fell on top of the seven dead.

Blood spattered the face of a soldier in the front row. He remained motionless, eyes wide.

Wertz holstered his Luger. "Now, this American that seemed to so easily meander about our headquarters appears to be the same American that was our guest about six months ago according to some of you. He managed to escape then as well while I was attending other business." Wertz stared toward the street again. "Tollwütiger Hund. That's all he is. A rabid dog. Well, we'll find the tollwütiger Hund and put him out of his misery."

NINETEEN

HEAVY SWELLS PRODUCED whitecaps off the Normandy coast. The chilly air and overcast sky presented a less-than-ideal *holiday at sea* atmosphere. The salty air and sounds of landing waves gave the beach a peaceful quiet. Pre-invasion bombing suggested that the war was coming to the Normandy coast, but perhaps not that day.

Two German soldiers manned a small machine gun emplacement just after dawn. The Allies had bombed the Normandy area for months in anticipation of an eventual landing. The concrete structure offered protection from the elements and, to some extent, protection from air attacks but not near as much as the larger casements that housed larger guns and larger crews.

One German took his turn peering through the binoculars into the early morning darkness over the ocean. "You think the Allies will come today, Sergeant Strom?"

"You ask that every day, and every day I say the same thing, young Erdmann. I have no idea." The old German sergeant sat back on a concrete ledge and lit a cigarette. His forty-two years and two wars showed on his face.

"Well, I want to be ready, that's all."

"Nothing really prepares you for combat, except combat.

You've never even shaven your face. Don't be in such a hurry to fight."

Erdmann looked back from his binoculars. "I'm sixteen years old. I'm a man. And I'll kill every one of the enemy I see. Maybe, even today."

The old soldier took a deep drag. "OK, young one. We'll see."

Lieutenant Jaeger ducked his head and entered the emplacement.

Strom began to pop up to attention.

Jaeger waved a hand. "Sit."

"See anything worth reporting?" Jaeger asked Erdmann. "An armada of fish or a renegade seagull? Perhaps a fisherman attacking us with an oar?"

Erdmann turned. "No, sir. Nothing to report."

Jaeger removed his cap and sat on the ledge. "You fought in the last war, right, Strom?"

The old soldier nodded.

"Is this what it was like in the trench? Just sitting and waiting for the enemy?"

Strom shook his head. "No, sir. Not quite. The difference is, they attacked. And attacked often. A whistle would blow and they'd come running and screaming. We'd shoot and kill several and then they'd retreat. Then our side would blow a whistle, we'd attack, they'd shoot, we'd retreat. This went on over and over. Occasionally, one of us would get a little further and gain one valuable meter of ground."

"My father said the same thing," said Lieutenant Jaeger. "Seemed so senseless."

Strom raised his mug and bread. "This here is the life. In the trench, we missed many meals. We slept sitting up with our feet in knee-deep water. Everyone was sick. A miserable existence. All that, and we lost. Humiliated."

"There's nothing humiliating about serving the Fatherland," the young Erdmann said.

Strom chuckled. "You're so idealistic. Did they teach you that in the Hitler Youth?"

"Don't be so hard on the young private, Strom. He is our future. He even has the blond hair. If the Führer were here, he'd pat him on the head and give him a medal." Jaeger stood and took a position next to Erdmann. He looked out through the binoculars. "Yes, Sergeant, it's soldiers like this young man that will bring us victory. If only our beloved Führer would let our commanders that have actually won battles make the decisions."

Erdmann and Strom looked at one another and then at Jaeger.

The lieutenant lowered the binoculars. "First, von Rundstedt is in charge. Then, Rommel. But neither of them can put on their boots without Hitler's permission. What does Hitler know? He fought in the trenches like a good German soldier in the last war, but what does he know about stopping an invading army?"

"But, sir. Look where we are? We own France. And Poland. And—"

"And what, Private?" Jaeger sneered. "We invaded countries that could not fight back. Not to any meaningful degree, that is. What happened when we invaded the Soviet Union? The Battle of Stalingrad? We lost. Hitler with his 'hold at all cost' orders. Overextended like the Romans. And yes, look at us now. Sitting and waiting for an army of well-trained, well-equipped, highly motivated soldiers. They will come from the sea and fall from the sky. And they will fight in great numbers. Do you think this elaborate wall we've built along the Atlantic coast will hold them? It might delay them. We are like that obstacle out there." He pointed to a large, X-shaped iron device known as a Czech hedgehog used to stop tanks and large vehicles. "But they will get through. And many of us will die. They aren't hampered by this dysfunctional command structure like we are. Roosevelt and Churchill let their commanders do their job. They let soldiers lead soldiers."

Strom jumped to his feet. "You see, Erdmann. This is what I've been saying. We are going to lose this war."

"No!" Jaeger shouted. "That's not what I'm saying. We will lose with Hitler in charge. If he will let those trained in the arts of war actually lead, we will win. But Hitler's too drunk with power to do that. He thinks he knows more than anyone. It's like a game for him, moving toys around on a map."

"I've heard things," Erdmann said.

"What things?" Strom asked.

"About the Führer having syphilis or something. People in the town say it's made him crazy. They say he rants and raves like a madman."

Strom scoffed. "You shouldn't listen to these people. Propagandists. They're filling your head with lies."

Jaeger held up a finger. "No, wait, Strom. It's not too far from the truth. I know an officer that experienced one of these tirades. The Führer went on and on about cold soup. That some Jew had made sure his soup would be cold by the time it arrived. That this Jew meticulously considered the preparation and timing of when the soup would be served to ensure the Führer had cold soup. He forced high-ranking officials to investigate as he obsessed over it." The officer raised the binoculars again and looked into the English Channel. "Hitler will lose this war. If he was removed from command, let's say, then we'd have a chance.

"And now, Rommel, our best general, has left Normandy for his wife's birthday. General von Rundstedt is in charge. And he doesn't even agree with Rommel. The Allies will probably attack in the middle of the night, but we will all die because the Führer will be asleep and everyone will be afraid to wake him." The officer paused and looked to the side. "Nero fiddled while Rome burned."

Erdmann cocked his head.

"Rommel has left?" Strom asked.

"Yes, he left. But look at this weather. The waves. It's supposed to be like this for days. The Allies won't be attacking in this weather."

Strom sat back down and lit another cigarette. "I don't think they will attack here anyway. It's too far across the English Channel. Pas-de-Calais. That's where they'll attack."

Jaeger nodded. "You're probably right. But we'd better be prepared for them to walk right up these beaches." Jaeger handed the binoculars back to Erdmann and walked to the exit. "Attack or not. Hitler or not. Calais or not. We'd better be ready when the Allies come. And I assure you, they will come."

Strom lay back on the ledge and tipped his cap. "Wake me up if you see the Allies."

The young Erdmann returned to his watch and scanned the horizon.

TWENTY

June 5, 1944
D-Day Minus One

MANY IN THE Resistance knew the Allies would launch a massive invasion force, but like the Germans, they remained in the dark as to when and where. There were far too many untrusted sources offering mere guesses. When the Allied attack would begin, where the landing would take place, and where reinforcements should be placed to support the coastal defense were all questions facing the German command. Rommel believed in stopping the Allies at the beach, knowing that the German army would suffer from a land battle. The Allies owned the skies and would be able to give ground troops tremendous support. He personally supervised the fortification of the vast Atlantic Wall with encased gun emplacements, anti-glider stakes, the flooding of fields, and thousands of mines.

The Allies offered cleverly designed misinformation to throw off the Germans. A phantom army of rubber inflatable tanks, equipment, and more were staged in England as if in preparation for an attack elsewhere than Normandy. Radio chatter and information further confused the Germans so that they considered attacks from the north, south, and west to all be plausible.

The French Resistance had prearranged secret announcements by the Allies to let them know when the invasion would begin. As the location was revealed, they could begin their work of cutting communication wires and conducting other minor acts of espionage.

The French not engaged in active resistance lived their lives as best they could, longing for the invasion and enduring the bombing. Allies dropped ordnance across the coast to weaken German defenses. Unfortunately, the sporadic nature of carpet bombing took many French lives and destroyed non-strategic property. The bombing stretched inland, wrecking property throughout farms and cities, including Caen. No one in Normandy escaped the war.

EIGHTEEN-YEAR-OLD HENRI DRAY had served Valère and the Resistance well. Nick Jordan appreciated his firsthand knowledge of the Caen neighborhoods. Like many Maquis, his hatred for the Germans and thirst to rid them from his homeland fueled his desire to fight. He'd seen friends and family suffer under jackbooted thugs.

He'd spent his youth in Caen living a normal and peaceful life. His parents, who had no other children, provided for all his needs. A decent student, he had a natural talent for art and hoped to study in Paris. As the war came, he watched those dreams fade away.

Henri had urged his parents for weeks to leave Caen and stay with friends in Molière away from Allied bombing. The conversation always began and ended the same.

"I'm not cowering in the woods like you and your friends," his father said as they sat at the kitchen table.

Henri stood, his chair screeching across the floor. "We're not cowards, Papa. We're doing important work. We're fighting the Germans like soldiers."

Henri's mother put her hands on his shoulders. "Sit, Henri. Calm down."

His father pointed his finger down toward the chair, order-ing him to sit.

"Sit, my son. Just listen to your father."

Henri sat and cupped his glass.

"I'm not suggesting the Resistance, or you, are cowards. Perhaps 'cower' was a poor choice of words. I mean that we should face the Germans head-to-head, like in the last war. We charged them, bayonets fixed." His father held his arms up, el-bows out, mimicking the action. "One time we—"

Shaking his head, Henri interrupted. "That was another time, Papa. The Germans have tanks and planes. They aren't in trenches. We tried that early in the war and they beat us in six weeks. The Allies are coming. We have to help them. We have to distract the Germans and disrupt their activities. Valère is a good leader. He knows what he's doing."

His father pinched tobacco and stuffed it in his pipe, offering no answer to his son.

Mother and son sat quietly awaiting a response from Henri's father.

The quiet was broken by a match striking the side of the table. Puffs of smoke exited the side of his father's mouth. "The Allies. Yes, our great hope. The Allies that we hoped were com-ing in '42. And then they were sure to be here in '43. And now we wait, yet again."

Bang! Bang! Bang!

All three turned to the door.

"Open up!" someone shouted in German.

Henri's father looked at his wife and son and slowly ap-proached the door.

"Right now, open up!"

He turned the knob slowly. As the door cracked open, a German soldier drove his shoulder through, forcing it open.

Henri's father was knocked to the ground, his pipe sliding across the floor.

Henri's mother screamed as Henri reached down to help his father.

Five soldiers filed in behind the first.

Henri's father rose to one knee. "Get out of my house."

A soldier brought the butt of his weapon down on his chest, sending Henri's father back to the floor.

Major Wertz slowly stepped in, rubbing his neck with the back of his gloved fingers. "I'm Major Wertz. Thank you for inviting me into your home."

Henri's mother covered her mouth with both hands. Most in Caen had heard of him.

His father crouched, hand over his chest.

Henri touched his father's shoulder and looked up at Wertz.

"You," Wertz said, pointing to Henri. "Sit." Wertz directed him to a chair at the kitchen table.

Henri obeyed.

The SS officer walked around and sat directly across from him. He wore a knee-length leather jacket, gloves, and a cap, all black. The outside air offered a chill, but not one necessarily warranting a leather coat. He removed none of them. Wertz placed his forearms on the table and locked his fingers. Lacking emotion, he stared at Henri.

No one else spoke. Henri's parents remained in position. They could do nothing but hope the Germans would leave.

The SS guards had seen this before. The Wertz stare. The ultimate in intimidation. No emotion. No noise. The victim left only to their thoughts. Thoughts about what might happen. Sweat dripped. Pulses quickened.

Henri suffered all these afflictions.

After an agonizing ninety seconds, Wertz broke the silence.

"Would you be so kind as to state your name?"

Straightening up in his chair, defiantly, the young man answered, "Henri Dray."

"Correct," Wertz announced. "You have spoken the truth. I know this because I am a lie detector. I know there are those that have this machine and hook up wires to your body. But I need no machine. I have a specific ability to read minds. So, I know what you're thinking right now. You think you're tough enough to take anything. That you can lie and trick me. I assure you that none of this will happen."

"Go ahead. Ask me anything. I'm not afraid of you," Henri said, folding his arms and looking to the side.

"I'm so glad you're agreeable. I will indeed ask you a few questions. How long has your father been working with the Maquis?"

"What?" His father blurted.

Henri shot a look back at Wertz. "That's a lie. My father's not a Maquisard."

Wertz pursed his lips and nodded. "I believe you. And I'm happy to learn that you know who is and is not a Maquisard. It's you that is actually a Maquisard. Isn't that so?"

Henri glanced to the side and back. "No," he said, matter-of-factly.

"That would be a lie." Wertz lifted his head, looking at one of his soldiers in the eyes.

The soldier struck Henri's mother's stomach with the butt of his MP40.

His mother let out a loud grunt and collapsed to the floor, coughing.

The father reached for her but was blocked by the same soldier.

"Nooooo!" Henri cried out and made a similar gesture

toward his mother.

Wertz slammed his hand on the table. "Silence!"

Henri rubbed the sides of his face and rocked in his chair. "No, no."

"Listen to me!" Wertz screamed. "Listen to me!"

The room fell silent as everyone resumed their positions.

Clearing his throat, Wertz locked his fingers again and rested them on the table. "Now. I told you I could tell when you're lying. I failed to mention that there are repercussions for lying. You know that now, don't you?"

Henri looked at Wertz with no reply and back at his parents, now both sitting on the floor.

"Don't you!" Wertz said in a loud, commanding voice.

The young Frenchman nodded and turned back to Wertz.

"I'm happy we have an understanding. I know you're with the Maquis. Why do you think we're here? You're with that same Maquis that's helping those Allied soldiers. The same ones that murdered my friends at our headquarters. And I know that your little group likes to run around and hide in the woods. I want you to tell me where that is. And you'll also tell me what their plans are. Their activities. You will be like my special, little helper."

"But, I can't do—"

Wertz nodded again at a soldier, who prepared to strike Henri's mother.

"No, wait!" Henri said, holding his hands out. He licked his lips. "I mean that I don't know if I can."

"You have lied to me again. You want to be difficult and say you cannot. You don't want to do this, but you will do it. You'll say anything to protect your parents. And to make sure you do the job as my special, little helper, your parents will be coming with us. Not so that I can kill them. I may do that eventually. If I find out you fail in any way, I will make sure they suffer for days. Another one of my special talents. I can torture someone for days before they die." Wertz leaned in and began to whisper, but everyone in the room could hear. "I like doing that to French pigs the most."

The stunned Henri sat quietly, offering no reply. He looked at his parents.

Mr. Dray's head hung low.

Mrs. Dray shook her head, tears rolling down her cheeks.

A GUARD STATIONED outside Henri's apartment walked over to Wertz's car. The driver leaned on his leg with one foot on the front tire. The smoke of his cigarette rolled into the air.

"What's going on in there? How long will this take?" the guard said to the driver.

The driver shrugged. "How should I know? I just drive where Major Wertz tells me."

The guard looked up at the building. "I've heard stories. That he plays with your mind. Sometimes he just stares. I hear his stare can make you go mad. Like hypnosis."

"Ha," the driver laughed. "You shouldn't listen to rumors. He's—"

"Not rumors. A friend of mine had this happen. He and another soldier were supposed to collect a package for the major, but they returned very late, claiming they got lost. He knew they were lying. The major just smiled at them and made them sit in chairs. He sat across from them and no one spoke for thirty minutes. Major Wertz read a book. He'd occasionally look up and smile. It was warm and they were sweating, but not the major. The only noise was the pendulum of a clock.

"Finally, my friend blurted out that they had stopped for a drink. That he knew this was wrong and that they deserved to be punished. The major closed his book and said something like 'thank you for your honesty.' He took the binding of the book and struck the other guard in the nose, breaking it. You've seen him. The one with the bandage. He told my friend to pick him up and leave. And that was it. You see. He's crazy."

The driver rolled his head left and right and stuck out his bottom lip. "Perhaps. That does seem crazy. I've heard these rumors, err, stories, as well. But if you think about it, the major sat in comfort, enjoying a good book, and got the information he wanted. Some would call that crazy; others might call that smart.

"Of course, he is ruthless. We were both in the garage during his rant about the American killing several of our soldiers. He shot one of the guys right in the head. Execution style. Like it was nothing. Then he holstered his weapon as if he'd swatted a fly." The driver dropped his cigarette and snuffed it out with this boot. "If I were you, I'd quit asking questions, and I definitely wouldn't discuss the sanity of our commanding officer."

TWENTY-ONE

COMDET SIXTEEN AND Valère's Maquis entered the cave following a successful, but costly raid on the SS headquarters. The French buried their fallen comrade in a shallow grave near the cave. A proper burial would have to wait, as the invasion loomed. Preparations had to be made. In a mere twelve hours, gliders would land and paratroopers would fall from the sky.

Jordan, all business, addressed the group. "It's time everyone was briefed on what will happen tomorrow."

The commandos lifted their heads.

"Pay attention," Valère said, calling the French to listen to Jordan.

"It's been a long time coming." Jordan paused and smiled. "The Allied invasion, weather permitting, will begin at midnight. Paratroopers will drop all over Normandy during the night. Troops will land in gliders across the countryside. They will come in boats from the sea. Our mission will be similar to some of theirs. Disrupt the Germans' communications, movements, and reinforcement of the coast. If they run, we'll get them there too. Unlike the regular troops, I have no interest in prisoners." Jordan's smile had turned to a stern demeanor. "Thousands of men are coming. They're highly motivated Americans, British, and Canadians. Many of them have never seen combat. Some will be scared. They'll be running up the beach under fire. Some of those paratroopers will drop in a field, all alone. We're going to do everything we can to support them. Our main area of operation will be Caen. Both preventing the Germans from leaving Caen for the fight at the beach and stopping those coming to Caen with supplies. We'll hold them."

Valère stood and pointed to the map. "Our focus will be here. The main road out of Caen to the coast. When the call goes for Wertz's troops to help out, we'll have a few surprises for them. Some of you will join the ComDet team and the rest will go with me. We lost a friend this morning. A brave young man that I will deeply miss. But we got another back. It's war and these sacrifices hurt." He paused, looked down and then back up. "Get some rest. Eat. Check your supplies. Tonight we leave. Tomorrow we fight. Tomorrow we take back our country."

The listeners dispersed.

Colette walked up to Valère, who stood next to Jordan. "Which group do you want me with?"

Valère shook his head slightly. "Neither. You've been through too much. You need to stay here."

Hands on hips, Colette protested. "I'm as ready as anyone else. I'm not going to sit around with the other women cooking and cleaning." She still wore the dress she used to woo Wertz, although it was ripped and dirtied. Her bruised nose still held dried blood in the nostrils and her hair remained looking like an old mop. Hardly fetching.

An older woman approached with a moist cloth and attempted to clean Colette but she swatted her away.

"You're not going. That is final. Remember what happened the last time you went against my wishes." Valère matched

Colette's hands on hips as the two faced off.

Jordan waved a hand between. "C'mon, Valère. She's as battle ready as anyone. You should have seen her in the SS headquarters firing—"

Valère shot a look at Jordan. "I'm not interested in your opinion on this matter, Captain. It doesn't concern you."

Jordan, now facing off against Valère, opened his mouth to speak but paused.

Valère and Colette looked at Jordan, awaiting a comment.

Why am I involving myself in this squabble? Jordan thought. Why would I want Colette in harm's way? Maybe Valère thinks the same? She might just be a distraction?

Jordan recovered and pulled Valère aside out of Colette's earshot. "I'm not telling you what to do. I only care about the mission. She's one of your best fighters. She's capable. Take her with you so you can keep an eye on her. You know that when we leave, she'll find a fight to get into. Might as well put her to work."

Valère looked at Colette and back to Jordan. "OK."

Colette threw her arms up. "Excuse me. I don't need big brothers making my decisions. I'm—"

"Fine, you can go with me," Valère said, holding up a hand. "Go. Change. Get something to eat."

Colette cocked her head back, in victory, and walked away mumbling.

Moody grabbed Jordan by the arm and pulled him to a corner, away from Valère. "We have to talk, Nick."

They both looked at the rest of ComDet Sixteen. Cummings tinkered with his equipment and Whitfield sharpened his knife. Jean-Pierre conversed with two older Maquis. The activity in the cave settled as many rested and recovered.

Moody folded his arms. "What are we doing here, Nick?"

"What do you mean?" Jordan asked.

"Why are we here? We're here for a mission. Not to run off and save the Colettes of the world. Not to get involved in the Maquis's arguments. We—"

Jordan held up a hand, recognizing the rhetorical question and lecture. "I—"

"Let me finish!" Moody said. "You snuck into SS headquarters. Managed to find Colette. Busted her out. Fought through who knows what. Incredible. No dispute. But think of the cost. I mean think about it. I've never been on a mission before. Something happens to you and I'm in charge. That was way too risky. No way you ever do that again. That's all I'm saying. Not trying to be disrespectful."

Jordan rubbed his face with an open palm. "Yeah. Probably not one of my most brilliant decisions. But it got the juices flowing, you know?" He smiled.

Moody, not smiling, said, "I'm not kidding, Nick."

"Alright, alright. I hear you. Besides, I'm not happy with the way it went down in there. We eliminated quite a few, but it was sloppy. Too many things could have gone wrong. Too many variables unaccounted for. And I fought this big guy. Could've gone bad. Way too sloppy."

"You're injured, and one of the Maquis died," Moody said, with raised eyebrows. "Costly maybe, but I don't know about sloppy."

"Yeah, well, I'll be fine. But I can't reconcile that Maquisard's death."

Moody leaned in and whispered. "Well, from what I hear, any one of these guys would gladly have given their life for Colette. Not to win her over—although that'd be nice—but because of the hell she's been through losing her family."

The same woman that attempted to clean Colette's nose

walked up. "Let me take care of that, sir," she said, pointing to Jordan's shoulder injury. "Take off your shirt, please."

Jordan stripped off his shirt, revealing a deep, three-inch gash across his left shoulder where a German bullet had likely grazed across.

She poured liquid from an unlabeled brown bottle, moistened a cloth, and dabbed the wound. "I'll need to sew this up."

He nodded.

She inserted the needle.

Jordan winced, barely, and then looked up at the map, thinking about the next evolution.

ONE HOUR BEFORE midnight, the five members of ComDet Sixteen and eighteen Maquis gathered around the map in the cave. Five Maquis would join Jordan's team and the remaining, including Colette, would follow Valère.

Jordan used a crooked stick for a pointer. "The Grand Crossroad on the northeast side. We'll control that intersection without anyone noticing. In other words, we'll allow traffic to pass when we want, divert it, or stop it. It's a vital point where the road to the west feeds other roads to the coast. The south and east directions offer access for reinforcement and supplies. And, of course, the north road goes straight to the coast, where thousands of Allied troops will be landing. We'd prefer they have a casual walk up the beach. Those boys will be defenseless against machine guns, will have to navigate through mines, and endure shelling.

"Valère's team will be in four separate groups at points on the outskirts of Caen with two-way radios to notify us of German reinforcements headed our way. Hopefully, we'll keep the enemy response to a minimum, slow down advances, and dam up retreats."

Henri held up a hand. "Who are you taking with you?"

"Well, Henri, I want you to go, and Valère is giving me others that know the Caen streets like the back of their hand. I'll need fast intelligence on every road that feeds toward the crossroad. We'll own this intersection." Jordan looked left to right at the group. "It's a privilege to serve with you. That is all."

The group began to disperse.

Cummings grabbed Jordan's arm.

Jordan turned. "Ah, yes. I almost forgot." Jordan held up his hands. "Hold up, everyone. I have forgotten that Sergeant Cummings has developed a little ritual of reciting this poem before we leave for a mission, if you'll indulge him." He turned to Cummings. "Floor is yours."

Ian Cummings didn't have the Oxford-like education of many of the other ComDet commandos, but he sounded as if he did. His natural accent sounded much more like royalty rather than a reflection of his Cockney upbringing. He could converse on history, politics, or literature with anyone. He didn't particularly care for poetry, but this piece carried special meaning.

An avid soccer player, Cummings had a secondary school coach who forced the players to memorize *The Charge of the Light Brigade* and recite it in perfect synchronization as a pre-game speech. The poem, as his coach had related, promised adversity. Each player may question the strategy, but they must still follow commands. They were to play on and serve the team. Only with that would they reach the greater goal.

Jordan loved that concept and had experienced something similar. His Yale football coach had attended West Point when Douglas MacArthur had taken over as superintendent. Stressing academics, MacArthur famously said, "Upon the fields of friendly strife are sown the seeds that, upon other fields, on other days, will bear the fruits of victory." The Yale coach had repeated it often in preparation for gridiron battle, so Jordan relished his ComDet team having their pre-battle ritual.

Cummings stepped forward. "With your permission, a recitation of a poem about a British light cavalry's valiant charge on a Russian battery in the Crimean War."

He stood, ready to present a formal recitation as if he were in school.

He cleared his throat. "Ladies and gentlemen! A poem by Alfred, Lord Tennyson. *The Charge of the Light Brigade*.

"Half a league, half a league,
Half a league onward,
All in the valley of Death
Rode the six hundred.
'Forward, the Light Brigade!
Charge for the guns!' he said.
Into the valley of Death
Rode the six hundred.

"'Forward, the Light Brigade!'
Was there a man dismay'd?
Not tho' the soldier knew
Someone had blunder'd.
Theirs not to make reply,
Theirs not to reason why,
Theirs but to do and die.
Into the valley of Death
Rode the six hundred.

"Cannon to right of them,
Cannon to left of them,
Cannon in front of them

Volley'd and thunder'd;
Storm'd at with shot and shell,
Boldly they rode and well,
Into the jaws of Death,
Into the mouth of Hell
Rode the six hundred.

"Flash'd all their sabres bare,
Flash'd as they turn'd in air,
Sabring the gunners there,
Charging an army, while
All the world wonder'd.
Plunged in the battery-smoke
Right thro' the line they broke;
Cossack and Russian
Reel'd from the sabre stroke
Shatter'd and sunder'd.
Then they rode back, but not
Not the six hundred.

"Cannon to right of them,
Cannon to left of them,
Cannon behind them
Volley'd and thunder'd;
Storm'd at with shot and shell,
While horse and hero fell.
They that had fought so well
Came thro' the jaws of Death
Back from the mouth of Hell,
All that was left of them,
Left of six hundred.

"When can their glory fade?
O the wild charge they made!
All the world wondered.
Honour the charge they made!
Honour the Light Brigade,
Noble six hundred."

Cummings, stoic, had offered the recitation in the Queen's English, pausing occasionally for emphasis. The Maquis listened intently, although many didn't understand the words. He had practiced it, and recited it a second time, in perfect French.

Those in the cave applauded.

Cummings politely nodded.

"You are the noble ones," Jordan said. "It's an honor to serve and fight with you."

TWENTY-TWO

MAQUIS CAMP
June 6, 1944

D-Day

I WISH WE could have run it a few more times," Jordan said to Moody as they walked along the path three miles from the cave.

Moody smirked. "We can only run it so many times. Ever since Tunstall gave us this assignment, we've practiced and practiced it."

Jordan shook his head. "But not these guys." He pointed with his thumb over his shoulder at two of the Maquis in the rear. "We had guys stand in as Maquis, but these guys haven't done it once. They've not run through successful scenarios or one of the hundred things that can go wrong. That's exactly why I wanted to jump sooner."

"You heard old Tunstall. Didn't want to risk us getting caught and tipping off the Nazis that an invasion was coming. Every minute we're here, we're a walking wealth of intelligence."

"Yeah, I know. Just like to be prepared," Jordan said. "Most of these guys have combat experience. But look how young they are. Damn near kids. Not trained soldiers. We don't even know their backgrounds, and think of all the sensitive information they have."

"Well, Nick, if everything worked out, it wouldn't be any

fun, now would it? We've got to keep things interesting."

Jordan smiled.

FORTY PACES AHEAD, Henri and another Maquisard, named Philippe, led the group down the path. Philippe had fought with Valère for over a year.

He barely looked sixteen years old and probably came to Valère at that age. He'd been telling others he was nineteen for over two years. He had made deliveries on his bicycle for his father's business in Caen and knew every street, alley, and shortcut. He had not experienced any particular family tragedy like the others. His parents and younger siblings remained in Caen and endured the occupation as best they could. They'd been spared of interactions with German soldiers and attempted to keep from being noticed. Swayed by the rhetoric of Jean Prene, Philippe chose adventure against his parents' wishes and joined the Maquis.

"Why are you walking so fast?" Philippe said to Henri.

Henri turned his head and shrugged. "What do you mean?"

"The others, the Allies, are getting further behind. Why are you rushing?"

"Just ready to get there. Ready to fight. Besides, they should keep up." Henri adjusted the sling for his Sten gun and bit the nail on his left ring finger.

Philippe looked over his shoulder at Jordan and Moody. "Those Americans are ready to fight. This is going to be a big one." Philippe raised his Sten and mimicked firing. "I'm going to kill so many Germans, they'll think I'm a commando. I'll be a hero. Probably get a medal."

Henri rolled his eyes. "Quit talking so much. We're supposed to be quiet."

"Quiet? We're all alone out here. Besides, we're practically whispering."

"Just stop talking. I don't want to talk. I need to think." Henri picked up his pace.

ONE HOUR AFTER Jordan's departure, Valère's group of eighteen departed the cave. Their journey, similar to that of Jordan's group, involved a few key friends delivering them to their appointed area of operation.

The final Maquisard soldier exited the cave, offering a wave to those left behind: one injured man and the two older ladies that served in domestic roles.

The group slung their weapons and made final checks before they would disappear through the woods. The mood was jovial despite the dangerous task ahead of them. One yawned but most were accustomed to the late-night departures in which they used the dark to hide their movements.

"I'm sorry I've been difficult, Valère," Colette said. She returned to her normal Maquis look of long pants and ponytail. Like the others, she carried a Sten gun with spare magazines in pouches strapped to her waist. Unlike most of the men, she wore no beret. No one confused Colette for a man.

"I was very worried those Germans might hurt you. And, you know. Something worse. I mean. . . . uh . . . assault you . . . or—"

Colette held up a hand. "No. They didn't."

Valère turned back. "I wish I could say you've been a pleasure to have around. You gave us all quite a scare. How about you think like a fighter, huh? Like them." Valère pointed at the other men gathered around the cave entrance.

Colette smirked.

Rat-ta-tat-tat-tat!

Blood splattered the outside of the cave and three men fell.

Valère, Colette, and the others crouched and scattered.

From the dark of the woods, German machine gun fire produced yellow flashes. The bullets sparked as they ricocheted off the cave's rock wall and bark flew from trees.

Several more French cried out from wounds. Attempts at return fire proved feeble.

Pockets of German soldiers moved up from clumps of bushes and trees and fired at will.

One German soldier met a Maquis bullet to the face and fell dead.

Two French tried to run back in the cave only to find another machine gun light up the entrance. They darted back to their position behind a large rock.

The French Resistance fighters had no escape. Except for three: Valère, Colette, and one other, Laurent. They had been standing away from the rest of the group. Valère returned fire and yelled for Colette and Laurent to make their way down a steep hill next to the cave. Seeing his comrades' cause lost, Valère scurried down the hill as well.

A teenage Maquisard tried to follow Valère but was cut down.

Another Frenchman made a mad charge toward one of the machine guns. His desperate attempt lasted a mere twelve feet.

The covering machine gun fire, number of troops, and advantage of surprise allowed the Germans to easily overtake the remaining French. Those that could lifted their hands and offered their surrender.

When the shooting stopped, six French lay dead and eight were on their knees with hands interlocked behind their heads. One other lay face down, alive but writhing in pain.

The Germans had entered the cave and forced the two older

women out to join the other prisoners.

Wertz approached. "Good evening, my friends. Or, morning I should say. I knew you little varmints were hiding out here somewhere." He wagged his finger at them.

The injured Maquisard on the ground cried out in pain.

Wertz lifted his head at a nearby soldier.

The German lifted his weapon and put three bullets into the wounded man, silencing him.

Wertz sat on a stump, removed his cap, and scratched his head. "So, where were all of you headed?"

The ten remaining French, on knees, said nothing.

A German soldier with a Luger pistol at his side took a position behind one of the women.

"Anybody feel like talking?" Wertz said. "You see, your friend, Henri, has been very gracious with information. Too bad he's not here. He might like to hear what we've done with his parents. You should share that same graciousness as Henri. He's already told me so much. I only need you to fill in a few blanks."

An agonizing eight seconds went by.

Wertz nodded.

The soldier raised his Luger and fired into the back of the woman on the end.

"Nooooo!" one of the men cried.

The other woman remained in position with her hands behind her head, but now, she screamed hysterically. "Wha . . . wha . . . wha . . . !" Her sounds making no sense.

One of the young Frenchmen jumped up to run away but was quickly dispatched by a German MP40.

"Now, where—"

The woman's screams interrupted Wertz. He nodded again.

The German executed the screaming woman.

Wertz shook his head. "Such a pity. Now, where were we?

Ah, yes. Where were all of you headed?"

The nodding and shooting continued until only three Maquis remained upright.

One bled from an earlier wound during the firefight, one stared defiantly into the woods, and one blubbered, next in line for the Luger.

The German removed the empty magazine from his pistol and replaced it with a full one. He raised his weapon toward the crying man.

"I'll tell you," the bleeding man said.

His friend next to him whipped his head. "No. You can't. It won't save us. They'll kill us anyway."

"I know. Just trust me," he whispered. "Calais!" he announced to Wertz.

Wertz replaced his cap and stood. "Calais? Why? Why were you going to Calais?"

"The invasion next week. Everyone is going to help. Caen is lost. No reason to stay. We were to go as far as we could and help protect the invasion force. But that's all I'm saying."

His friend, playing along, shook his head in disgust.

The other one's tears dried up.

"When exactly is the invasion?" Wertz asked.

"The Viking likes to sleep," the man said. He winced from the wound on his neck that oozed blood.

"What?" Wertz asked, approaching methodically.

"The radio message yesterday. 'The Viking likes to sleep.' That's our signal that the invasion will be at Calais next week, depending on the weather. Had they said, 'The Viking is tired,' it would mean the invasion is next Monday at dawn. But that's all we know, I swear." He began to weep. "I'm so ashamed. I don't want to die. Please . . . please spare me."

Wertz approached the man slowly. He knelt and faced him

within inches. Wertz stroked his own neck. Neither spoke.

The man slowed his pulse and took deep breaths. He returned Wertz's stare.

The Nazi major had mastered the art of reading body language. To know when someone was lying. To pick up on the most subtle cues. He didn't know that he stared at a classically trained actor. One renowned locally for his stage presence and convincing performances. Who had decided to play a French Resistance fighter that had received a message to travel toward Calais. And he gave the greatest performance of his life.

Wertz broke the silence. "He's telling the truth! Let's go!" Wertz hopped up and walked briskly toward the opening in the woods from where they had arrived. He turned and waved his arm as if swatting away a fly.

The German with the Luger finished off the last three Maquis.

A junior officer ran up to Wertz. "We found a map on the cave wall, but nothing more. No useful information."

"Burn it," Wertz said. "Burn it all. But not these French pigs. Leave them for the wildlife."

The dutiful SS soldiers set fire to the interior of the cave and then followed Wertz through the woods.

One of the Maquisard's feet twitched. He'd been shot at the beginning of the ambush and lay near the cave. The Germans, assuming him dead, spared him of the *coup de grâce*.

TWENTY-THREE

C ACKLING CHICKENS WOKE a French farmer. He threw off the covers and stood.

"What is it?" his wife asked.

"Probably a damn fox again. I'll get it this time."

He reached for the shotgun propped next to the front door and headed toward the coop in a nightshirt and bare feet. As he reached for the latch on the coop, he noticed an object falling slowly from the sky just above the tree tops. He switched from anger to bewilderment. As his sleepy eyes cleared, more and more floating objects appeared.

Is that a parachutist? he wondered.

"Don't move!"

The farmer, not understanding the phrase, turned slowly to find a soldier pointing his weapon.

"Put that gun down, right now." The soldier used his other hand to point at the farmer's shotgun.

The soldier spoke no French and the farmer knew little English.

It didn't matter, the farmer was too paralyzed with fear to speak, but he managed to lower his shotgun to the ground and rise back up with hands raised.

"Now, we won't have any trouble from you, will we?" The soldier looked barely old enough to shave.

The farmer cocked his head. "American?" He pointed at the soldier. "You American?"

"No, British. All of us," he said, looking past the farmer to the left and right.

The farmer turned around to find two more soldiers. He smiled. "Merci, merci!"

Realizing the farmer presented no danger, the soldiers huddled for a moment and then began to walk away.

The farmer took a few steps toward them and whispered. "Merci. Merci."

The soldier turned back. "Secret, OK?"

The farmer nodded. "Oui, oui. Secret."

"And you're welcome, sir." The Brit smiled and disappeared into the trees.

The farmer rushed into his bedroom. "Mon cherie, mon cherie, get up, quickly."

She leaned up on elbows. "What?"

"They're here. The Allies. The British. The soldiers. The invasion has begun."

While many of his neighbors may have feared the unfolding events, he smiled at the dramatic arrival of those that would help to free France from the German invaders.

He ran back out and leaned a ladder on his house. Climbing to the roof, he sat as if watching a sporting event. He noticed several more parachutes fall all around him as well as silent planes gliding toward the ground. In the far distance, bursts of flak littered the sky. He experienced a strange but peaceful quiet on his farm as he imagined the violence that must be occurring near the sea.

NORMANDY COAST
June 6, 1944

D-Day

SERGEANT STROM SLEPT on a ledge inside a German bunker at dawn. His body had accustomed to sleeping through aerial bombardment.

"If they hit us, they hit us. It will be our time to die," the two-war veteran would often say.

His sixteen-year-old partner, Private Erdmann, winced at each explosion, some of them caused by Allied bombs detonating German-laid mines.

Immediately outside his concrete window, sand and clumps of grass surrounded the front of the casement under strands of barbed wire. Behind him, an abandoned holiday home stood in desperate need of repair. His fellow soldiers used it often for shelter, but most preferred an escape into the nearby commune of Lion-sur-Mer.

Erdmann had secretly vied for the affections of a young French girl his age but had been rebuffed at every attempt. He spent the long nights on watch thinking of a German victory, marrying that girl, and living in one of the houses by the sea.

He was too naïve to understand that she hated him. Not so much personally, but she hated all Germans that had stolen the last five years of her life. They stole those years during which she should have been enjoying school with friends and reading by the sea. Instead, she spent her days dodging Allied bombs and inappropriate German soldiers. She wanted nothing to do with Erdmann or any other Nazi. And they were all Nazis to her.

Strom coughed and struggled to a sitting position. "Well, any Allies today?"

"Not yet. Just beach and sea." Erdmann picked up his field glasses and peered toward the rough waves.

The sun, to his right, began to break through. For many days, he saw nothing but the occasional fishing boat. This day, like the past few days, showed rough waves and an overcast sky. But something was different. Hundreds of black bumps appeared through his lenses. He wiped his eyes and looked again. He scanned left to right and still saw more bumps.

"Sergeant. Come have a look. There's something out there on the water. A bunch of small black things."

"Probably birds or something," the sergeant replied through a yawn. He stood and walked over to the opening, taking the field glasses.

"Those are not birds, my young friend," Strom said, once he'd taken hold of the binoculars again. "That would be the Allied armada coming right at us."

Erdmann's eyes widened and his mouthed opened.

Strom turned to him. "Run, go get the lieutenant."

As Erdmann reached the exit, Lieutenant Jaeger burst through. "The Allies are coming! Check your weapons and ammunition."

"Yes, sir!" Strom replied.

Jaeger put his hand on Erdmann's shoulder. "This could be a diversion. The main attack could be somewhere else. Be ready for anything. And remember your orders. Fight to the death."

Jaeger exited to check the other emplacements along the beach.

Erdmann's teeth chattered.

"Calm down, Erdmann. This is what you trained for. You have good cover. All you need to do is shoot at everything that tries to come up that beach. Kill as many as you can. Our defenses are sound. We'll cut them down before they step one foot on the beach."

The sounds of planes above were followed by those of bombs dropping. These and the bombs from ships at sea wreaked havoc around them. The old German soldier and his young, idealistic partner could only wait and hope that they'd survive the explosions.

Over the next hour, the bumps turned into ships. Hundreds of them as far as the two soldiers could see. As the bombing along the beach died down, smaller boats emerged from the larger ones and headed directly toward them.

The silence was broken by the whirring of landing craft. Heads poked out over the walls of the tiny vessels.

"Here they come!" someone shouted in a nearby casement.

"Here they come!" Erdmann repeated.

"When I say, fire at that one," Strom said, pointing to a particular boat.

The whirring became louder. Incoherent commands, shouted in English, could be heard from the boats.

Erdmann focused on the one Strom had pointed at. It rose up on a wave and made a splash as it stopped. The front began dropping with a cranking sound. As the door opened parallel to the water, there was a brief moment of silence.

One brief moment.

Men yelled and emerged from the craft, dropping waist deep in the water.

"Fire!" Strom yelled.

Erdmann closed his eyes and squeezed the trigger. He quickly opened his eyes and noticed his tracing fire was far left. He corrected and directed it at the opening of the landing craft. Three men fell and others crouched back in the craft while several others pressed forward. He fired wildly, unsure if his MG42 machine gun was killing the enemy or his fellow machine gunmen were getting the job done.

The weapon stopped and Strom reloaded.

Six more landing craft opened their doors as men spilled out. Tens of them became hundreds working their way from the water to the sand.

Erdmann tried to hit the individual soldiers that headed for the protection of the dunes between him and the water.

"No, shoot at the masses coming out of the boats!"

Erdmann's fire proved little resistance as many ran up the shore. Several others made it to the seawall. It seemed his was the only gun left.

The bombs must have taken out the other positions, he thought.

Strom poked his rifle out of the opening and attempted to snipe a few of the enemy.

Several of the Allied soldiers were a mere forty yards away.

One man screamed in agony from injuries.

More and more boats appeared and hundreds of soldiers scattered across the shore and into the water.

To Erdmann's right, one of the big gun casements burned. Lieutenant Jaeger ran out, his right side on fire, and was shot at point-blank range by an enemy soldier.

The shouts in English grew louder and clearer although Erdmann and Strom understood none of it.

"What can we do?" Erdmann shouted.

Strom looked at him, calmly. "We can run or we can fight to the death. You are so young. You should run. I will man the gun."

"No!" Erdmann cried. "I will fight! I will fight to the death for the Fatherland!" He turned to his gun and placed his finger on the trigger.

A round object flew through the opening.

Strom instantly recognized it as a grenade. The two

Germans looked into one another's eyes.

Strom closed his.

Erdmann took one step toward the exit as the grenade exploded.

Moments later, British soldiers entered their casement. "They're dead," one of them said.

The beach, which would later become known to the world as Sword Beach, was a vital point for the British to land in and control. The enemy offered sparse resistance for the initial landing, but the Germans would not easily relinquish Caen, and reinforcements were sure to head toward that beach. Caen's waterways and roads offered numerous strategic advantages for both sides. The British hoped to liberate the city on the day of the invasion but met much stiffer resistance. Moving beyond the Atlantic Wall, they fell short of the city by a few miles. The Battle of Caen would linger.

TWENTY-FOUR

CAEN OUTSKIRTS
June 6, 1944
D-Day

A DARK GREEN sedan rumbled down the old Molière road toward the outskirts of Caen. Because of its unimproved surface and winding route, the Germans rarely used it, and thus the Resistance often did. The early morning darkness required the driver to keep his headlights on.

"Stop the car here," Valère said, pointing toward a clump of trees.

Colette leaned up. "Why here? We're supposed to be at the main road out of Caen."

The vehicle came to a stop and Valère jumped out.

Laurent, the other Maquisard that survived the cave ambush with them, followed Valère out from the backseat.

Colette held out her arms. "What are we doing?"

"Just trust me, Colette." Valère curled his finger.

The elderly Mr. Frère looked over his shoulder to the backseat. "Please, dear, I cannot sit here too long. You must go."

Colette grabbed the barrel of her Sten gun and stepped out.

Mr. Frère backed up, turned, and headed back down the path.

"So, what are we doing?" Colette asked.

The trio began walking along a line of trees that led toward an industrial section of town and offered a stealth entrance into the city.

"We're going to the warehouse near City Hall where the Germans have those stores of supplies and explosives," Valère smiled. "We're going to blow it up."

"What?" Colette stopped. "Are you mad?"

Valère and Laurent stopped and turned around.

Colette shook her head. "We're supposed to be on that side of town," she said, pointing in the opposite direction. "Nick is expecting us to be there and radio him information. We're supposed to contact him as soon as we reach our position. We need to tell him about the ambush. About the others."

"Nick?" Valère said. "You're suddenly on a first-name basis with Captain Jordan."

Laurent rolled his eyes.

"What does that have to do with anything?" Colette repositioned her gun to the other shoulder.

"Nothing," Valère said, sarcastically, and began walking again. "Those plans were abandoned when the Germans ambushed us and took out all our fighters. We need to do something big to distract the Germans. This will keep many of them from leaving Caen."

Laurent remained silent, too young and inexperienced to offer an opinion.

"I know what you're doing. You're jealous of Captain Jordan. You think you have to do something big so that he doesn't get all the credit." Colette quickened her pace and got in front of Valère. She slapped the back of her hand onto her other open hand. "You're quick to act without thinking of the repercussions."

"Really, Colette? Do you hear yourself? I'm the one to act without thinking?"

"Exactly. I have learned my lesson. If I've learned anything, it's that we have to consider how our actions can put others in danger."

"I know what I'm doing. This will help our Allied friends." Valère walked defiantly.

Colette looked to the side as she walked.

"Maybe we should at least contact them," Laurent said, breaking his silence. He held up the radio that he carried in his pack.

"Yes, I agree," Colette said, with a mocking smile.

"No!" Valère made a side-to-side slashing motion. "There's no need to break radio silence until we're in our new position. Then, we will tell them what we're doing."

"They need to know that not one of the four groups will be in position. The commandos may need to completely alter their plans." Colette took the radio from Laurent's hand and held it toward Valère.

He grabbed the radio from her hand. "Don't you understand, Colette? Jordan's commandos don't need us. They were just keeping us busy. We're like their innkeepers."

"You've gone mad, Valère. You're not making any sense," Colette said.

He handed the radio to Laurent. "Put this away. Let's go."

Colette and Laurent watched for a moment and then reluctantly followed.

JORDAN'S TEAM RESTED in an abandoned office building at the Grand Crossroad on the northeast side of Caen. The recently built brick structure had suffered damage to the top floor above them, including several broken windows due to an Allied shell. Surrounding buildings seemed untouched by the war. Although far from downtown Caen, the area offered numerous shops and cafés for those choosing to be closer to the sea.

From their fourth-floor vantage point, they could see in every direction. Heavy drapes concealed their position. They already noticed some commotion within German units, presumably a reaction to invasion reports, but nothing worth ambushing and revealing their position. Bigger fish lay ahead. The enemy troops seemed alarmed but unsure of any coherent assignment. Otherwise, the locals went about their morning routine as many walked or rode bikes following the same direction as the vehicles and working their way through the crossroad.

After a long evening of slow, methodical travel to avoid detection, the five members of ComDet Sixteen and five Maquis checked their weapons and equipment. A few ate the rations that the older Maquis women had prepared. No one slept.

Jordan and Lieutenant Dick Moody used the thick layer of dust on a desk to draw out potential scenarios. Their work required a great degree of flexibility and freelancing should conditions change. Their orders were to disrupt the Germans on their way to the beach to intercept the invading Allied army, and to slow up retreating soldiers. Major Tunstall's "Ten-to-One" philosophy would be in full effect. ComDet teams were expected to carry the advantage due to superior training, surprise, and help from indigenous forces—the Maquis.

"Anything?" Jordan asked Sergeant Ian Cummings as he tried to reach Valère and other Maquis on the radio.

"Nothing, sir. It's as if they have them all turned off or something."

The bulky radios were difficult to operate. The ComDet team depended on one Maquis group toward downtown Caen and another toward the beach to warn them of oncoming Germans.

"Must be your radio. I can't imagine yours is working and

both of theirs are not," Jordan said. "Keep trying the backup frequency."

"Well, we can't wait for them," Moody said. "That means we'll have less time to react, but we know the Krauts will be coming right through here." He pointed toward the intersection.

Jordan glanced at his watch. "Fifteen minutes and we're moving into positions."

Henri bit his fingernails, sitting against a wall next to Philippe. Three other Maquis sat across the room.

"You have to tell him," Philippe whispered. "You have to tell him what you just told me. You should have told him last night. You should have told Valère before that the Germans might know where the cave is."

Henri shot him a look. "I told you that I can't say anything. They will kill my mother and father. I just told you in case something happens to me."

Philippe leaned forward and up to one knee. "You tell him or I will."

Jean-Pierre overheard them. "What are you two whispering about?"

Henri looked at Jean-Pierre. "Nothing."

Philippe maintained his stare at Henri. "Tell them."

Henri stood. "Ca . . . Captain Jordan."

The young French fighter commanded the attention of the entire room.

Tears began to flow from Henri. "I was so scared. I didn't know what to do."

Jordan and Moody stood on each side of Henri.

"Calm down, son. Take a breath. Just tell us," Jean-Pierre said with his hands on the eighteen-year-old's shoulders.

Henri proceeded to tell the group of the valuable information he gave Wertz. None of them knew the true costs of his betrayal but imagined the worst.

One of the other Maquis rushed toward Henri. "Traitor!"

Henri winced, expecting a blow.

Moody stepped in and held back the attacking Maquis.

"Stop it!" Jordan said. "There's nothing we can do about that now. We have to assume the worst. That no one else made it out and we're on our own. And that's why we can't reach anyone on the radio."

Corporal Rance Whitfield turned from peeking through a draped window. "Captain. If one of our friends here were to take that motorbike parked outside, they might get to the cave fast enough to warn them. At least we can do that one thing."

"Yes! I will go," Henri said.

"Humph. I think you've done enough," the Maquisard that had lunged at Henri said. "I will go."

Jean-Pierre nodded. "That's a good plan, Captain. There's a reason Henri's here. He knows this area better than any of us. He should stay and let the other one go."

Jordan threw his arm back, thumb extended.

The Maquisard headed for the door.

"Can you ride?" Whitfield asked.

The Maquisard turned back and smiled.

Careful to avoid too much commotion with the moving of drapes, a few of them looked down at the motorcycle. The Frenchman walked up to it, started it, and rode away as if it were his. A couple of German soldiers watched him ride by as he nodded back.

Jordan's group now consisted of nine men: five ComDet members and four Maquis.

"I have to get to my parents. I have to save them," Henri said, collecting his things.

Moody grabbed his arm. "Listen, kid. Wertz is going to be

very busy today. He probably got all out of you he wants for now. I doubt he'll be worried about you or your parents."

THE RIBBON-CUTTING FOR the new Caen City Hall was well attended in the previous century. For seventy-three years, the town had considered it a great achievement in architecture. A large church, one hundred years older, stood to the left, and an even older building to the right housed the museum of fine art. Once the Germans took over City Hall, they pillaged the museum of its most valued assets and murdered the curator. They left the church untouched and allowed the priest to continue his work, but closely monitored him and his congregants' comings and goings. In essence, Caen's enemy controlled the three most prominent structures, exerting authority over Caen's government, culture, and religion.

In addition, they confiscated the property of many businesses, but they left many others in place to keep the city running. Down the block from City Hall, they used the Renaud Fabric Company's warehouse to store military goods, in particular, explosives for anything from small arms to howitzers. It had been lightly guarded, but recent events with attacks and infiltrations of the German headquarters at City Hall forced Major Wertz to replace the regular army troops around the storage area with his own SS.

The warehouse, which stood on the end of a row of connected buildings, had a typical front door entrance facing the main street. Just inside, an office, once busy with Renaud workers, typically had one middle-aged woman working at a desk. Two large doors on either end of the back were guarded by four German soldiers each. A truck backed partially into the side opening as soldiers loaded boxes onto the truck.

Valère, Colette, and Laurent blended in with morning

commuters. They chose a table at a café across the street from the Renaud warehouse and sipped cappuccinos. They had stashed their weapons and other Maquis-related gear behind a dumpster two blocks away. This included a knapsack full of explosives. Laurent had turned off the radio at Valère's instruction.

Colette wore her hair down to cover her appearance, possessing the one face among the three that some of the German soldiers might recognize. She sat facing the café's rear and occasionally turned to view the warehouse when the other two told her it was safe.

Laurent, being practical, suggested they order breakfast.

"How can you eat at a time like this?" Colette asked.

Laurent shrugged. "I'm hungry."

"He's right." Valère raised a hand, signaling for the waitress. "We do need it for strength, and it will keep us from looking conspicuous."

Colette stroked her hair. "So, what exactly is this grand plan of yours, Valère?"

He nodded. "Right through the front door. There's no guard. I've been in there before and a door leads into the warehouse. It's piled high with boxes. I can sneak in there and set off the explosives. The chain reaction will set off everything."

Colette rolled her eyes. "With all those guards. They'll hear you. They'll catch you."

"No. They'll be distracted."

"By what?" Laurent said, shoving food into his mouth.

"By you two," Valère said, sneering. "You two will come around the corner to the building across from the warehouse's two main doors and have a lover's quarrel. A loud, embarrassing quarrel. One that will attract and entertain all the guards. I only need two minutes. You'll end in classic fashion with a slap across his face." Valère made a tiny slapping motion over his plate of food.

"Sounds too easy," Colette said. "Besides. We all know Mr. Renaud. He's given so much. He's lost two sons to the war and most of his business. Now we're going to destroy his building, not to mention the building next to it."

Valère leaned back. "We must all make sacrifices."

TWENTY-FIVE

CAEN GRAND CROSSROAD
June 6, 1944
D-Day

S ERGEANT IAN CUMMINGS held the most forward spot of the ambush location. He sat amidst several small crates in the back of a broken-down truck. He had strategically stacked the boxes to conceal himself. A small slit remained for him to see everything coming down the main road from downtown Caen. The largest invasion force in history was landing mere miles from him at the beach, and Wehrmacht and Panzer forces were all around him. However, he saw no signs of either. Other than the morning hustle and bustle, it remained relatively quiet. Most of the buildings were unoccupied due to heavy bombing. Pedestrians and commuters traveled through the crossroad, as few lived or worked there. The citizens around him had no idea that the most significant day since the start of the war had begun.

The Maquisard in the truck cab, whom the French called Rud, could see Cummings and would relay his signals to Jordan. Without the advanced warning by radio, Jordan quickly developed a hand signal system. It was simple: done on one hand with a signal of one to five. A one meant the sighting of a vehicle, a two that they would let it pass thinking it offered no great threat to the landing troops and that it was not worth exposing their position. A five meant an overwhelming force that they'd attempt to slow down, an attempt which would reveal their location and impel them to flee. It was far from perfect but gave them the chance to extend their mission as long as possible.

Cummings lowered his field glasses and rubbed his eyes. He'd slept little in the last twenty-four hours. A familiar rumble caused him to raise the field glasses.

A German staff car approached, leading a convoy of other vehicles. Behind the car were two trucks and one motorcycle with a sidecar. As one of the trucks came around a slight bend in the road, Cummings noticed that it pulled a howitzer—a powerful weapon against soldiers marching up a beach. He flashed three fingers to Rud, who relayed that signal to Jordan.

A three meant they'd attempt to disable the oncoming force, clear wreckage, and hope no locals would alert other Germans. Then, they'd reset for another ambush. The crossroad area was known to be Resistance-friendly and would likely help, rather than hinder the ComDet team.

Corporal Rance Whitfield created a sniper's perch on top of the building where the commandos and Maquis had rested early that morning. He had a clear view in every direction. He built his perch so that he could swing his M1903 Springfield sniper rifle for a direct shot at targets on any of the four roads leading toward the intersection.

Jordan and Henri knelt in a café to Whitfield's left. An Allied bomb had destroyed the interior of the café and they knelt behind a window with all the glass missing. Jordan could see all the other positions, and they could see him. He played the quarterback.

"Listen to me, Henri," Jordan spoke to the young Frenchman while looking straight ahead. "I know you feel bad about what you did. You probably think you need to do something to make up for it. That would be a bad move. Just help us here as you normally would, survive, and go home to your mother and father." Jordan looked at Henri. "Understand?"

Henri nodded. "I do. I just hope they're still alive."

"When we're done here, I'll do my best to help you find out."

Moody and one of the Maquisard pretended to move boxes out of a truck owned by a friend of the Resistance. Moody was careful to glance at Jordan every few seconds for any signals. They would use their machine guns to kill as many of the enemy as possible.

The initial assault would fall on Jean-Pierre and the young Maquisard Philippe. Their position behind the last remnants of a once large building gave them several duck-and-cover opportunities. The road slightly curved from Cummings's point to theirs. The oncoming convoy would lose speed while navigating the turn.

Jordan flashed three hand signals at Whitfield: three fingers, cupped hands for the letter O, and an open hand across the neck.

Whitfield interpreted this as a level-three assault that would begin with him killing the officer in the lead car.

Moody and his Maquisard set their boxes down and picked up their weapons. The Maquisard jumped into the back of the truck and pointed his Sten machine gun out of an opening over the cab. Moody knelt near the rear of the truck with his Thompson machine gun.

The convoy entered the turn and slowed to 20 miles per hour. The lead car contained a driver and one SS officer in the passenger seat. The officer lit a cigarette, leaned his head back, and blew out smoke.

Cummings and Rud turned and pointed their weapons toward the trucks now passing by. Several German soldiers in the back wore the familiar SS uniforms. The second truck pulled the howitzer. Two soldiers, on a motorcycle with an attached sidecar, brought up the rear with no obvious strategic reason.

Whitfield looked through his telescopic sight. His right index finger pressed against the trigger. He slowed his breathing.

The SS officer turned to the driver. "Speed up."

The driver glanced over. "Yes, sir."

Crack!

The officer's head came apart.

The driver, who had just accelerated, took his foot off the accelerator, looked over, and pulled down on the wheel. The car popped up on the sidewalk and into a streetlamp.

Bystanders ran into shops and ducked behind anything that would cover them.

Two hand grenades flew through the air toward the first truck. Jean-Pierre threw one that rolled under the engine. Philippe's landed on top of canvas covering the truck, but it rolled over the far side and exploded one foot down. Jean-Pierre's detonated less than one second later. The truck screeched to a halt. Three soldiers jumped out of the back, met by gunfire from Cummings and his fellow Maquis.

Jean-Pierre and Philippe threw two more grenades at the second truck but both overshot their target. The truck kept rolling and swerved around the disabled one.

The driver of the first truck stumbled out and looked up just as the second truck mowed him down. Realizing he ran over his fellow soldier, the driver slammed on his brakes.

"No! Go!" the passenger-side soldier screamed.

He shifted gears and pressed the accelerator to the floor.

The stunned Germans failed to return fire and were quickly cut down by commandos and Maquis to the front and rear.

Jordan and Henri had yet to fire a shot.

The motorcycle and sidecar had sped up and drove onto the

sidewalk.

Jean-Pierre fired at the soldier in the sidecar, killing him, but the rider survived with a wound in the back.

The truck pulling the howitzer grazed the truck that Moody hid behind, knocking him to the ground. The Maquisard that was in the back had jumped out and approached the truck.

The passenger leaned out as the truck slowed and shot the Maquisard in the chest with a Luger.

Jordan and Henri began firing as the truck sped up into the intersection. One of Jordan's rounds hit the driver in his left shoulder, but he roared past him.

The motorcycle trailed the howitzer by thirty feet.

Jordan jumped out of the window and ran directly at the rider, firing.

Riddled with bullets, the rider slowly veered off to the side and ran into a parked car near Moody.

Jordan stood in the middle of the intersection and watched the howitzer getting smaller as it headed toward the beach. They had halted the convoy but failed to stop the most important piece.

Cummings, Jean-Pierre, and the Maquis fired a few final shots at the remaining survivors. Taking prisoners was not practical and none offered their hands in surrender.

Moody pulled the dead German off the motorcycle and backed it up. "C'mon," he yelled at Jordan.

Jordan ran over and lifted the dead German out of the sidecar.

Moody revved the accelerator while Jordan still had one leg outside of the car. Henri, standing in the middle of the intersection, watched them ride away.

A disabled truck and car, and several dead SS, littered the street, as did one dead Maquisard. French locals slowly poured out of buildings and other places where they'd hidden.

"Hold your positions! Some may still be alive," Jean-Pierre yelled. "Henri, see if he's still alive," he said pointing at the French fighter with a blood-covered chest.

Whitfield kept his sniper rifle pointed toward the chaos.

Cummings had Rud resume the watch down the road.

Jean-Pierre and Philippe approached the back of the truck. Jean-Pierre nodded to Philippe as they ran up to it, ready to fire.

"All dead," Jean-Pierre said. "Help us get these vehicles and bodies off the road," he said to several bystanders. "We'll hide them in that warehouse down the block."

Henri walked around the truck. "Our friend is dead. What are we going to do if more Germans come?" he asked.

Jean-Pierre looked at him matter-of-factly. "We'll stop them."

"Where are the captain and Lieutenant Moody?" Cummings said, out of breath.

Jean-Pierre looked down the road leading to the beach and shook his head. "Off on another great adventure, I suppose."

MOODY FOLLOWED THE trail of dust churned up by the truck pulling the howitzer. Its driver had veered off the paved road and onto a gravel-covered one. Driving much faster than ideal for that type of road, the howitzer swayed back and forth.

"I can't see it," Jordan yelled. He rolled up to his knees for height.

Moody leaned left and turned the bike off the road and out of the haze from the dust.

The bumpy field knocked Jordan back down.

The truck rolled along sixty yards ahead of them at forty miles per hour. A barrel poked out of the canvas that covered the rear of the truck followed by muzzle flash.

Pow! Pow! Pow!

Machine gun rounds hit the ground in front of the motorcycle. Moody steered back toward the road using the haze for concealment.

The truck increased its speed to forty-five miles per hour.

"We have to get closer," Jordan said.

Moody rolled back on the accelerator as the motorcycle lurched ahead and pulled within ten feet of the howitzer.

The German machine gun fired again, causing Moody to veer off. He recovered and moved within six feet.

Jordan returned fire from his Thompson machine gun, forcing the German deep inside the truck. "Get me up to the truck," he yelled.

Moody sped up to the right side, becoming parallel to the howitzer.

A German soldier leaned out of the passenger side of the cab and fired his Luger. His first shot missed, but the second hit the sidecar.

Jordan fired, sending the soldier inside the cab.

The soldier in the back appeared again and pushed the canvas aside with his machine gun.

Moody switched his hold on the accelerator to his left hand and pulled out his 1911 pistol with his right. He pointed and put down the soldier with a shot to the right cheek.

The Luger-wielding soldier emerged and fired three quick rounds. One hit the front tire, blowing it out. The handlebars twisted out of Moody's hands, and the motorcycle with the sidecar slid sideways toward the howitzer.

Jordan, who stood on top of the sidecar, leaped onto the howitzer, landing at its base.

Moody kept rotating and was thrown off the bike as it slid to a stop. Unharmed, he looked up to see Jordan riding the howitzer.

Moody shook his head. They didn't teach us that at Camp Delta, he thought.

The driver corrected the truck to the center of the road, causing the howitzer to swerve. Jordan fell off the opposite end. His feet dragged on the road while he held on to a piece of the axle. The barrel towered over his head pointing to the rear.

The Germans, thinking they'd lost the two commandos, looked straight ahead down the road.

Gravel and dirt splattered Jordan's face. He reached for a higher point and pulled himself up. One leg still dragged as his other knee reached a secured position. He inched his way up the huge weapon and navigated his way across the left axle. Much like walking on a moving train but one that was only six inches wide. He extended his arms for balance. At the halfway point, he paused.

I wonder if there's anyone else in the back? Probably would have stuck their head out and fired by now, he thought.

The truck hit a rut.

Jordan crouched and braced as the howitzer wheels hit the same rut. He fell between the two axles and straddled across the entire frame. Counting to three, he released the right and grasped the left, shimmying the remaining few feet to the rear of the truck.

He hopped onto the bumper and pulled out his sidearm. Jordan's eyes widened as two German soldiers stared back.

One had no life left in him after meeting Moody's bullet, but the dead man's eyes remained open. The other sat holding his side, with blood covering the area. His head moved up and down from heavy breathing as he looked at Jordan helplessly. He posed no threat.

Jordan lifted his 1911 to end the boy's misery but paused.

Poor kid, he thought. A mortal wound. He'll die anyway. I don't want to be the one to do it.

Jordan collected the wounded and the dead man's weapons and dropped them out of the back so they wouldn't be noticed by those in the cab.

The only access to the cab would be over the canvas covering, supported by a metal framework.

Jordan climbed to the top and crept toward the front. He considered throwing his one grenade but abandoned the idea, realizing he'd need the truck intact to hide the howitzer as well as its boxes of munitions. He planned the quickest and cleanest path. Shoot the passenger, swing into the cab, kill the driver, and take over the truck.

He quietly slid on top of the cab. Pulled himself to the edge of the passenger side and readied his 1911 pistol.

The rut that had knocked him off the axle was dwarfed by the next one. His pistol flew from his hands and slid down the front windshield and across the hood.

Both Germans swung their heads left, right, and up. The driver sped up to just over fifty miles per hour.

The passenger-side German crawled through the window and set both hands on top of the cab, his right hand grasping his Luger pistol.

Jordan bent his index finger into a point and brought it down on the back of the hand holding the Luger.

"Ahhhh!" the German cried as the Luger followed Jordan's 1911 down the windshield and across the hood.

Jordan followed the strike with another to the back of the other hand and then a closed fist to the soldier's face.

The German leaned back, parallel to the ground with his lower half in the cab.

The driver grabbed his ankle to save his comrade from

falling out.

Jordan rotated on his belly, facing the driver side.

As the German pulled himself back up, Jordan drove his heel into the man's face.

Failing to hold on, the soldier back-flipped to the ground. The truck tire missed his head by inches, but the howitzer swerved and crushed him.

Jordan dove through the passenger-side window, feet first, and landed in the seat.

The driver swallowed hard, pointing a Luger at Jordan's face. *Click.*

The gun jammed. The driver released the wheel and attempted to clear the jam.

Jordan struck the driver's throat with an open-handed knife strike.

The driver dropped the Luger and grasped his neck.

The truck veered off the road, through a fence, and into a field.

Jordan reached for the Luger on the floorboard as the driver kicked him in the face.

As Jordan lunged for the Luger again, the driver attempted another kick, but Jordan intercepted it with a punch to the calf.

Jordan grabbed the Luger, pulled the slide, cleared the jam, and fired at the driver's other thigh after the driver had pushed Jordan's arm.

"Ahhh!" he cried.

Jordan fired again into the German's chest as the truck plowed into a hedgerow.

The commando paused for ten seconds, collected his breath, and remembered the wounded soldier in the back.

He pulled the driver from the truck and hid his body in the hedgerow.

With the only remaining weapon, the Luger, he checked the back to find that the young man had succumbed to his wounds. He placed both dead bodies next to the driver, backed up the truck, and headed for Moody and the crossroad.

At the point where the passenger had fallen out, a farmer had already collected the body and put it on a cart. Perhaps a friend of the Resistance or maybe just somebody clearing his land from the leftovers of war. Jordan drove by, nodded at the farmer, and kept going.

He found the crashed motorcycle and slammed the brakes. The howitzer hitch clanked.

Where's Moody, he thought. Did he come after me? He should have headed back to the crossroad to help them.

Moody's training would have told him to stay off the road but that made it harder for Jordan to find him.

Jordan hopped onto the hood and scanned the horizon.

"What are you doing, looking for Nazis?" a voice said from behind a hedgerow.

Jordan recognized it as Moody's and smiled.

"I figured you'd be back. I'm a little disappointed it took you so long." Moody jogged up with two Thompsons slung over his shoulder.

"Well, I forgot to say 'please' when asking for their howitzer and they took offense at that. My skills of persuasion overcame the situation."

Moody hopped into the cab. "Old Ten-to-One Tunstall would be proud."

"Well, well," Jean-Pierre said, seeing the two Americans drive up with the howitzer.

The crossroad had been secured from the previous ambush.

Whitfield had remained at his sniper's perch and Moody took the advance lookout position.

Jordan parked the truck and climbed out, extending a hand to Jean-Pierre. "Good work."

"We've received some reports from locals coming from downtown of several more convoys preparing to advance this way. Much larger ones. Ten times larger. I don't think we'll be able to stop them. Maybe slow them a little," Jean-Pierre said.

Jordan rubbed his chin.

"Something else." Jean-Pierre put his hand on Jordan's shoulder. "Cummings finally received a radio call from Laurent. I'm afraid it's very bad news."

Jean-Pierre relayed the story of the ambush at the cave, during which Valère, Colette, and Laurent were the only known survivors, and of Valère's plan to blow up that SS warehouse.

Jordan threw his hands up. "Valère is reckless. We need to call them back. Tell them to wait."

Jean-Pierre shook his head. "I already tried to tell him, but he got off quickly. That's another thing. Valère purposely did not want us contacted. Laurent snuck in the call while retrieving plastic explosives they had stashed."

Moody put his hands on his hips. "We've got to get there. Might as well help them. Cut the snake off at the head."

"You're right. Let's take the fight to them," Jordan said. "We'll take this truck." He looked at Henri. "Can you take us up some back roads to downtown?"

"Of course, Captain."

"I'll have some of our friends here hide the howitzer and munitions."

Jordan swirled his finger in the air.

Whitfield grabbed his gear and rifle and headed down from the top of the building.

Moody and Rud exited their disabled truck and ran toward the group.

An elderly woman handed them a basket full of biscuits and fruit. "God bless you, boys."

The five commandos and remaining French fighters loaded onto the truck and headed for the heart of the 12th SS Panzer Division.

TWENTY-SIX

WERTZ PACED IN his office, rubbing his neck. "Call them again!"

The sheepish soldier nodded.

Wertz ordered him to call the German High Command for a fourth time that morning. Since invasion reports had come in, no commanders were able to advance major divisions without Hitler's approval. And no one had the courage to wake him. Once awake, Hitler sat in disbelief that Normandy was the real attack and insisted it was a diversion from the real attack at the Pas-de-Calais. The German army remained immobile.

Wertz's information about the invasion was far from perfect. He chose a reactionary tactic to stop the Allies from gaining a foothold. He ordered his troops to begin readying for a trip to the sea and to leave a skeleton crew behind. Every fighting unit should mobilize in his mind.

"Well?" Wertz screamed at the soldier on the phone.

"They . . . they said to hold our position, sir."

Wertz grabbed the receiver from the soldier. "What the hell is the matter with you? What are you idiots waiting for? Hello?"

The line was dead.

Wertz slammed the phone down. "Idiots!"

"What?" Valère stared at Laurent with hands on hips.

"I told them about your plan," Laurent said.

Valère slapped the top of Laurent's head. "I specifically told you not to radio them. We don't need their help. What all did you tell them?"

"About what happened at the cave. About the warehouse."

"I told him to call them," Colette said. She hadn't really, but wanted to spare Laurent from Valère's anger. "They should know about the ambush. We're supposed to be working with them. They don't do any operations without us. And we could use their help now."

Valère swatted away her comments. "Let's go. We need to get this done. They've already loaded two trucks in the last hour. Go get in position."

Colette and Laurent made their way around the block and toward the rear of the warehouse. They waited in a doorway for Valère's signal from the café. Once he smoothed back his hair, they were to walk up and begin their argument as he slipped in the front door.

"What is he waiting on?" Laurent asked.

Colette shrugged. "Who knows. Are you really in a hurry? He's likely to get us killed."

"I'm in a hurry for this war to end." Laurent folded his arms and looked up and down the street. He looked back at Colette. "I was going to the Olympics in 1944, you know. Boxing." He performed a left jab and right cross in the air. "I'm really good. Even after the war started, I kept my training up. My uncle worked with me. He was a great boxer in the twenties. We had a gym set up in the garage behind his house. But the Germans took him away two years ago to a work camp like many of the other Jews."

"Maybe you can train again when he gets back," Colette said.

"I hope so. The last thing he said to me was, 'don't drop that left hand.'" Laurent smiled. "He always got onto me for dropping my left hand before my right cross and thus lowering my guard. Even as he was taken away, he was teaching me. When he gets back, I'll get better than ever. There will be regional matches and national competitions. Worlds and then the '48 Olympics. You'll see. I'll be on the podium wearing a gold medal as they play *La Marseillaise.*"

Colette lightly applauded as Laurent took a gold medal podium posture.

"What about you, Colette? What will you do after the war? You're a good fighter. Maybe you should box."

Colette scoffed. "Very funny. But, no. I'm sick of fighting. I want to go to the university and study literature. I want to study all of the works of the Brontë sisters. I want to write novels like them. And meet a man who loves to read. And marry. And have children. And never see war again." Her cheerful demeanor at those plans faded. She looked neither happy nor sad.

"I bet you'll be a great writer," Laurent said.

"Unfortunately, I know more about a Sten machine gun than a typewriter."

"I've seen those notebooks you write in. I'll bet you have lots of stories."

Two German soldiers walked by. One smiled at her and kept his head turned in her direction as his friend babbled on. He winked just before turning his head.

"I hate them," she whispered. "They think they can do anything. I hate every one of these Nazis. They're all sheep following Hitler. I hope we kill them all or at least send them back to Germany with their tails between their legs. Disgusting pigs."

Laurent shook his head. "Sometimes, before I fall asleep, I think about boxing Hitler. I'd jab, jab, jab and then—" Laurent glared at the café. "The signal."

Valère ran his fingers through his hair and walked across the street toward the warehouse. A satchel slung over his shoulder held plastic explosives. Two years before, he had used the power of the pen as a journalist to fight the Germans and fuel the fire of the Resistance. Now he used a Sten gun and explosives.

As he stepped up on the sidewalk, a German soldier looked in his direction.

Valère took a few steps past the front door.

The German turned back, dismissing him.

Valère spun and walked into the warehouse office. As he had suspected, the office was empty except for one woman, the secretary that had occupied the office for twelve years.

"You should take a break," Valère said.

She cocked her head.

He lifted the strap to reveal his satchel. "You really need to take a break."

Her eyes widened. She reached for her handbag and darted for the door.

Valère eased toward the doorway from the office to the warehouse. He split two of the blinds to peek through the window that looked into the warehouse. The large overhead door was open and five SS soldiers stood guard, smoking and talking. Boxes of ammunition and various supplies filled the remainder of the warehouse. Twelve feet of open space existed between the door and the closest stack of boxes. He planned to slide through the door, place the explosives behind the stack, activate a detonator with a ten-minute delay, and sneak out. In and out in under one minute. Valère needed those guards distracted.

Colette and Laurent strolled down the street with her hand

clutching his bicep. They noticed Valère enter the front door as they turned the corner parallel to the open overhead door of the warehouse. Five SS soldiers stood in the doorway.

Colette pulled her hand down. "What?"

All five Germans, along with two older ladies that were standing nearby, whipped their heads toward the couple.

Laurent held out his hands, palms up.

"Why were you with her? Why would you even be talking to her?" Colette turned her head up, indignant, hands on hips. Anyone within a block could hear her remarks.

The Germans laughed and one pointed.

Laurent smiled. "Please, dear. Listen to me. I'm in love with you." He reached for her arm.

"I've seen the way you look at her."

He cocked his head. "Dear, it was one little mistake."

Colette's eyes widened and she slapped Laurent.

The soldiers laughed.

"You teach him," one said.

In the warehouse, Valère made it through the open space undetected. Kneeling down, he pulled the explosives out of the satchel and began to set the fuse.

Click.

"Can I help you?"

Valère slowly turned his head.

A Luger pistol stared back. At the other end, an SS soldier sneered. "Get up," he said, waving him toward the overhead door with the barrel.

Apparently, there was a sixth soldier, Valère thought. He held up his hands.

As they walked toward the opening, the other five Germans laughed at the spectacle across the street.

One of them turned and noticed his fellow soldier and the

prisoner. He whipped his weapon around and took aim. The others followed suit.

"Which one of you fools was supposed to be watching the front door?" The guard kept his pistol pointed at Valère. "What do you think Major Wertz will say when he hears about this?"

The other guards looked at one another.

"He doesn't need to know," one of them offered. "He's crazy. He'll shoot us all."

"We need to show him we dealt with this," another said. "Let's execute this French pig. There's so much else going on with this supposed invasion, Wertz won't care."

Valère turned his head back and forth following the conversation but understood none of it. He didn't speak German and had no idea they were debating his demise.

Colette and Laurent watched from across the street. They watched the guards point their weapons at Valère. He stood helplessly with his hands in the air.

Their lover's spat ploy had effectively distracted all the guards . . . save one. The one that decided to use the toilet at the worst possible time for Valère.

And thus revealed the error in Valère's judgment. A sabotage operation like this required more planning and more fighters. A few hours, if not days of preparation, would have revealed how many guards worked at that time of day. Where they stood or walked and at what times. And a suitable plan to rescue anyone caught. Many times, the French Resistance worked in small numbers, but Valère, Colette, and Laurent were far too few. It was a risky operation from start to finish.

"What should we do?" Colette asked.

Laurent shook his head slightly. "Nothing. There's nothing we can do."

One of the soldiers turned his gun up and smashed the butt

into Valère's face.

Another brought his gun's butt down into his stomach.

Valère grunted in pain.

The rest jumped in with rifle butts and kicks.

Valère attempted to cover himself to no avail.

Colette and Valère looked on in horror as did several bystanders.

One mother covered her young son's eyes and hurried him away.

"Stop. Stop it!" the soldier that had captured Valère shouted. "Pick him up."

Two soldiers lifted Valère up from the warehouse floor.

Valère, barely conscious, hung in their arms. Blood oozed down his face.

The German soldier in charge raised his Luger once again and pointed it at Valère's head. "We should handle this as Major Wertz would." He smiled and pulled the trigger.

Valère's head snapped back and the two soldiers dropped him.

"Noooooo!" Colette screamed.

Three of the soldiers whipped their heads in her direction.

Laurent grabbed her arm, pulling her away. "We have to go."

The Germans gave her no further thought, likely assuming her shocked at the event.

An old French man that had been sorting vegetables at his stand stared at Valère's body. He'd seen this many times. After a moment, he shook his head and returned to his vegetables.

TWENTY-SEVEN

COLETTE HURRIED DOWN the sidewalk with Laurent six steps behind.

"Slow down, Colette. You'll draw attention." Laurent reached for her arm.

She pulled it away and wiped a tear. "I don't care. I'm sick of fighting. I'm sick of it all."

Laurent sped up and put his arm around her as they stepped off the sidewalk curb between two buildings. "We need to—"

A hand reached around both of them and pushed them into the alley. It was Nick Jordan. He put his finger to his lips, shushing them. "Follow me." Three of his knuckles were bloodied and he had a scrape on his forehead.

As they moved down the alley, Jean-Pierre brought up the rear, ever watchful, with Philippe a step ahead of him.

"How long have you been here?" Colette asked.

Jordan frowned. "Long enough. The three of us came to get the three of you. We walked up just as Valère was shot." He slowed and looked into her eyes. "I'm sorry."

"Where are the others?" Laurent asked.

"At a safe house. We're headed there now to regroup," Jean-Pierre said.

The group zigged and zagged through several blocks and buildings.

"I want to go back and kill them all," Colette said.

Laurent scoffed. "I thought you just said you were sick of fighting."

She shot him a look. "Well now we're not alone, are we? I suddenly have my confidence back."

After twelve minutes, they reached the safe house. Rickety stairs led to an apartment over a garage. An old French man with a long gray beard and oil-stained hands nodded as he opened the door. The three other ComDet members and two remaining Maquis looked up from their seats.

The Germans exerted great effort but failed to find and eradicate the numerous safe houses, farms, shops, and other locations where Resistance members and Allies could hide. These locations also offered rest, food, supplies, intelligence, medical help, and a morale boost for French fighters, who typically lived in less than ideal circumstances. As the German increased patrols, the Maquis found it more challenging to travel into Caen. A few hours or a few days in a safe house allowed safe passage from one act of sabotage to another.

Henri jumped up. "Colette! Laurent! I'm so happy to see you. Thank God, you're alive." He looked past the others as the door closed. "Where's Valère?"

Laurent dropped his head.

Colette folded her arms and walked to a corner of the room.

Jordan looked from the left to the right of the group. "I'm afraid our friend Valère is gone."

Philippe covered his mouth.

"I must have killed him too," Henri said.

Colette and Laurent both looked at him.

"What does that mean, Henri?" Colette approached him.

"Nothing, dear," Jean-Pierre said.

Colette looked at Jordan and back at Jean-Pierre. "What does he mean?"

"They have to know," Henri said. "I have to confess to everyone, especially them."

Henri proceeded to tell of Wertz's interrogations, the unknown fate of his parents, and his offer to sacrifice himself if he could.

"I understand," Colette said, almost void of emotion. She cupped Henri's face with her hands. "If I could have saved my parents, I might have done the same thing. I can tell you're sorry." She looked at Jordan. "We should go get them. We can go right now."

Moody held up a hand. "We received word this morning that they were let go. We don't think Wertz ever intended to keep them. Just a little insurance to pressure Henri."

The old man that owned the garage lit his pipe. "So what's your next move?"

Jordan nodded. "I'm glad you asked."

The entire room looked up at Jordan.

"Our mission remains the same. Disrupt German advances, or retreats, in reaction to the invasion. Based on what we're seeing, Wertz and his near 200 troops will be moving out soon. They'll probably leave a skeleton crew behind, but the rest will go."

"I guess this will be a five," Sergeant Ian Cummings said, referring to the hand signal system Jordan had improvised.

The old man pulled his pipe from his mouth. "First Winter Snow."

"First Winter Snow," Jordan said, nodding.

The reference had nothing to do with snow, winter, or when it would occur. The Resistance created the term as a call for everyone, including non-combatants, to arm themselves and fight from wherever they were. During the Spanish Civil War, nationalist General Emilio Mola told a journalist of elements within the city operating as a fifth column in support of four columns of his troops. Jordan looked to locals for their own fifth column.

Once ordered, First Winter Snow required little planning, and by its nature, was designed for situations where time was short. It was more a level of action rather than a type or location of the action.

"Henri. Philippe. Go spread the word. First Winter Snow at Rue Vence," Jordan said. "Barricades and bullets."

Jordan noticed several trucks lining up after Valère's execution and assumed that Wertz would order his troops to depart at any moment for Rue Vence, the main road from City Hall toward the Grand Crossroad and the beach. The small Allied force would make their stand at Rue Vence.

Moody stood. "I'll take Whitfield and gather our downtown stash."

The team had three locations in Caen where they'd hidden extra ammunition and explosives.

Jordan nodded, then continued instructing Henri. "Tell them to set up a barricade at the end of the big curve on Rue Vence and also on all of the side streets as they approach the curve. They'll be moving fast in a column of vehicles. Once they turn the corner, they'll see the barricade and stop. We'll have them boxed in. Then we'll give them hell. Grenades, explosives, gunfire, everything we've got. I want every Caen citizen that can shoot to have a rifle or Sten in their hands. No escape. No prisoners."

Henri nodded and headed out of the door. He'd begin knocking on doors and telling Resistance-friendly homes that First Winter Snow would take place immediately at Rue Vence along with the other instructions. Then, their sons and daughters would knock on doors and spread the word.

The elderly and young children would gather in a safe location. It wasn't necessarily meant to be all-out warfare, but it was serious enough that fathers and sons (and a few mothers and daughters) would drop everything to join the fight.

The old man walked across the room and knelt down. He opened a loose floorboard and pulled out a rifle. He worked the bolt action and loaded a round. "First Winter Snow," he said out of one side of his mouth as his pipe occupied the other side.

WERTZ PULLED ON his leather gloves in the garage of City Hall. "Are we ready?" he asked a junior officer.

"Yes, sir," came the reply.

While Wertz's company of the 12th SS Panzer Division numbered 189 men and officers, pockets of German troops harbored in and around Caen. But none had better training, leadership, and organization than Wertz's group. Most of his troops operated on fear rather than out of a patriotic fervor for the Fatherland. Some grew up in the Hitler Youth or had fathers that fought in the previous world war. Some hoped for a greater German nation or a continuation of the turnaround Hitler had led.

However, many had become disillusioned with the Nazi party. They saw the worst of the party in their very own leader—Wertz. His violent tirades confused them as to who was the real enemy. They had little choice but to suffer under a tyrant or face execution.

On this day, their training kicked in and they followed orders. Sixteen different vehicles lined up from the City Hall garage to the warehouse. Most of them were trucks full of troops or ammunition. Two trucks pulled howitzers.

Wertz chose to ride in a truck in the middle of the pack. Some leaders may have chosen the front vehicle to lead their troops into battle; some the back to avoid risk. Wertz wanted to see his entire force spanned out in each direction.

"Shall we leave a few to guard our headquarters and the warehouse?" the junior officer asked.

"Just that one." He pointed to a soldier with a bandage around his head from Jordan's previous visit. "That's all that's needed. These French pigs don't have the guts to come in here. And I'm sure those others, like that American, are long gone."

AT RUE VENCE, the French had tightly parked cars and carts across the main road and at side roads. People threw furniture out of windows to add to the pile. Shopkeepers along the street constructed cover for their firing positions with stacks of items they felt would stop German bullets. Fathers pointed and showed sons where to aim and when to fire. The Germans had attempted to confiscate guns when they first occupied Caen, but the Resistance had managed to smuggle many guns back in.

A well-dressed businessman walked out of his office and approached the barricade. "What is the meaning of all this? What on earth are you doing?"

"Nothing. Go back to your office," one person said.

The businessman was not a friend of the Resistance, but rather, a supporter of the Vichy French Regime and therefore a collaborator. He, like other appeasers, was not told of First Winter Snow. If told, he wouldn't have known its meaning, but might alert the Germans to suspicious activity.

"What do you mean, 'nothing,'" he protested. "You're obviously up to something. Does this have to do with these invasion reports?"

One of the Resistance nodded. "Uh . . . yes, yes it is. We don't want the Allies coming through here and fighting on our street so we're putting up this barricade. Let them fight out in the country."

The businessman opened his mouth and rolled his head back. "Ahh, yes. Well, let me help you then." He began throwing furniture on top of the pile.

Two of those in the know smiled at one another.

In the back of a shop, several women prepared bottles with petrol and cloth wicks and lined them against a wall. Those Molotov cocktails would rain down on stopped German vehicles. On a normal day, these ladies might be crocheting, but it was no ordinary time.

The ambush area stretched for six city blocks from the bend in the road to the barricade. As the final German truck passed the bend, three French trucks would move across the road and form a barricade in the rear.

Once the Germans were trapped, ComDet Sixteen, the Maquis, and every willing French participant would fight. But the Germans would fight back. Whether motivated by fear or loyalty, once fired upon, human nature would require them to fight back. They'd be a compelling force. Most of these troops had endured brutal training to join this elite force. As combat veterans, being fired upon would not shock many of them.

Should the Germans hold off the attack, offering them a retreat route might be a wise choice, as long as they returned to their headquarters rather than the beach. But they would be back, more prepared, and seeking retribution. The ComDet team, and the French, had to make their stand at Rue Vence.

Few of the French were young, able-bodied men. Most of them had already joined the fight elsewhere. Other than the commandos and Maquis, these were older men, teens, boys, and women of all ages. These were citizens that had endured years of German occupation and sought to rid themselves of that scourge once and for all. They were far outmatched by the German troops, but these French knew what they were fighting for.

TWENTY-EIGHT

RUE VENCE IN CAEN
June 6, 1944
D-Day

N OTHING SIGNIFICANT RESIDED at the end of Rue Vence where they formed the barricade. No one influential or famous. No crucial business or building. Nothing strategic for either military other than convenient access to the shore from downtown Caen. Dozens of side streets fed into the main road from a working-class neighborhood where families made their livings in various warehouses and manufacturing facilities providing everything from bed coverings to kitchen tables. Most of the shops that lined the streets served those families. A large market offered produce from surrounding farms. Lower and middle-class residents from miles around congregated in the area to discuss news of the war. In another time they'd discuss family, farm, and local items, but the war took precedence over all other news. The market had remained open every day since the start of the war—a testimony to this groups' resiliency—although the fruits and vegetables were greatly reduced in quality and quantity.

Few bombs had found their way to this neighborhood, and no rubble or pockmarked buildings could be seen. The local citizens quickly cleared any damage from the war. A bank building that had endured a direct hit was now an empty lot and served as a children's playground with unorthodox equipment. A broken-down Renault tank became a favorite. Children of all ages climbed on the tank, journeyed inside, and hung from the turret. Several months earlier, some men carted in a Messerschmitt plane that had crash-landed. Kids took turns making whirring noises as they sat in the cockpit, ignoring the missing left wing. Everyone had to make do in time of war including the children with their toys and imagination.

"PAPA. I'M SCARED." The twelve-year-old boy held a rifle that was nearly as long as he was tall. He rested the barrel on the ledge of their second-story window. He'd been one of those children who had played in dilapidated military machines and pretended that he was at war. Now he was, far earlier than any person should.

The father knelt next to his son and placed his hands on his shoulders. "Don't worry, son. I'll be right here next to you shooting from the other window. If it gets rough, you can stop and move back. Like I told you before, you just get off a few shots while the Germans are confused. Retribution for your brother and cousin.

"You just shoot like I've taught you. Aim for the largest part of the body, exhale, and squeeze the trigger. You'll do fine."

The boy practiced his aim. "What's it like to kill someone?"

The father looked out the window. After a long pause, he lit a cigarette. "It's a terrible thing. But a necessary evil."

"When are they coming, Papa?"

"Anytime, son. Anytime."

The boy looked up and down the street. He saw no Germans. He saw no war. He reached into his pocket and placed several toy soldiers on the window ledge. The Napoleonic War soldiers were made of tin and had long ago lost their paint. They'd seen hours of imaginary battles. The young boy collided two toys and made a crashing sound but with much less enthusiasm than in times past.

ACROSS THE STREET, and two floors higher, Corporal Rance Whitfield rested his rifle against a chair. Unlike the boy, he had no fears. Jordan placed him at approximately the middle point of where the column of vehicles would stop. The flat offered him a clear shot from the front of the column to the rear. Jordan had given him clear orders. "I'd love to take him out myself, but if you see Wertz, kill him." He had given Whitfield a vivid description of the SS major.

Whitfield's host, and owner of the flat, was a woman in her sixties that lived on her own. Her husband had died before the war, and her two sons had volunteered during the Battle of France. One gave his life for his country, and she hadn't heard from the other son in two years.

She walked over to Whitfield with a serving tray. "Here, son, you need this."

"Merci." He thought this surreal. He was about to be in the battle of his life, and this sweet French woman was offering coffee and bread.

"Don't forget the jam," she said.

Whitfield winked, ate every bite, and drank his coffee.

She offered a motherly smile of satisfaction and prepared to vacate the flat for a safer location.

JORDAN TOOK A position on the ground below Whitfield at a bakery. The commandos and Maquis worried little about blending in or concealing their weapons. They merely needed to hide long enough for this section of the column to pass them. There was little planning in First Winter Snow. They had no way for him to communicate with the rest of the team, other than Philippe, who sat across the street in a café. He gave his team a simple command. "Kill as many as you can. If you're overwhelmed, make your escape down a side street."

Each of them planned an escape route either out of the back of a shop and into an alley or down a street. But none planned to leave too early. They knew the townspeople carried significant risk.

Jean-Pierre and Cummings placed themselves at the rear, where they thought the column might end. Jordan tasked them with providing the most firepower. Since the column could not move forward, or down side streets, the Germans might seek to retreat. The two commandos planned to disrupt that along with Henri and Rud.

Henri's father, Mr. Dray, joined the fight as well. "I owe the Germans a little payback for their treatment of my family," he said.

Lieutenant Dick Moody took the lead of the column with help from Colette and Laurent.

Jordan knew better than to keep Colette from the fight. In the old man's flat, he had offered a feeble, "You want to stay? No one would blame you after what you've been through."

"No, I'm going," she replied.

He only nodded.

The commandos checked their gear. The Maquis paced. Over forty residents along Rue Vence nervously waited. Men and women of all ages.

While ComDet Sixteen was assigned to work as a small elite force in the most dangerous areas behind enemy lines, they also could be a force multiplier. Indeed, they worked with the Maquis to make them even better, the theory being that a Maquis force could greatly increase their effectiveness under a ComDet team's leadership.

Jordan's team had no time to train the townspeople. They only hoped they could each pick off a few Germans when the fighting broke out. The group of fifty or so believed the element of surprise and some clean shots would allow them to kill over half the German force in the immediate fight.

"JUST LIKE JESSE James," Whitfield said to the elderly woman.

"Pardon," she said.

Whitfield's French had greatly improved since their first mission. Jordan made sure his entire ComDet team crammed the language and spoke it daily leading up to their current mission.

"Non, seulement parler en français," he'd say, admonishing them to speak only in French when they uttered English. They also picked up enough German for mission-related items, but not near enough to pass themselves off as German.

Whitfield cleared his throat. "In the States, we had these out-laws about seventy years ago who robbed banks and trains. They were called the James–Younger Gang led by this Jesse James. He and his band would ride into a town, steal all the money in the bank, fire their guns in the air, and ride off."

The woman took a seat. "That's terrible. How could they get away with such a thing?"

"Well, that's just it, you see. This one town in Minnesota set an ambush to catch them. They figured—"

"Minnesota?"

"Yes, ma'am. It's a state up in the northern part of America." She nodded.

"The townsfolk figured they might be coming into that town to rob the bank one day pretty soon. So, the whole town thought that if the bank was getting robbed, they'd all take cover

and fire away. But these gang members were tough and experienced. A bunch of them had fought in the war, kind of like these
Maquis folks."

She covered her mouth but then lowered her hand. "War?
What war?"

"The War Between the States. When Americans fought each
other."

She lifted her head. "Ah, yes. I read about that in school. The
Civil War."

Whitfield looked out the window to check for activity but
saw none and looked back. "While some of the outlaws were
in the bank, the rest were outside with the horses. The shooting started and the outlaws realized they had to get out of there.
They were shot up really bad and confused. The town sent out
a posse . . . err . . . like policemen to go after them. A couple of
them died, and all the Younger brothers were caught. They never
caught Jesse James, but somebody shot him years later. The gang
was pretty much finished after that."

"Incredible," she said.

"And, you see. That's what we have right here, except we're
outnumbered. But the Germans, just like those outlaws, aren't
expecting an ambush. They're used to doing what they want here
in Caen. Having their way with no resistance. If we can shoot a
bunch of them really fast, and some turn tail and run, then we
can finish off the rest. Especially here in the middle. We want
those in front to think they're all alone, and the ones in the back
to think the same. Sort of a divide and conquer situation."

"Then we must do it!" she said, defiantly. "I need one of
those guns."

"No, ma'am. You've given so much already. Survive and find
your other son. That's all I want you to do."

"Thank you, son. You're so brave."

"You better leave now, ma'am. And, you're welcome."

TWO BLOCKS AWAY at the main blockade, Lieutenant Moody and Colette occupied a second-floor room of the Hotel Marius. No one had rented the room in months. This part of Caen rarely had tourists visit and certainly not in a time of war. They surveyed their view from windows and planned to use that elevation to wreak havoc on the first two trucks. Laurent would do the same from across the street. Moody and Colette, if needed, would be able to escape out of a side window, onto a roof, and down to the alley behind the hotel.

Colette's eyes closed and her head slowly lowered.

Moody smiled. "Tired, dear?"

She perked up and opened her eyes. "I . . . I'm fine."

"No, you're not," Moody said. "I'm trained for this and have experienced plenty of sleep deprivation over the last couple of years. You should be worried about which boy is taking you to the theater. Not sitting here waiting to fight Nazis."

"I'm as ready as you are, Lieutenant."

"Relax. I'm just saying you shouldn't have to be ready. Trust me. We respect your skills as a fighter. You're the epitome of the Resistance. You are the Resistance."

She nodded. "I don't think Nick Jordan thinks that. And neither did Valère. They didn't understand that I will give my life for France. For my parents and brother. I'll do whatever it takes."

"He does. He knows." Moody lifted his Thompson machine gun for a sight check. "But you never seemed to realize they're sweet on you."

"Sweet. What do you mean, sweet?"

Moody shook his head. "Never mind. We need to focus on what's about to happen."

Colette looked at Laurent and lifted her head to acknowledge him. He did the same from his spot across the street. "Yes, when is this going to happen?"

"Well, I imagine any time now. Assuming our fearless leader was correct about the Krauts coming through here."

"What makes him so certain?" Colette asked.

"Well, he thinks Major Wertz is cocky. But Jordan is confident. There's a difference."

"What do you mean cocky?"

Moody looked to the side in thought and then over to Colette. "Some people are cocky while others are confident. Cocky people might have success at this or that, but they get arrogant and overconfident. That's when they make a mistake. They're so consumed with thinking they're right or that they'll win, they don't consider the consequences. That's Wertz.

"Then you have confident. They make decisions or perform actions based on a result that is known or likely given what they've done before. That's Jordan."

Colette scoffed. "I think Nick is cocky."

"Well, he might be a little risky at times. Hardheaded and quick-tempered even. But I don't think Nick is cocky. The smart play for Wertz would be to hold his ground, but the man is itching for a fight. Someone in his position would send his troops out in three groups through areas where they have multiple escape routes. But not Wertz. He's like a dog going for fresh meat on a bone. He wants to get there fast. Get into the fight and get a medal. If we're wrong, then we failed to keep a major force from attacking those boys landing at the beach. So that's risky. We could fight them at their headquarters, but we'd be greatly outmanned and outgunned. This is the smarter play. This is the confident play."

"So you think Nick is smart?" she said, raising one eyebrow.

Moody grinned. "Yeah. I do think he's smart. Off-the-charts

smart. And tough. He's not just a commando. He's everything a commando should be. Athletic. Quick. Brave. Unbelievable in hand-to-hand combat. Nobody bested him in the circle."

"Circle?"

"It's where we trained in hand-to-hand fighting back in England. Jordan was the best. So, he's got a lot to be confident about. But he never tells you that. He's also humble. No bragging from him, and he's got a lot to brag about."

"Let's just hope he's right about the cocky one."

As ONE JUNIOR officer ran to the front vehicle, another walked up to Wertz. "Excuse me, Major. I was thinking. Perhaps we should split up our column. In case the Resistance heard we're leaving and plans on stopping us. I could lead a group along the western route and meet you on the south side of town."

Wertz's sneer cut through the junior officer. "Do you think they would challenge me? They wouldn't dare. Besides, we would crush them. If you see any French Resistance along the way, run over them as if they were a little rabbit running across the road." Wertz touched the front of his cap to secure it on his head. "We're going in one column. We're going fast. And we'll mow down anyone that gets in our way. Now get back to the last truck in the coward's position. That's why I put you there."

"Yes, sir," the junior officer said as he scurried off, defeated, with a slow roll of the eyes.

Wertz stood on the side step of the truck he planned to ride in. He looked to the rear of the column and then the front and waved his arm forward.

The first truck pulled forward and the rest followed suit.

TWENTY-NINE

THE YOUNG BOY'S toy soldiers began to move on their own from their standing position on the window ledge. A few of them rotated and one fell over. The boy looked at them, curiously. He lifted his head and caught one before it fell to the ground. He turned to a rumbling coming down the street.

"They're coming! The Germans are coming!" a middle-aged man said from below. He used a whispering yell as he moved down the street.

The boy opened his mouth and turned to tell his papa but his father stood tall behind him.

"Get ready, son. This is it."

The boy watched as others below scrambled into shops and homes or behind vehicles. Several picked up weapons that had been resting against ledges. Three teenage boys stood on a roof across the street with Molotov cocktails lined up in rows.

The rumbling of the trucks grew louder but he couldn't see them. Urine trickled down his leg and his teeth chattered. He squeezed his thighs together and regained his composure. Lifting the rifle, he took aim at an empty street that the enemy would soon fill.

JORDAN FOCUSED ON the noise of the approaching trucks. He nodded, content that he'd been right about the Germans using this route. The smell of freshly baked bread filled his nose in the small bakery where he sat. His position was far from safe. He'd face the Germans head-on from the ground. It wasn't exactly an every-man-for-himself situation but not far from it.

Moody had suggested he take a higher position with Whitfield directly above him. But Jordan felt that plenty of others would fight from there and the Germans needed to receive some fire up close and personal.

Three blocks down, Jean-Pierre, Henri, and Mr. Dray leaned back from the windows of their ambush position as the trucks approached. Across the street, Sergeant Cummings and the Maquisard fighter Rud crouched behind a street vendor's cart.

The first truck reached Jean-Pierre's position. An officer sat in the front passenger seat. As it passed by, Jean-Pierre noticed troops sitting in back. One looked up at him but had no reaction. There was nothing odd about a man looking out of an open window at a convoy of trucks. He and the other commandos were dressed as local French.

"Sixteen," Henri said.

Jean-Pierre nodded, agreeing with Henri's count of the trucks in the column. From their vantage point, they could see the whole group of Germans. The rolling power of these trucks, weapons, and highly trained men made for an ominous tone.

With his left eye squinted, Whitfield used his right eye to look through the crosshairs of his sniper's scope at each driver and passenger as each truck came into view. He measured every breath, preparing to squeeze the trigger. Despite Jordan's description of Wertz, the major would be hard to distinguish from other officers, and Whitfield had no idea if he'd ride in the cab of one of the trucks or in the back. Jordan reasoned he would be near the front and wanted Wertz dead as the first shots rang out. However, Whitfield couldn't fire too early. The ambush team wanted the entire group of trucks trapped in the barricaded area. One of Whitfield's greatest traits, and a requirement for any sniper, was patience. The officer in the lead truck lifted his chin, looking left and right. Whitfield thought him too young for Wertz and noticed his epaulets. He dismissed the possibility of him being the SS major.

One floor below, Jordan concealed his face but watched each truck pass by. He wore a light leather jacket to conceal his extra magazines, pistol, and knife, worried that one of the drivers or passengers might recognize him after his two visits to the SS headquarters. He picked out one face that had been particularly rough with him in custody, but he was looking for Wertz.

"Conserve your ammo. Point and shoot in short bursts at the torso. Got it?" Moody said to Colette.

"Got it," she said with confidence.

THE GERMANS FAILED to notice the eerily empty streets, how the closed shops and parked vehicles had replaced the normal hustle and bustle. One young man ran across the street and an older man shut his door. A caravan of soldiers often sent locals scrambling for cover in hopes the Germans ignored them.

The lead truck pointed directly toward Moody and Colette's location as it turned the corner and sped up. One by one, trucks full of Germans turned the corner along with two howitzers in tow. The noise grew louder. The vibration grew stronger. The degree of men and firepower became abundantly clear. Echoes of Blitzkrieg.

The officer in the lead truck reached into his left inside pocket for a cigarette and his right pocket for his lighter. "Ah. I forgot my lighter. Do you have one?" he asked the driver.

The driver pulled his out, lit it, and held it over so they both faced each other. In those few seconds, as they took their eyes off the road, they missed the enormous barricade in front of them. Although less than ten feet high, it had a thickness of thirty feet of steel and wood from trucks, cars, carts, and an old piano. It packed tightly against buildings on both sides. Citizens had thrown several smaller items on top, such as chairs and crates, but they'd have little effect. The real strength lay in its ability to keep the German trucks from plowing through. There would be no room or maneuverability for any of the trucks to build up sufficient speed to challenge the barricade. Due to Rue Vence's numerous manufacturing facilities, plenty of large crates, vehicles, and machinery could serve as cover for First Winter Snow.

The French had lined up several trucks to the right so, as drivers turned the corner, they'd fail to see the barricade.

The driver clicked his lighter closed and looked back to the front. "Scheisse!" he cried.

The officer next to him widened his eyes. His cigarette dropped to his lap as his hand braced the dashboard. "Halt!"

The driver slammed the brakes. The wheels locked up and began to skid. The impact barely moved the barricade. The driver grunted as he collided with the steering wheel.

The officer hit the windshield, cracking it, and rendering himself unconscious.

Eight soldiers in the back crashed toward the cab with most of them falling to the floorboard.

The driver lifted his head to a wall of wood and metal.

The second truck's impact into the front truck caused similar reactions and a second jolt for those in the first truck.

The third truck's driver slammed the brakes, stopping the vehicle within inches of the second.

Screeching and skidding tires replaced the massive rumbling of the convoy.

Drivers and soldiers stepped onto the running boards or emerged from the back end. They traded glances and held out their arms with palms up. Those farther behind yelled to those ahead in the pack, things like "What's going on?" or "Why did we stop?" They failed to notice rifles emerging from windows all around them. They didn't see young men on top of buildings lighting Molotov cocktails. The soldiers bringing up the rear in the final German truck didn't realize that four French trucks had quickly parked tightly behind them.

For a few seconds, quiet enveloped the street.

The driver in Wertz's truck looked up and down the street. "Major. Where are all the people?"

Wertz, standing on the road, looked up to his right. His position prevented a clean shot from Whitfield's Springfield sniper rifle. The major noticed a few small flames and realized they were held by men on top of the buildings. A rifle barrel rotated toward him. He mouthed, "Ambush." He whipped his head toward his driver with eyes widened. "Ambush," he screamed.

The back of the driver's head came apart and splattered on the rear window of the cab. Whitfield's bullet had entered the man's left cheek.

Wertz had just begun to dive into the cab and dropped to the floorboard. He looked up. The remaining half of the driver's face stared back. Gray matter coated the seat.

Six Molotov cocktails rained down on the convoy. While four landed on the street, missing their targets, two landed on trucks. All six burst into flames and shocked the German soldiers.

One SS trooper jumped out, on fire, and ran down Rue Vence. A French baker, wearing an apron, leaned around a corner and fired into his chest. He had offered his little establishment for Jordan's position.

What began as single gunshots now became indistinguishable. The French fired from every angle as several Germans fell. The rest scrambled in, around, and under vehicles. Two trucks burned brightly as another round of Molotov cocktails burst all around them.

In the rear, Jean-Pierre and Cummings, along with their Maquis counterparts, Henri and Rud, unleashed a massive burst of firepower from their Thompsons and Stens. Jordan had tasked them with rendering the last truck not only immobile but so devastated that the Germans would realize they couldn't move to the rear for a retreat. Jordan wanted them spread out. Panicked. Unsure of where to run.

The German officer in the last truck attempted to run down the alley, Luger in hand, directly toward Cummings and Rud's position. He approached so fast, he ran between them before they had a chance to shoot. Rud simply looked up at him amazed.

Cummings darted out from behind his cover of stacked crates and tackled him.

The Luger fell inches from the officer. He kicked Cummings in the face and reached out for his pistol.

Cummings pulled his Thompson around and fired a deadly burst of rounds to end him.

Down the alley, three French teenage boys stared back, mouths open.

Cummings gave them one look and returned to his position.

The boys ran to the German and looted his body of the Luger, wallet, and cap.

JORDAN HAD SEEN Wertz when they stopped. He had watched Whitfield's deadly round take out the driver but now couldn't see Wertz, and assumed Whitfield could not either.

Nick Jordan had never been a vindictive person. He considered himself more an arm of justice. His duty was not to seek vengeance but, rather, to rid the world of tyranny. He knew no greater tyrant in his area of operation than Wertz and considered him the epitome of Nazism. Jordan wouldn't torture him. He didn't seek to deliver the SS major a long speech of his atrocities. He simply wanted him dead.

Jordan fired several rounds from his machine gun to the left and then right, providing his own cover fire as he made an attempt for Wertz in the truck. He took three steps on the sidewalk as several rounds splintered the wooden crates near him. He took cover behind a car.

Wertz popped his head up while remaining in his truck.

As Jordan began another step, he noticed four German soldiers entering the dress store three doors down where several women worked. An hour earlier, he had cautioned the women to move to another location a few streets over. They chose to stay and assist with nursing, or fighting if needed.

Jordan looked back at Wertz's truck but chose the dress shop.

So many bullets flew in so many directions that no one on the street was safe. Glass broke over his left shoulder, and a truck burned to his right.

A German soldier looked up at him from under his truck but made no attempt to shoot. Others did make an attempt as Jordan ran toward the shop.

The commando dropped to a knee and returned fire.

An SS soldier ran around from behind a truck and raised his MP40 to fire at Jordan's back.

Whitfield rotated his rifle and fired into the soldier's torso, saving Jordan.

Jordan turned and, realizing his fortune, looked up at Whitfield, nodded, and then ran into the dress store.

Expecting a fight, he darted in and swept left to right, careful not to fire in case the women were downstairs. He saw no one. No Germans. No French.

"Ahhhhhhhhh!"

The high-pitched scream came from upstairs. Jordan noticed a stairwell in the back. He loaded a fresh magazine in his Thompson and headed for the stairs.

A TOY SOLDIER fell to the street. The boy didn't notice as he fired his rifle, wildly, for the sixth time. He'd yet to hit anyone but kept aiming and shooting. The recoil of each shot pushed his right shoulder back, producing the inevitable bruise. He was normally a decent shot, but this wasn't a rabbit eating grass in the woods. This wasn't a serene scene. This was war.

His father had already killed three SS soldiers and wounded numerous others. The boy looked down the street at the final truck in the convoy as it burned out of control. This somewhat peaceful street, seemingly untouched by war, was now ablaze. Germans ran in every direction. Some, however, began firing back.

The first shots hit the wall above the boy. He winced and crouched inside. The second shattered the raised window. Glass fell down around him. He felt a pinch on his left cheek. He touched and noticed blood on his fingers. Am I shot? he thought.

No bullet found the boy, but the broken glass had.

"Uhhh!"

The grunt came from his father, who fell back from the window.

The boy cried, "Papa!" He dropped his rifle and reached for him.

Blood oozed from the father's right shoulder.

"Papa, no." His eyes watered.

His father looked up. "I'm OK. I think I'm OK." He winced and grabbed his son's arm. "You go to Mrs. Olivier next door. You go to her. You'll be safe there."

The boy shook his head. "No, Papa. You come with me."

"It's not that bad." The father sat up. "See. I can get up. I just want you to be safe. I should never have had you at the window. It's too dangerous and you're too young."

The boy grabbed a towel and touched it to his father's shoulder. "There's blood on your back, too!"

"That's good, son. It means the bullet went right through." He winced again. "Feels like someone hit my shoulder with a sledgehammer."

"You can't shoot now, Papa. You come with me to Mrs. Olivier's. She will fix you." Tears rolled down his cheeks.

The father smiled. "Alright, son. I guess we're done fighting for today."

COLETTE'S ROUNDS LANDED several successful targets. She'd taken out four Germans to Moody's six. With Laurent's shots from across the street, and a few citizens firing, they had killed or severely injured every German in the front two trucks.

One soldier crawled under the barricade, attempting to sneak below the stacks of assorted items. His bulky torso prevented him from sliding under a car at the bottom of the pile. As he pulled his upper half under, his bottom half stuck out. Laurent's bullets riddled his lower half. Enough bullets reached his midsection, killing him.

Moody looked at Laurent and pointed toward the third truck, instructing him to concentrate his fire there.

He leaned back from the window and stood. "Colette. You and Laurent keep firing and working your way back."

"Where do you think you're going?"

"I saw Jordan fight his way into that dress store down the block after some Germans. Those women are hiding upstairs. I'm going to check it out."

Colette pulled her Sten back from the window. "I'll come with you."

"No. I need you here. Keep firing. I don't know if these people can hit much more. You're tearing up the Krauts. Keep at it." He reached the doorway and turned back. "If you need to, head out the window and use the escape route to the fallback position."

She shook her head. "Cowboys."

THIRTY

B LACK SMOKE ROSE over Rue Vence. Molotov cocktails
had set six trucks on fire. Gunfire erupted in every direction. The Germans now produced more firepower than
their opponents, but the citizens' cover in buildings and behind
barricades protected most of them. Bullets ricocheted off buildings and broke windows.

Dead soldiers littered the street. One body burned on the
sidewalk, no longer recognizable as human. Another German,
who'd caught on fire, ran into an office building and collapsed on
file boxes. A French businessman struggled to extinguish the fire.

Jordan had worried that, when the shooting started, many
of the citizens might flee. In particular, if they saw their friends
and neighbors fall, they'd weaken. The Germans killed a few
French on the street and some in second- or third-floor windows.
One of the young men on top of a building that had thrown several Molotov cocktails was hit and fell five stories to the sidewalk.
But to their credit, most stayed and fought.

In addition to the sounds of bullets, German voices rang out.
In the chaos, they attempted to organize. Few of them cowered
in fear, while most of them made an attempt to organize. Their
training emphasized them doing the ambushing, not the other
way around. They were completely surrounded, had fire coming
at them from every direction, had opponents with good cover at
higher ground, and had no means of escape. Twenty percent of
their force initially died due to the element of surprise.

Near forty were wounded. The commandos, Maquis, and civilians gave no quarter.

"Help me, please. Oh God. Please help," a German cried as he dragged his body along the sidewalk. His lower half riddled with five wounds. He pleaded for anyone to help him. The baker obliged and put him out of his misery.

Although the community along Rue Vence had seen little war come to their street in the past, they had suffered many German soldiers visiting their neighborhood. The Germans had stolen from their stores, laughing as they walked out. They ate in cafés and left without paying. They drank their liquor and acted like drunken bullies. They took advantage of several women and committed numerous assaults.

They had murdered one businessman who failed to give them the information they wanted. The brutal scene occurred, ironically, in the same location as the main barricade. They marched him into the middle of the street, announced his alleged crime, and an SS officer shot him in the head with his Luger. Before the incident, citizens argued over whether they'd participate in First Winter Snow. After that incident, they begged for that day.

These citizens knew of German atrocities not only in Caen but throughout their homeland. They had seen Jews sent off to work camps. They lost sons in battles. Today, the citizens of Rue Vence had their chance for retribution. For some this meant revenge, but others saw it as an opportunity to end the war. They knew a massive Allied invasion was coming. They hoped for it. The Germans' continual preparation for an invasion confirmed it. Those in the Resistance affirmed that the Allies had landed. This was their chance to take out a group of SS soldiers that posed an imminent threat to France regaining its liberty.

One of the German trucks had turned down a side street,

attempting to ram the barricade. It ran over a teen girl that had attempted to run away. She lay dead. Her mother pulled her to the side and cradled her. The truck rammed the barricade over and over. The driver backed up and attempted to break through a fifth time. Each effort moved the barricade a few feet. Two more runs would be enough. He rammed it again.

As he backed up for a final attempt, a young French man leaped onto the bumper and fired a German MP40 he had picked up. The windshield shattered and bullets riddled the driver and passenger, the downed German truck now becoming part of the barricade.

Several soldiers jumped out of the back only to be met by guns shooting back. One soldier prevailed in surviving the assault. He fired his weapon and killed three citizens. His helmet had come off and his eyes widened as he screamed. He stood six feet seven inches tall with thick blond hair. An Aryan giant. A man possessed. He stepped over the three dead and fired one way down the street and then turned his weapon upward, firing at the building across the road. He spun the other way to fire down that end of the street, letting out another maniacal scream.

Jean-Pierre fired back, stopping the soldier's motion.

The big German looked toward him, almost puzzled at his flawed invincibility. He dropped to his knees and lowered his head.

Jean-Pierre had turned away but noticed his barrage had failed to end the big German's assault as the man lifted his weapon.

Jean-Pierre squeezed his trigger.

The big man fell sideways to fight no more.

MOODY REACHED THE back of the dress shop. The alley seemed

almost peaceful aside from the noise of the hell on the other side of the building. A dog tore into garbage seeking a meal, oblivious to the sounds of gunfire and screams.

The rear door to the dress shop dwarfed him. A bank once occupied the location and they had installed a door that, when locked from the inside, became impenetrable, even for a commando with rudimentary lock-picking skills. No windows existed for the rear first floor and both sides had connecting buildings. He'd have to find a way through to the front and possibly fight his way in.

The window above him opened. A woman stuck her head out and screamed. "Help!"

An arm pulled her back in and shut the window.

Moody noticed a ledge that ran beneath the row of second-floor windows. He swiveled his head in search of a ladder. To his left, the connecting building stretched further into the alley than the dress shop building did. A metal bar protruded near the ledge. It stuck out for no reason. Perhaps an unfinished construction project.

A Major Tunstall saying popped into his head. "When there's no way, find another." He'd continue with something like, "There's no quitting. You overcome."

Moody slung his Thompson and backed up several steps. He eyed the wall, the bar, and the ledge. He darted quickly. His left foot landed four feet up the adjoining building wall and his right boot hit the dress shop building two feet higher. He grabbed the bar, but his right hand slipped. He dangled with only his left hand grasping the bar.

He swung his right leg against one building and pressed his back to the other, gaining enough contact to worm himself up. With his knee on the bar, he reached for another higher up and then managed one foot on the ledge.

Another scream came from inside the building, muffled by the closed window.

He crept along the ledge to the first window, peeking inside. He saw no one. Struggling to maintain his balance, he lowered himself down the wall to find the window unlocked. He inched it up and stepped inside.

The door to the hallway was closed. He moved across the room slowly and turned the knob.

THE FOUR SS soldiers held six women hostage. They forced them upstairs and into one room. The oldest, a feisty, gray-haired lady made a run for the window, but a soldier pulled her back in and pushed her to the floor near the others. The others, four adult women and one teenage girl, cowered in a corner.

"What are we going to do?" one of the soldiers asked his sergeant.

"How am I supposed to know?" he answered. "Our lieutenant was just killed if you hadn't noticed. We're on our own." He paced. "It's just like we've been saying. The major would get us all killed."

Another walked to the window and looked outside. "We may need to jump."

The sergeant looked out of the window. "Are you insane? We'll all break our legs."

"Ahh! Ahh!" A young SS soldier held a hand over his shoulder where a French bullet had landed. The blood dampened his jacket.

"Quiet!" the sergeant barked.

The fourth German spoke. "There must be hundreds of them out there. Thousands."

The teenage girl cried.

One of the women put her arm around her. "It'll be OK.

Don't cry. Be brave, dear."

Another told her, "Don't worry."

The women spoke in French and the men in German. A blur of sounds with gunfire in the background.

The sergeant removed his helmet and rubbed his head. "Everyone, shut up. Just shut up. I can't think."

The Germans stopped.

The French women didn't understand him and kept talking.

He dropped his helmet to the floor and lifted his weapon, pointing it at them.

Two of them screamed. They all hugged one another.

Jordan took the steps slowly. He heard the screams and shouting but assumed that was better than gunshots and measured his approach. He reached the second-floor hallway and had yet to spot a single soldier or dressmaker. The shouting and screaming had muffled.

He took one step into the hallway and saw the first-door knob turning. He raised his Thompson and pointed to where, presumably, a head would pop out.

The door creaked open. A barrel emerged.

Jordan instantly recognized it as the barrel of a Thompson machine gun rather than a German MP40. He slightly lowered his weapon as a head followed the barrel. "Moody?"

Moody, startled, looked back. "Hello, Nick," he whispered and formed a slight grin.

Jordan lowered his weapon. "How the hell did you—what are you—?" He shook his head. "Never mind." Jordan lifted his chin to point to the next room. "There are about four Germans in there. I think they have all the women in there as well. I haven't heard anything coming from the other rooms."

Moody shrugged. "What's our plan?"

"I don't know. Just got here. Same as you. I don't even know how many people are in there—SS soldiers or women." They both continued to whisper.

"How about we ask them nicely to come out?" Moody said, sarcastically.

Jordan shrugged and then looked to the door. "Come out of there with your hands behind your head, fingers locked. Leave you weapons on the floor," he shouted in German.

The voices inside the room stopped, including the women's.

One of the ladies broke the silence. "Help!"

"Silence," the sergeant yelled.

After a whimper, the women became quiet.

The sergeant approached the door but didn't open it. "We are not coming out. You drop your weapons and come in with your hands in the air."

Jordan shook his head. "Nope. If I have to come in there, I'm going to kill every one of you."

"Ha! You're very funny," the sergeant said. "How about I begin killing these women one at a time and throw them out of the window?"

Gunfire continued to erupt outside along with muffled yelling.

Moody leaned in. "Maybe we need to get a better look at the situation."

"How do you propose we do that?" Jordan whispered.

"I can climb onto the same ledge I used to get in through this room." Moody thumbed toward the room down the hall. "I'll tiptoe along that wall and sneak a peek. See exactly how many are in there, how they're fixed for weapons, and all that."

Jordan backed up and looked through a nearby empty room. "What if they see you and start shooting? You'll have no cover."

"It's cinder block. I'll be fine. If I have to, I'll jump."

"How do you feel about playing the decoy?"

"You mean draw fire while you burst in?" Moody asked.

"Yeah, something like that. But we need a signal."

Moody slung his weapon. "You mean a signal other than me getting shot at."

"You have your smoke pack?"

Jordan referred to a special pack of Chesterfield cigarettes that each of the ComDet members carried. A few of the cigarettes near the opening of the pack were real, but the rest of the pack contained a special concoction created at the shop near Camp Delta where inventors and tinkerers created gadgets for the commandos to use. The pack had a mini fuse at the bottom. When lit, it produced enough smoke to cause a diversion or provide concealment for movement.

"We'll run with two plans. Both have the same results. I assume that room is just like this one. We'll divide it into four quadrants." Jordan walked their sample room and stood in four different spots. "One, two, three, four. I'm hoping you can get a sneak peek and then tell me quietly from the window. You'll give me the quadrant number or numbers I need to avoid. I'm thinking they have the women huddled in one corner. So, if you give me a four, for example, I'll be able to shoot at will in the other quadrants. I'll fire two shots at the window first and give you an opening to fire through. You take the no-go quadrants since you'll have the advance look. Me shooting out the window will be your signal to lean in and fire."

Moody nodded. "And what quadrant is the door you'll come flying through?"

"That's neutral territory. You avoid that, and I won't shoot at the window after those initial two shots."

"And if I can't tell you quietly?"

"That's plan two. Just shout it out. I'll be through that door in seconds. I'm going to keep talking to them. Distract them from the window while you get the lay of the land in there. Once you give that to me, you can light your smoke pack on the ledge. Then they'll be looking there when I come through the door."

Moody put one leg over the window ledge. "It's risky. And I don't mean for us. For those women."

"I agree. We need to get this done and get back out on the street. Pistols only. Less likely we'll fire off a wild bullet." Jordan slung his Thompson and unholstered his 1911 sidearm. He pulled back the slide and noticed a round was chambered. He lowered the magazine ensuring it was full and returned it. "Let's do it."

WERTZ FIRED HIS Luger at a second-floor window as he exited the cab of his truck. He ducked, fired, and ran down the sidewalk, stopping behind a fruit stand.

A small boy looked out of the window in disobedience to his father's order to stay in the storeroom of their shop. He saw Wertz wave his pistol and yell at German soldiers. He noticed the scars on the back of his neck. The disfigurement ran from his right ear and halfway across, from the hairline and down under the collar.

What the boy could not see was that Wertz's scars ran halfway down his back. Remnants of another war. What many called the war to end all wars.

Twenty-seven years earlier, barely old enough to shave, Wertz fought against the French. An order came for him to leave the trench and charge the enemy. A haze from explosives covered the battlefield, impairing his vision. He could barely see down the line of troops to his left and to his right. As he raced across, machine gun fire rang out. He noticed his comrades falling, but the young Wertz kept charging. Eventually, he outran them all until he was all alone. He dropped to a knee and fired at the enemy's trench. The head he aimed at popped back. Presumably, he'd killed the enemy. He stood to charge again but an explosion burst near him, throwing him to the ground.

Wertz opened his eyes to see the French enemy leaving their trenches. He dragged himself behind a dead horse. The putrid smell of death invaded his nostrils. The haze thickened as he recognized the poisonous gas moving toward him. He reached into a pouch strapped to his side and donned his gas mask. Whistles, explosions, gunfire, and screams added to the chaos.

The view back toward his lines cleared, and he noticed most of his fellow troops retreating. He stood and ran toward them. He stopped once, turned, and fired a wild shot at the enemy.

"Help!"

Wertz saw a soldier with a hand in the air as the deadly gas moved toward them. The man had no mask on. Wertz ran and knelt down. It was his friend, Emil, who came from the town neighboring Wertz's home. They had met in training where they became fast friends.

He pulled Emil's mask from the pouch and placed it over his face. Three French soldiers in gas masks lowered their weapons to fire.

"Run!" a fellow German soldier yelled.

Wertz looked at the unconscious Emil. His midsection oozed blood through his clothing. Wertz applied pressure, but the blood surged between his fingers. Emil's eyes rolled back, and he passed out.

He lifted Emil over his shoulders and stood. Though a boy of sixteen, Wertz had already grown into the size of a man. He shifted the rifle to his left hand and moved toward his trench as the gas neared. Wertz's fellow soldiers fired past him as he reached the trench and lowered Emil to those below.

Climbing down the ladder, Wertz noticed another soldier crawling toward them. He left the trench despite the bullets flying past him and repeated the same rescue as he had with Emil. The second rescue forced him to run into the gas. He didn't know if his side or the other had released the deadly poison.

He returned to the trench with the wounded man on his shoulders.

Three days later, he lay in a hospital ward. The bed to his left was empty. Emil had been there but died from his abdominal wound the night before. To his right, the other soldier he had rescued slept. Bandages covered several parts of his body including his eyes. The mustard gas had left him blind.

Wertz lay on his stomach. Although his mask had saved his lungs, his eyes, and his life, the blisters formed within a day on his neck and back. The treatment for chemical burns only added to the pain and left scars that would remind him of that day, every day, for the rest of his life.

The Iron Cross made him a hero in his hometown but that did little to comfort the loss of Emil. Whenever he rubbed his neck, he hated the French, and thirsted for revenge.

THIRTY-ONE

M OODY STEPPED FULLY on the ledge. Now he had no bars to grab and his foot rested on a ledge that protruded just four inches from the building. Another ledge ran one foot over his head. Both served as decorative veneer for the old building. He crept along, moving inches at a time.

Jordan returned to the hallway and addressed the Germans inside. "How we doing in there?"

"Ready to kill these women. How are you?" the sergeant said, sarcastically.

"Now why would you want to do that?" Jordan answered. "Won't help you any. You do that, I've got thirty guys ready to shoot you. Just waiting downstairs for my signal. You let those women go and you get to go to a nice Allied prison camp in the States. No more war. No more Wertz."

"I don't think so," the sergeant said. "Major Wertz is very clear with his orders. We don't get taken prisoner. We fight to the death."

"Wertz is dead," Jordan lied.

"How do you know that?"

"Because I killed him. Shot him dead right when his truck stopped. He was about halfway back in your convoy."

The sergeant, knowing the major rode in the ninth truck, found Jordan credible.

One of the other soldiers spoke up. "You hear that? Wertz is dead. We don't have to worry about him anymore. We can get him some help." He pointed toward the wounded soldier.

"Shut up!" the sergeant said.

The oldest woman stood. She'd developed a certain moxie over the last few years. Before the war, she had up to thirty women working for her, making the finest dresses in Caen. She made several trips each year to Paris to sell her latest creation and the wealthy hired her for custom-made wedding dresses. As with many entrepreneurs, her business waned and she was reduced to providing the average French citizen's annual allotment of clothing. The occasional German would stop in and force her or her workers to fix a hem or button. She earned a few bumps and bruises by demanding they pay like anyone else.

The sergeant whipped his MP40 toward her.

She lifted her hands. "Let me help your friend. His wound looks very bad."

"He doesn't need the help of a French pig," he said with a scowl.

The young, wounded soldier looked up at her with pleading eyes.

"Are you that arrogant, you fool, that you won't let me help him? I know what I'm doing. I served as a nurse in the last war. I even treated a German or two."

The sergeant swatted at her. "Fine. Do you what you want." He looked back toward the door.

Jordan paced from the hallway to the window of the empty room to check on Moody's progress. This little altercation took valuable time when all those French citizens on Rue Vence needed his leadership. He popped his head out of the window. He weighed saving these few women compared with the potential of the ambush failing. It was one of those difficult command decisions. Choosing who lives and who dies.

Moody inched along the ledge, more than halfway there.

Every step tempted a twelve-foot fall. Survivable, but he didn't need a broken leg or busted shoulder. There was the mission, dozens of shooting soldiers on the opposite side of the building, and several women in jeopardy of execution. He looked back at Jordan with a pained expression and pressed on.

Three feet from the window, a loose piece of the ledge gave way. Moody's foot shot straight down. He lost the grip with his right hand on the upper ledge but his left held on.

"What was that?" one of the Germans said.

The sergeant looked to the window. "Check it out."

The soldier stepped toward the window.

"Ahhh!" the wounded man cried, distracting the entire room.

"What did you do?" the sergeant said to the woman treating him.

Everyone forgot about the noise outside, as plenty of gunfire continued to sound on the other side of the building.

The woman pulled a bandage from his shoulder. "There's no exit wound. The bullet must still be in his shoulder. It's very dangerous. You need to get him to the hospital. It's only a few miles away."

"Are you mad, woman?" the sergeant replied. "Do you not hear what's going on out there? You think I'm going to risk all of us for one wounded man?"

A boy, really, she thought.

"Besides, we have many wounded men out on the street. I can hear their cries for help." The sergeant paced. "I doubt your French doctors will be in the mood to help us."

Another one of the women stood. "That hasn't stopped you before. I was there many weeks ago. You brought in one of your soldiers that'd had an accident. Sliced his hand open. It was minor in the scheme of things. You barged in and threw truly sick people aside and demanded the doctors treat him."

The sergeant darted toward her and brought his open hand down on her face. She fell, cupped the side of her face, and looked up at him with surprise. "In case you haven't noticed, Caen is our town now."

The older woman stood and held her hands in front of her chest. "Listen, Sergeant. There's another way."

Her real motive began to manifest unbeknownst to the others.

She walked to the window. "Look. There's nothing happening out in the back alley. It's not that high. You can jump and then lower your injured friend down. You will be at the hospital in no time." She didn't notice Moody on the ledge.

"You hear that man in the hallway? He's not going to let us just walk out of here," the sergeant said.

"Take me as a hostage. He won't shoot if I'm in front of you. I'll tell him to let you go."

The sergeant curled his lip. "There are four of us. I think we need four hostages."

Moody stepped over the missing part of the ledge. One more step and he could see into the room.

Jordan, who had returned to the hallway at the wounded soldier's scream, was back at the open window and leaned out.

Moody saw five women crouched in a corner. He moved his face across for one quick look. One German stood near the door to the hallway, two in the center of the room, and an older woman knelt near a German sitting in the corner.

One of the women looked at him with eyes wide.

He put his finger in front of his lips, signaling her to keep quiet.

The two-second look would have to suffice. He backed up one pace on the ledge.

Jordan held up a palm, looking for an answer.

Moody flashed him two fingers and then four. The signal meant that Jordan could not fire in quadrants two or four.

The plan, which called for Jordan to kick the door in, shoot the window to give Moody an opening, and then kill every German, worked perfectly, in theory.

"She's right, Sergeant," one of the fellow soldiers said. "Let's get out of here."

Boom!

An explosion came from the street, reminding them of the chaos on Rue Vence.

The sergeant nodded. "Hey! You, outside. We're coming out with the women in two minutes. If you shoot at us, you'll kill them first."

Jordan ran through the scenarios in his head. Go in now or wait the two minutes. If they come out with the hostages, there'd be too many to shoot around. A possibility, but that might present too great a challenge. Let the Germans make it downstairs, out the back door, and to the back alley with the hostages. They might then shoot all the women. They're too scared and vindictive. They'd definitely shoot them. Since the German said they were coming out in two minutes, the quadrants would likely remain the same for a moment longer.

Jordan needed to resolve this quickly and return to the action on Rue Vence.

Five women huddled in one corner.

The older women crouched over the wounded soldier in the opposite corner.

Two SS soldiers stood in the middle of the room.

The sergeant stood near the door and rubbed his forehead before putting his helmet on.

Jordan remembered one of Major Tunstall's simple

principles. "Before you kick a door down, see if it's open." It sounded so simple. "You men are trained in combatives, but remember to fight smarter, not just harder. Many times, brains prevail over brute force."

The only issue remaining was noise. Jordan chose to do a lightning-quick turn of the knob. If it remained locked, he'd step back and kick the door in.

He ran through the empty room, stuck his head out of the window.

Moody looked at him with his smoke pack and lighter in hand.

Jordan gave him a thumbs-up and returned to the hallway.

Moody lit the pack and waited the eight seconds for it to begin smoking.

Jordan approached the door with his Thompson slung tightly around his torso. He gripped his 1911 pistol firmly, but not too tightly, cupped it with his left hand. He stepped lightly.

He heard whispering inside the room.

The fake cigarette pack began smoking and Moody placed it on the ledge. Smoke billowed up.

The youngest woman noticed first and cocked her head. She elbowed the woman next to her who produced the same puzzled look.

The wounded German glanced toward the window. He pointed with the finger of his non-injured arm. "Fire!"

Two of the Germans took a step toward the window.

Jordan reached for the knob with his left hand. He turned it and the latch recessed. He kicked at the bottom of the door to swing it open. As the door swung one inch past 90 degrees, Jordan fired two shots at the window, blowing out the top right of four panes.

The sergeant turned his head and followed his body around

with his MP40.

Moody swung around, lining up his 1911 with the opening.

Jordan stepped left so Moody's aim would point toward an empty quadrant. His bullet centered on the sergeant's forehead. The man's knees buckled and he fell dead.

The five women in the corner screamed and covered their heads. All except the one nursing the wounded man. She'd seen war.

The other two Germans turned to fire at Jordan.

Moody fired two rounds, near point-blank range, in one of the men's torsos. The man coughed blood and fell on his face.

The other met a similar fate as his sergeant with a bullet to the forehead from Jordan's pistol.

The three Germans never fired a shot.

The older woman looked up. "Thank God."

Jordan pointed his 1911 toward her head.

She looked up in shock. She winced as the pistol fire rang out. Her hand had been clutching the wounded man's bicep to support the shoulder. Feeling the young German convulse, she looked over to see his right eye missing. The bullet blew it through the back of his skull.

"What have you done? Why did you do that? He was injured?" She stood.

Jordan looked at her matter-of-factly. "Because he was about to shoot me."

She looked down. The MP40 that had lain on the floor was in the young German's left hand.

The other women held one another, crying.

The older woman leaned against the wall and looked to the side.

Jordan moved over and opened the window, giving Moody a hand.

"Let's go," Jordan said.

The teenage girl spoke up. "Thank you!"

Jordan had already left the room.

Moody stopped in the threshold and winked. "You're welcome."

THIRTY-TWO

A MIDDLE-AGED FRENCH man with a handlebar mustache had watched the German officer leave his truck and move to a concealed position behind a fruit stand. He didn't know Wertz, but he knew that killing an officer would further disrupt the German response. Other than a corner of the officer's head, the French man had no clean shot. He left his second-floor perch and hustled down the stairs, carrying his army-issue rifle.

After serving in the early years of the war, he had returned to civilian life, choosing to leave combat for younger men. He had kept his weapon, memories, and a few scars.

As he burst through the downstairs door to the sidewalk, he lifted his weapon and charged Wertz, half a block away.

At first, the major didn't notice him. He continued to fire his Luger at random and bark commands to nearby soldiers. Wertz paused shooting to load a new magazine into his Luger.

The French man remembered a glorious day on the battlefield when he had charged a machine gun that had pinned down his fellow soldiers. He snuck behind shrubs and ran to the German soldiers' side. They looked up at him as he fired his rifle, killing them both.

This would be the same. He approached with confidence. Twenty feet away, he dropped to fire at Wertz.

A young boy looking out of the window distracted him. A concern that one errant bullet could kill the child. The French man returned to the aim on his rifle.

The major turned to see the Frenchman. He lifted his Luger and fired twice into his chest.

The Frenchman's eyes closed as he fell to the side on top of his rifle.

Wertz showed no emotion and turned to his front.

UNLIKE THE GERMANS, and even the citizens of Rue Vence, the commandos had slept little in the last forty-eight hours. Nothing more than a quick nap or two. They had the opportunity for more sleep the night before in the cave, but their adrenaline kept them awake. The five men had escaped serious injury. They each had a few bumps and bruises, but their training kept them from even noticing annoyances like minor injuries, hunger, and fatigue.

As Jordan returned to his position, Moody worked his way back toward Colette and Laurent.

Whitfield continued picking off Germans as they poked their heads out from behind trucks. Philippe, directly across the street, made sure no one went after Whitfield.

Meanwhile, Cummings and Jean-Pierre held down the rear of the convoy with Rud, Henri, and Mr. Dray.

Those in the rear began to notice what Wertz was doing. At first, it seemed as if he gathered his soldiers to protect himself. But he was no coward. He had no fear of death. He was organizing a defense.

Approximately thirty SS soldiers and one junior officer gathered around Wertz. To his left, a truck's fuel tank had exploded from a Molotov cocktail and the blast had thrown it sideways. One truck remained in front of him. He directed a driver to reposition another truck to cover his right. He had essentially barricaded himself in along with thirty others. Those in the buildings directly behind them had fled, and a blast of several MP40s had cleared the windows in the floors above.

Wertz's soldiers confirmed that escaping through the back of the two buildings behind them seemed a poor choice. The French had braced the doors closed. Even if the Germans could break the doors down, they didn't know what waited for them on the other side. The alley across the street would force them to leave the covered position and face fire from both directions and above. The alley up the street was equivalent to three city blocks. One block down, where Cummings and Rud sat behind heavy cover, seemed their best option.

Jean-Pierre picked up their visual cues that they intended to come their way. A junior officer near Wertz and six soldiers lined up to fire down the street toward the alley.

"Henri. You and your father keep firing up the street. I've got to speak with Cummings," he said.

The fire from the last truck in the barricade still burned. Jean-Pierre covered his face from the heat of the flames. One dead and burning body sat in the back, presumably where that soldier had been sitting when the Molotov cocktail made its direct hit.

A bullet hit the pavement in front of him as he stepped across the sidewalk and reached Cummings.

"How we doing, mate?" Cummings said.

Jean-Pierre exhaled. "You see what they're doing?"

"Yes, I do. They're coming this way. Wertz is cutting his losses and escaping through this alley with the few troops he has left."

Jean-Pierre placed his hand on Cummings soldier. "We can't let them through."

"No way, mate. They're not coming through me." Cummings lifted his head and looked left and right. "Rud and I will hold our ground for a short time, but then we'll move down this alley. They'll think we're retreating. But I'll have a little surprise rigged up."

The two commandos looked down at a plastic explosive device.

Jean-Pierre nodded. "I'll have Henri and his father slow them down, and I'll come in behind. It'd be nice to have more help, but there's no time for that."

Although Jordan, Whitfield, and the others were close by, they had no means of communication. The scene remained chaotic, and they likely had their own skirmishes to fight. They had no time to instruct the few French citizens near them. They could only hope they'd take out a few Germans attempting to escape.

"Cover me," Jean-Pierre said.

Cummings and Rud raised themselves above their cover and sprayed bullets at the German, allowing Jean-Pierre to make his run back across the street.

"They're going to kill us all! We're all going to die!" the young SS soldier cried out.

Another next to him grabbed his lapel. "Shut your mouth. You're supposed to be a soldier. A man."

The two SS soldiers fired up the street next to their disabled truck.

On the sidewalk near them lay a dead French citizen with a handlebar mustache.

The young man fired and looked to his friend. "Well, what are we going to do? They have us pinned down. The major got us into this mess and now he's going to get us killed."

A bullet pinged next to him off the side of the truck, causing him to wince.

Although guns fired at them from several directions, they managed to clear the doorways and windows behind them, and trucks gave them cover in the other directions. Several of their comrades maneuvered to reach that spot and many more fought for their lives up the street.

They'd seen combat but always as the aggressor. Over half of their force had perished and many others suffered wounds.

Yet, Wertz remained optimistic.

"We're going that way." Wertz pointed down the street toward Cummings's position. "When I give the command, I want you to direct your fire in that direction. Then we'll move as one."

The one other officer, a lieutenant, knelt next to Wertz. "Major. What about the others? There may be at least forty or fifty others up the street. It's hard to say."

"They'll need to fight their own way home. If we stay here, we'll die."

The lieutenant fired his pistol at an open window, killing a mannequin. "This must be the invasion. They're everywhere."

Wertz scoffed. "This isn't even close to how many Allies are coming. This is the work of that American and his French pig friend. They've been lucky so far. But they have superior cover. We have to show a retreat."

"But, Major. The Führer says to never retreat. To fight to the death."

"Well, Lieutenant. The Führer isn't here, is he? Besides, we're not leaving. We'll make it look like we're running away so they'll let their guard down. We're going to take out their force down the street, then come back. Reduce the angles of fire around us. I want these Allies dead and every citizen on this street will wish they were dead."

As Moody worked his way back toward his original position with Colette, she continued to fire. Now that several minutes had passed since the original assault, she measured her bullets. She chose to group her rounds at one German at a time. She occasionally looked across the street at Laurent, who fought from a similar second-floor window.

Fewer and fewer Germans remained in her area as they moved toward the middle of the caravan, assuming they'd fare better there and regroup.

Laurent looked at Colette and furiously pointed to a position under her window.

She held up her hands in confusion as an awning blocked her view of the sidewalk immediately under her.

Several bullets hit the window and wall around Laurent. He fell back and didn't return.

"Laurent!" Colette cried. She lowered her Sten and exposed her head out of the window.

Still, Laurent didn't get up.

Although Colette saw several SS dead or dying, she saw none in the immediate vicinity that posed a threat. She pulled up her weapon and scurried down the stairs past a mother covering her child for shelter. She began to dart out of the door when Laurent's warning popped into her head.

What was he pointing at? she thought.

She chose a more cautious exit. She leaned out of a doorway, looking left and right but still no Germans. No danger. She stepped out and made a run for Laurent.

The concrete exploded around her into chips due to gunfire. A ricocheting bullet nicked her calf, leaving a long gash.

She grunted in pain and fell to the ground. She turned to see three Germans in the deeply recessed doorway of the building next to the one she'd just run out of. And then she knew why Laurent pointed so emphatically.

The Germans posed no immediate threat but their position would soon be enveloped.

Colette dragged herself back toward them, behind one of the parked cars. The distance between her and Laurent's side had too much open space.

She shook her head and chuckled. What have I gotten myself into now?

She ripped off the sleeve of her shirt to use as a bandage.

The three Germans pointed and argued, likely unsure of their next move.

Rue Vence remained in chaos. Few had secure positions. Certainly none of the Germans. They'd lost the vast majority of their force, were scattered, and their wounded had no hope of rescue.

ComDet Sixteen and their Maquis partners had all survived significant gunfire and their positions held. Other than Laurent, perhaps.

The citizens of Rue Vence remained defiant. Some had perished. Some had seen their businesses or homes heavily damaged. A few had retreated to the back of their buildings or run from them altogether. Their initial attack had been admirable, and it was left to Jordan and friends to finish the mission.

They began First Winter Snow, and in essence their entire mission, with the understanding that they could not take prisoners. The intention was practicality rather than brutality. Since they couldn't house prisoners, they either had to kill them or let them go. Letting the local French deal with them as they saw fit seemed acceptable. The SS troops at Rue Vence presented a more challenging dilemma. They'd seek revenge. Unless the Allied invasion was extremely swift, the people living on Rue Vence might face a reprisal. A few leading citizens had approached Jordan with their preference. Even in the best case, a soldier or two might escape, but their goal had to be the elimination of the entire force. Every single German—dead.

THIRTY-THREE

N O ONE EXPECTED a decisive victory for First Winter Snow. No one thought it would win the war. It would be little more than a skirmish. Not even a footnote in future works of history.

The barricade and ambush at Rue Vence surprised the SS unit, disrupted their mission, and depleted their force. Irregular warfare in action. One of Donovan's visions for the ComDet teams saw guerilla forces, resistance fighters, and even civilians as assets in the Allied war effort. Those assets, like wild horses, needed taming. The ComDet provided the bridle, harness, and saddle.

This force multiplier required a willingness of both parties to see the end in mind. The ending of the German occupation in Caen provided all the incentive that Valère's Maquis and the citizens of Rue Vence needed. Their motivation complemented Jordan and his fellow commandos' expertise and leadership. Either party, on their own, could barely have provided more than an annoyance to the 200 strong SS force. Together, they held their own.

This required dirty fighting: biting, scratching, and clawing their way toward victory. The generals of old preferred gentlemanly warfare of pitched battles. Ranks of soldiers concentrating their fire. Looking their enemy in the eye. Extracting the Germans from Caen and preventing their trip to the beach required a dirty, bloody street fight.

Yet, Wertz planned an equally ungentlemanly response. He'd go down fighting. He'd kill women and children if necessary.

The major didn't have the luxury of gathering his officers and men for a formal strategy. He gathered the twelve soldiers and one officer nearest him protected by the three-truck barricade they'd created.

"You men listen to me. These French pigs are weak. They will not defeat us. We're going to act as if we're retreating. They'll applaud and pat themselves on the back. They might even allow us a path out of here. Well, we're not doing that." Wertz lifted his head and looked about him. "When I give the command, concentrate your fire down the street. We'll move that way as a unit. Once we kill everyone down there, we're going to fight our way back up the street. That way, we won't be completely surrounded.

"I've seen a few kids popping their heads out. Some women shooting at us. If you can, snatch them, and use them as shields. Remember, our enemy has a weak mind. They cannot stomach shooting at women and children. We'll use them as much as we need to win this fight. We're going to kill everyone on this street whether soldier, fighter, businessman, woman, or child."

One soldier's mouth was agape, while another widened his eyes. No doubt, Wertz shocked several others, but most knew he didn't mince words. He tolerated nothing less than robotic compliance.

JORDAN MADE HIS way to the position he had for the start of the ambush. He ran upstairs and called out. "Whitfield. It's me. I'm coming in."

The precaution made sure Whitfield would not turn and shoot Jordan with his pistol.

"Roger!" Whitfield yelled out of the side of his mouth. He kept his eyes on the street through the scope of his rifle.

Jordan took a knee. "How's the shooting?"

Whitfield squinted his left eye and maneuvered his rifle from left to right. "Slim pickings. Most are dead or have good cover. But we have an interesting development several blocks down. A pocket of Germans have corralled themselves in. Made their own little barricade."

"Let me have a look." Jordan slid over and looked through the rifle scope.

"As far as I can tell, that's our last big pocket of the enemy. Rest are pretty well scattered," Whitfield said.

He saw the Maquisard Philippe across the street looking back and forth.

Jordan backed away from the scope. "I need a closer look. Hold your position. If they scatter, you can pick off the ones headed this way. If they move the other way, pack it up and come help."

"Yes, sir."

Jordan moved cautiously down the sidewalk, pausing occasionally behind a car or in a doorway. He'd holstered his pistol and kept his Thompson at the ready. Aside from the occasional wounded German lifting a hand for help, he saw little threat. When he spotted a Rue Vence resident looking down from a second-floor window, or offering a nod through a storefront, he returned the gesture.

Far up the street where Colette and Laurent fought, infrequent pops of gunfire rang out. In the direction Jordan headed, the gunfire intensified as a major fight continued. Most of the Allied fighters directed their shots at a horseshoe-shaped group of trucks where several Germans embedded themselves. Neither side seemed to do much more than waste bullets.

Jordan provided his own covering fire as he ran a short distance behind a car with four flat tires and every window shot out. He took in a deep breath and looked at the ground. A toy soldier looked back. He shook his head at the oddity. Even toy soldiers suffered casualties in this battle. Although mentally and physically tired, he wasn't exhausted. Far from spent, he could go on much longer than a normal man or even an average commando. He was human, however. He wiped sweat from his brow.

Across the street next to a truck that had exploded, a dead German lay with his dismembered foot next to his head. The carnage gave him pause. An image of Harvard entered his mind. He would have been halfway toward his Ph.D. in history by now and considering his dissertation. Probably on some aspect of the Civil War. Military history had always fascinated him. Jordan's father had once taken him to Gettysburg. He walked the land and wondered what it must have been like as smoke rose from muskets and cannon balls raced across the field. As leaders pointed and ordered men to advance. He had never considered the death and destruction.

Now he'd not only seen it but had given the order to cause it. Those few seconds, however, gave him no consternation. His mission remained clear.

He lifted his head above the car's quarter panel and peered through the openings. That's when he saw him.

Wertz's peaked cap bobbed up and down. He pointed and barked commands at his troops.

Flashbacks ran through Jordan's mind. Wertz raising a pistol and shooting Farrington in the head. The dried blood in Colette's nose from his punch. The atrocities he'd heard many witnesses testify to.

And there he was. Across the street. Nothing stood in the way of Jordan eliminating Wertz. His 1911 might be a tough shot, but he could make it. A burst from his Thompson gave him another option but he'd need to expose himself.

He chose the pistol. He rested the butt in his left palm and his left forearm on the car door. He lowered his head to aim.

Wertz moved his head twice but then sat still.

Plop. Plop. Plop.

The footfalls startled Jordan. He missed a man running up to him because he'd been hyper-focused on Wertz.

"Sir! Jean-Pierre sent me." Henri paused to catch his breath. He pointed toward Wertz's group. "We think they're about to make a move toward Sergeant Cummings's position. Maybe try and escape." Another heavy breath. "He's hoping some of you can slow them down."

"Well, you and I will have to do it, Henri," Jordan said. "I don't see many residents around to lend a hand."

Wertz stood and prepared to move down the street. Several of his men followed suit. Bullets from their weapons led their way. They moved in a mass.

Jordan and Henri shuffled to the front of the car and began firing.

Three soldiers that stayed behind fired back, forcing them to retreat behind the vehicle.

Wertz stopped and shot out a storefront window. He stepped up and entered, then found the child behind the counter. A child that had disobediently been watching the day's actions. His father and mother had told him to wait in the back.

Wertz reached down and grabbed the boy—four or five years old.

The child screamed.

"Silence!" Wertz shouted.

The major and the boy reached the shot-out window.

"Hey! Stop! That's my son!" a man wearing a vest and tie

yelled out. He darted to the window and grabbed Wertz's collar, yanking him back.

Wertz struck his chin with the butt of the pistol as two teeth flew out of the man's mouth.

The father immediately attempted to regain his footing, but Wertz shot him in the neck. He writhed in pain, unable to get up.

Wertz, holding the small child against his torso, jumped out of the window.

Eight soldiers waited for him while several more had moved down the street with the junior officer.

There were few Rue Vence residents on the streets. Most had shot from second-floor or higher windows. A few fought out of street-level locations. Some, solely for the notion of protecting their property. Nearly all of them favored the Resistance and hated the Nazis but didn't want to make their homes and businesses a battleground. They'd hoped to escape the fight with their furnishings and livelihoods intact.

A local jeweler, who'd already seen his sales plummet during the war, had converted his business to a pawn shop. Moments before the SS trucks came rolling in, he vowed, "I'll shoot anyone that comes near my store, whether German, British, American, or French."

Others scoffed, but he stood resolute. A German bullet ended his stance in the first moments of the ambush.

A few teens, out of sense for adventure, came down from the rooftops after throwing their supply of Molotov cocktails and vowed to join the Maquis.

The seemingly retreating Germans sought out children, teens, and women for their human shields. They found few at street level. By now, nearly no Rue Vence residents occupied the streets though a few mocked the Germans from upper-story windows with shouts of "coward" and "dog." Exhausted of bullets, they threw dishes, lamps, and other household items at them.

The occasional burst of a German MP40 sent the French back into their flats.

Other than Wertz's shield of a child, only three others had managed to secure a hostage. One found an older woman and the other two had teenage boys.

"HERE THEY COME!" Cummings shouted.

Rud lifted his Sten gun.

Jean-Pierre and Mr. Dray did the same from across the street. Although the Germans moved down the opposite side of the street, the two Frenchman held their position in case the Germans crossed.

A mass of SS ran toward Cummings with the four civilians.

"What do we do?" Rud shouted.

Cummings and Jean-Pierre had spent hours shooting all types of weapons in various situations. They could typically shoot around the innocents with their pistols, but not their Thompson machine guns. That issue, and the few French with them unwilling to fire, greatly reduced their firepower.

Cummings had planned to hold them a half-block away with their gunfire while he set off an explosive he'd rigged and hidden on the sidewalk. The explosion would certainly kill or maim the four hostages that the Germans prominently displayed in front of them.

Cummings looked over at Jean-Pierre, who only replied with a head shake.

The Germans approached, now a little more than one block away.

BLOOD STREAKED DOWN Colette's calf. A tragedy for a young woman any other day, but a mere annoyance in her current situation. She remained pinned between the open space behind her and the three Germans in the doorway across from her only twenty feet away. A car gave her adequate cover. She considered running but didn't know how well her injured leg would hold up. She couldn't stand to test it. The thought of rescue never entered her mind. She refused to be that girl again.

She pulled the magazine out, checked her number of rounds, and reinserted it with confidence.

Colette rotated around and lay flat on her belly. She watched the three SS in the doorway continue to argue and point, seemingly regarding their next move.

A block away, Dick Moody double-timed his way toward her direction. She realized he would run right in front of them.

She had confidence with her Sten, but a direct assault with a questionable leg gave her doubts. She knew who these men were—SS troops. Valère had said many times that they were well-trained and fierce fighters. "Don't underestimate them," he'd say.

Her family had given so much. First, her parents, and then her brother, François. She'd have to give herself for Moody. She barely knew the man, but could see the way the other team interacted with him. He was one of the good ones. She made her decision. She'd sacrifice herself. As he reached a few feet from their doorway, she'd stand and scream to distract them. And she'd fire. She'd go down with a fight.

Moody was one building away.

She took a deep breath, stood, and secured her grip on the Sten.

"Heeeey!" she screamed.

Two of them looked at her, then looked at one another, eyes widened.

Moody stopped, ten feet away.

The third German lifted his MP40 to fire.

Colette, limping, moved toward them and sprayed a burst from her Sten before he managed to pull his trigger.

The other two soldiers stepped out of the doorway.

Moody lifted his Thompson to fire.

She continued her maniacal yell. "Heeeey!" Colette stopped yelling and squeezed her trigger again as the two SS fell into each other, arms flailing.

They dropped, landing next to the first one that perished.

Moody never spent a round. He ran up to her.

As he got within one foot of her, she fired again at the dead bodies on the ground. Her shoulders convulsed and she breathed heavily.

Three SS Panzer soldiers lay dead at the hand of a young and wounded French woman. Their disbelief at her as a threat coupled with her reckless abandon put them in an inferior position.

Moody held up his hands in surrender. He slowly and slightly pushed her Sten down and to the side with one hand and put his other hand on her shoulder.

She looked at him with steely eyes.

"You got 'em," he said.

She gave a hesitant but firm nod.

"Now what do you say we go get some more?"

She nodded again.

He cocked his head at her injury. Kneeling down, he pulled the makeshift bandage back and looked up at her.

"It's nothing," she said. "I'm ready. Let's go."

Moody stood and smirked. "Alright, tough guy."

They took a few steps, hers a little less graceful. She paused and looked back.

Laurent ran up.

"I thought you were dead!" Colette said.

"Yes, me too. All those bullets came through the window. Not a scratch on me. What happened to you?"

"Nothing," she said.

THIRTY-FOUR

THE FEW GERMANS left at the head of the street had locals surrounding them. They were disarmed and too wounded to fight. The locals either beat them or shot them and otherwise ended their war. One young man begged for his life. A few in the crowd showed mercy but one declined and shot him with the soldier's own weapon.

Moody, Colette, and Laurent made their way to the bend of Rue Vence with zero resistance. The pockets of gunfire intensified the further they moved.

A whistle sounded overhead. Philippe looked down from his second-floor window. "What's going on? Did we win?"

Moody waved a hand. "C'mon down."

Across the street, Moody saw Whitfield double-timing down the sidewalk with his sniper rifle slung.

Seven Germans that Wertz had ordered to stay behind at their makeshift bunker continued a valiant fight. They faced no great military threat, other than Jordan across the street. Most of the locals had run out of ammunition or moved away from the fight.

"There!" one shouted, pointing at Whitfield running down the street.

Three SS pointed their MP40s toward Whitfield.

At the first burst, Whitfield dove behind a newsstand, its papers strewed all over the street.

Jordan, a half-block down, saw the encounter and yelled,

"Whit!"

The sniper looked up.

Jordan gave him a signal that he'd offer suppressive fire. He looked at Henri and nodded. They both rose and aimed at the Germans.

The soldiers pulled back the weapons and ducked.

Whitfield rose and darted past Jordan, proceeding one block farther. A howitzer with one flat tire remained hitched to a truck with the cloth canopy burned away. He quickly set his rifle in a position for sniping the last group of combatants. His barrel lay across the enormous howitzer barrel.

"Go!" Jordan said to Henri.

The Frenchman ran down the street, past Whitfield, and back toward his father and Jean-Pierre.

Moody's group ran up more cautiously.

As the Germans felt confident in resuming the fire toward Jordan's side, Moody and friends made them reconsider. Those final seven spread themselves in a half-circle, firing up, down, and across the street. Their backs faced the building behind them—a bank with no apparent threat.

Moody diverted Colette and Laurent toward the newspaper stand where Whitfield had taken cover. Philippe joined Moody as they hugged the buildings and doorways to move closer. With Jordan across the way, they could attack the pocket of Germans from two of their three sides.

Jordan could only communicate with Moody by hand signals and head nods. Jordan gave him a five-count at which the Allied team would end the small German stand.

Jordan looked left and right and then counted down to five with his hand in the air. As he flashed "two," the door to the bank behind the Germans burst open. A pudgy man, wearing a three-piece suit, held a revolver in each hand.

The same man, a banker, had been the one to help Colette identify Wertz in the café the day of her capture. Wertz indeed had not forgotten him. He believed that he carried value in his connections and hoped to turn him from the Resistance to an agent for Wertz. Months earlier, Wertz had shot the banker's wife in the head and carried off his fourteen-year-old son as a hostage.

Pointing the barrel of his Luger at his dead wife, Wertz said, "That's punishment for helping that stupid Maquisard girl." He then pointed the barrel at his teenage son. "That will happen to your boy if you don't comply with my orders. Every last one of them." Wertz and his goons dragged the boy off, leaving the pudgy banker helpless.

Whenever Wertz forced the banker to give him information, he developed clever ways of offering just enough to make Wertz happy, but not divulging so much as to endanger his fellow Frenchmen. He made sure the Germans needed him enough to keep his son alive as leverage, but their need for him soon waned. He'd given up hope of ever seeing his son again and plotted revenge. First Winter Snow gave him that opportunity and he had already killed two Germans at the beginning of the attack.

"Bastards! You bastards!" he shouted, repeatedly. He pointed with his right to shoot and hit one German in the back. He then pointed with the revolver in his left and hit another in the leg. He wobbled and moved slowly, showing no signs of any training with firearms. Resolute but awkward. Repeating the action, he managed to squeeze off five shots before one of the SS turned and put several rounds into him. His body contorted and he fell back into the doorway. He landed still clutching both guns.

While his last three shots missed, he offered the perfect diversion for Jordan and Moody to move in.

The two commandos lobbed grenades in sequence, one

second apart. As the Germans turned back from the pudgy man, the grenades exploded in succession. The two that still moved were met with a massive arsenal of Thompsons and Stens firing into them. With their deaths, only one pocket of German soldiers remained.

WERTZ LED A group three times larger than the one he'd left behind. All other soldiers under his command had perished.

The child screamed, only pausing to take short breaths. Wertz let him scream so his opponents could recognize his protection.

The only other officer in the group clutched a woman who fought relentlessly. She spit, clawed, and attempted to bite the officer. Twice, she knocked off his cap, and he chose to leave it on the ground the second time. Refusing to move, she dropped to her knees. He brought the butt of his Luger down onto the small of her back.

Her mouth opened with a dull scream.

The Nazi officer clutched a chunk of her hair to pull her up. She complied.

The other two hostages, two teenage boys, moved along more willingly.

That pace was slow, as Wertz's group moved ten feet, stopped, looked ahead, and moved again.

Three soldiers walked backward, protecting the rear.

Whitfield remained in position but found no clear shot.

Henri and his father remained in position while Jean-Pierre had moved up for a better look. Although far fewer people moved about on the street, the carnage and smoke made it difficult to survey the area. Less chaos but still confusing.

As the French commando moved between two trucks, he

saw the small boy in Wertz's arms. The major carried him, loose-ly, on his hip. And so close, Jean-Pierre could sneak up and snatch the boy in mere seconds. Perhaps, before Wertz even noticed someone had approached.

All of Wertz's men looked up or down the street. They paid little attention to the sides. As they made another slow move-ment, Jean-Pierre mimicked them under concealment of a truck. His situational awareness waned as he fixated on the child.

The ComDet team had always wondered about Jean-Pierre's silence on family matters but were careful not to push him for answers. The mere mention caused him depression. What they didn't know was that when he returned from battle in the early days of the war, his flat was ransacked with his wife Claire and young son Pascal missing. He noticed his son's toy truck and picked it up.

As he searched for answers, his elderly neighbor appeared in the doorway. "They're gone."

"Gone," he replied. "Gone where?"

The old man took two steps in. "No longer with us, I'm afraid. Claire was accused of spying or something. I think the Germans just made something up."

"Spying? That's crazy. Wha . . . what happened?" Jean-Pierre asked.

"I pleaded with the Germans. I told them this was crazy. I told them that I'd known you and Claire for years. But they just pushed me down. They took her into the street along with others. This was, maybe, six months ago. My wife tried to take Pascal from her before—"

Jean-Pierre stepped quickly toward the man. "Before what?"

"Before she was shot. She refused to let the boy go. They shot them both along with many others. I'm so sorry to have to tell you this."

Jean-Pierre dropped the truck to the wood floor. He then slowly sat next to it and wept.

The child crying in Wertz's arm looked to be the same age as Jean-Pierre's son would be now.

The Germans approached the area where Cummings had set his explosive. He had decided to let the front group with the hostages walk by. He would save it for the rear of the group. The amount of plastic explosive compound was light, and the bodies in the back would shield those in the front. Hopefully, he, Rud, and Jean-Pierre's group could hold down the rest and not injure any hostages.

Jordan and Cummings's group approached but was still blocks away.

Cummings held the two wires. He would only need to touch them to set it off.

Wertz looked left and right as he moved forward.

Jean-Pierre darted out from between two trucks and approached the group of Germans. His bravery unquestioned but his commando training relinquished. He lifted his 1911 pistol and fired at one soldier to Wertz's left and another on the right, killing both.

Wertz turned and looked him in the eyes.

Cummings moved the wires far apart. "What the—"

"Give me that child!" Jean-Pierre shouted.

Wertz, along with the soldiers around him, looked at Jean-Pierre in disbelief.

Jean-Pierre reached for the boy and brought his pistol up to Wertz's head.

The young child screamed.

Another soldier grabbed Jean-Pierre's arm, pushing it and the barrel upward.

Wertz whipped his Luger around but Jean-Pierre kicked the

SS officer's thigh, forcing him to drop and release the child.

Jean-Pierre swirled his arm, freeing himself from the other soldier's clutch. He took three steps toward Cummings.

Cummings noticed the entire group of Germans begin a push toward him and Rud. He touched the wires.

Boom!

The plastic explosive sent one SS soldier straight up into the air. He rotated, and came down to the sidewalk on his head. The display-case glass of a men's clothier blew up and sent shards into the Germans. Nearly a third of the group fell.

Jordan and Moody's group moved close enough to begin firing.

"Careful with your fire. They've got hostages," Jordan said.

A soldier quickly stood, recovering from the blast, and stepped toward his fellow soldiers. His head whipped back as Whitfield's bullet dropped him.

Wertz, a lieutenant, thirteen soldiers, and three hostages ran after Jean-Pierre and the young boy, not in pursuit, but to escape the blast and others firing at them.

The lieutenant and Wertz attempted shots at Jean-Pierre.

Jean-Pierre ran, and crouched, protecting the boy, who continued to wail.

"We're about to be overrun!" Cummings said to Rud.

"What do we do?"

Cummings looked left. The distance to Henri and his father seemed too far, and they were literally backed into a corner. Their escape path would now expose them too much. Cummings looked to his right down the alley that remained relatively quiet compared to what headed toward him. "There." He pointed to a small garage door that was partially open. "You and Jean-Pierre go there. I'll cover and be right behind you."

Jean-Pierre, a half-block away, looked at Cummings.

Rud took a final shot and began running.

Cummings pointed at Jean-Pierre and then at Rud. Jean-Pierre nodded, acknowledging that Cummings wanted him to follow Rud.

Pointing just past Jean-Pierre, Cummings fired covering bursts as the Frenchman ran by him with the child and turned left down the alley.

Cummings fired two more bursts and followed.

Wertz's group stopped at the corner where Cummings and Rud had been for the entire firefight. He now saw the rear of Rue Vence and the hastily assembled barricade. "I've been a fool," he whispered to himself.

The barricade before him gave no opening of escape. Behind him, several with guns closed in. Across the street, a tall building stared back. He saw movement in front and realized more firepower awaited him. He looked down an alley at yet another barricade. This one just as hastily assembled but smaller. Several rows of crates stacked five-feet high lined the right side.

At the end, a garage door slammed shut.

Mr. Dray, who had procured a rifle for the ambush, lowered his head, closed an eye, and fired.

A bullet zinged past Wertz.

Henri fired his Sten.

The next bullet hit the German lieutenant's right knee, causing him to drop and squeal in pain.

"This way!" Wertz shouted, pointing down the alley with his Luger.

Fourteen Germans moved down the alley as one of their members in the back dropped from a shot to the back.

Wertz helped his hobbled lieutenant.

As they awkwardly moved, they each looked left and right. The occasional door and window gave no opening of relief.

"Behind those crates," Wertz shouted.

The Germans slid into what seemed a maze of stacked boxes.

"You men stay in the front and protect us." Wertz quickly pointed at six men.

They lined themselves behind crates in semblance of trench warfare.

One soldier pulled up on the garage door, but it didn't budge.

Another checked a metal door with the same result.

A few in the rear began an attempt to deconstruct the barricade.

"I can't even see the other side," one said, throwing a suitcase behind him.

One of the teen boys darted from the crates and sprinted toward the street. He ran twenty feet before an SS soldier cut him down with a burst of bullets.

The other teen jumped up and ran the opposite way towards the barricade. He leaped and caught a piece to begin his climb. One of the Germans reached high to grab his leg and yanked him down. The boy fell back and banged his head on the concrete, which rendered him unconscious.

The lieutenant wounded by Henri's bullet rocked side to side. His chest raised and lowered.

"Ahhh. Ahhh."

He clutched his knee, the cap of which was missing. "What are we going to do?" he said to Wertz.

The major looked at him with no emotion. "I'm still working on that plan. It would help if you remained quiet."

"This is your fault," the lieutenant said. "You got us into this. I told you we should have divided the column and used different routes. You didn't listen and now look at us."

A nearby soldier overheard and quickly turned as if he hadn't witnessed the blatant insubordination.

Wertz, still lacking emotion, looked at the lieutenant and slowly cocked his head. He raised his Luger and placed the barrel at the young officer's forehead.

The young man closed his eyes.

Click.

The final round jammed.

"Isn't that unusual?"

The lieutenant opened his eyes.

Wertz pulled back the slide as the failed round ejected. He dropped the magazine and loaded another from his pocket. "There we go."

The lieutenant's eyes widened.

Wertz placed the barrel back on his forehead, ending the young man's war.

JORDAN REACHED CUMMINGS'S original position and knelt down behind his cover. Moody joined him as the others remained safely at the corner of the building.

Moody looked at Jordan. "What do you think Wertz will do now?"

Jordan looked back. "I don't know. But I'll bet he never went to old Ten-to-One's school of getting yourself out of a jam."

THIRTY-FIVE

CUMMINGS SMELLED OIL as he paced between two cars in various states of repair. He'd successfully led Rud, Jean-Pierre, and the rescued child to safety but the walls of the auto repair shop boxed them in. Only an overhead door and a metal office door gave access to the garage. They had quickly closed them both and locked them.

Rud walked up. "Nothing. I see no way out. No way up or to the building next door.

"Well. Isn't this a brilliant plan?" Cummings muttered to himself.

The child, still holding on to Jean-Pierre, had stopped crying. He held out his hand toward Cummings, and it had streaks of blood on it.

Jean-Pierre slowly set the boy down. Blood soaked his mid-section. He leaned against a car and slid down to a sitting position, placing his hands over the wound.

"You're hit," Cummings said as he rushed to Jean-Pierre's side. "How bad?"

"It's very . . . very bad I'm afraid." His breathing was labored.

Cummings helped him to a lying position and ripped open his shirt. He pulled a bandage from his pocket and held it over the belly wound. He rolled his fellow commando up and noticed another one on his back, presumably an entrance wound. The blood quickly filled the bandage and he pressed harder.

Jean-Pierre grabbed his forearm. "It's useless."

Cummings looked at him. "I'm sorry, old friend."

The boy stood and stared at the shocking scene.

Jean-Pierre curled his finger for him to approach.

The child shuffled his feet toward him.

"My little Pascal. Are you alright?"

The child nodded. His bottom lip quivered.

"That's good. This is Ian," he said pointing to Cummings and then at Rud. "And that's Mr. Rud. They are good men. They will take you home. Understand?"

The boy nodded again.

He looked deeply at the child. "My little Pascal." Jean-Pierre closed his eyes.

Rud reached for the boy and pulled him away from the dead body.

Cummings folded Jean-Pierre's arms across his chest.

THE OTHER THREE members of the ComDet team, the Maquis, and a few Rue Vence residents converged at the corner behind the cover of the convoy's rear truck. Others stood, concealed around the building corners. For the first time since the caravan had stopped, no one fired a shot. The occasional cry of the wounded and shouts of several French attempting to extinguish a fire produced the greatest noise. Dozens of residents entered the streets. Some to begin the cleanup but many to sightsee. The women that Jordan and Moody saved had begun the work of triage and nursing. A small boy placed a German helmet on his head, nearly covering his eyes. He looked down at his feet, picked up an MP40, and began to squeeze the trigger.

"Drop that!" his mother yelled.

He let it go, and it banged on the pavement.

Weapons of war, as well as its victims, littered the street.

"Poor kid," Moody said, looking at the dead teen that tried

to run away. He lay in the middle of the street with arms out-stretched as if reaching for safety. He was sprawled between the two belligerents and an untold amount of firepower.

Jordan shook his head. "Henri's dad said that Jean-Pierre, Cummings, and Rud ducked into that garage on the right side. Said Jean-Pierre had a little kid with him."

Moody stood and looked through the broken-out driver and passenger windows. "I saw Krauts tugging on the door. It's sealed up tight. Not sure if they were trying to get to our guys or just looking for an escape."

"We better assume they were trying to get our guys," Jordan said. He waved over Henri. "See if you can find a back way in there. See if they're still in there."

Henri's dad held up a hand. "There isn't. I know the owner and have been in there many times. It's very small with no rear entrance."

"We're a bit trapped ourselves," Henri said.

"What do you mean?" Jordan asked.

"I'm afraid the barricades are so complete, we'll have to dig our way out."

"Yeah, but we can make our way through buildings and the back doors."

Moody backslapped Jordan's bicep. "But if that last pocket of Krauts decides to attack, we'll have drawn them into the buildings. Still a lot of civilians in there."

"Right," Jordan said. "We won't do that. We're going to end this here."

Down the alley, Germans moved about, popping their heads up. Those near the barricade gave up their feeble attempt to break it down.

"How many did you see run down there?" Jordan asked Henri's dad.

"About fifteen. Plus one hysterical lady. Looks like they killed the two young men. You see the one lying there and there's another lying near the barricade."

Jordan shook his head. "Damn."

Henri's dad continued, "And that major. You know, Wertz. He's down there. I'd very much like to get to him."

"There's a long line for that," Jordan said.

Moody stroked his cheeks. "They have pretty good cover. We'd be sitting ducks on a direct assault."

"That's for sure. And if we pelt them with grenades, we're not sure we won't kill our guys in that garage," Jordan said. "The shrapnel might tear right through that garage door unless it's thick."

"Ask them to surrender?" Moody asked.

Jordan looked at him, incredulously. "I don't think they'll surrender. Waste of time to even ask. I wonder how much ammo they have left."

"Hard to say," Moody responded. "They were likely loaded up for their attack at the beach and who knows how much they carried down the alley. We should probably assume they have plenty. Maybe some grenades."

Jordan nodded.

Whitfield walked up with his Springfield rifle slung over his shoulder. "What's the plan, Captain? If I get up in that building, I might be able to pick a few off." He pointed to a three-story building across from the alley.

Jordan looked down the alley. "We need to finish this. I need you here. I have an idea."

Moody walked up with a musette bag. "Cummings left his goody bag."

"Any smoke grenades in there?" Jordan asked.

"Three." Moody handed him one.

"Perfect." Jordan cupped the grenade. "Whitfield. Secure me one drivable truck and one dead Kraut," Jordan said.

THE WOMAN RUBBED her ears and rocked. Her hair was mangled and tears poured from her eyes. "Uhhh. Uhhh," she mumbled as if she were a mental patient in a padded room.

"Will you shut up!" Wertz yelled.

"What are we doing, Major?" one of his troops asked.

Wertz shot him a look. "I'm thinking."

The woman's eyes widened. She banged on Wertz's back with the bottom of closed fists. "Bastard!" she repeated the invective with rising fervor.

He placed his hand on her chest and pushed her down.

She sprang up and repeated the blows and insults.

Another soldier turned around toward Wertz. "What's the plan?"

"Everyone shut up!"

The soldier lowered his head and cowered on the other side of the crate.

"Bastard!" she cried.

Wertz grasped the back of her hair and yanked it back.

Her head cocked up, silencing her.

He placed his other hand under her chin. He pulled hard left with one hand and pushed in the opposite direction with the other.

The slightest crack sounded. Her cries ended as the life left her body.

Wertz continued to hold her as her body went limp, almost aiding her down but then thrusting her aside. He looked up.

Three of his men stared back with looks of shock.

"Pay attention to the enemy, you imbeciles."

They quickly turned away.

Wertz stared at the crate in front of him. Words in all caps were stenciled, MADE IN FRANCE.

He folded his arms and shook his head at the irony of the one thing protecting him. "French pigs," he muttered.

"How did it come to this?" the SS trooper whispered to the man next to him. "I told you so many times something like this would happen. Major Wertz has a wish to die and take us with him."

His companion shook his head. "You're right, and I was so wrong. Here, we cower behind wooden crates. I believed in him. I fought for him as much as for the Fatherland, but now I want nothing to do with him."

"We should surrender," the first man said. "We can just throw our weapons down and run to their side."

"He'll shoot us before we get three meters. Besides, your family will be shamed at your cowardice."

"Better a living coward than dead for no reason."

Clink, clink, clink.

Clink, clink.

The smoke grenade canisters landed near each other and about halfway between Jordan's team and Wertz's remnants. Red smoke billowed up from each container, creating a wall.

"Here they come," Wertz yelled. "Fight to the death. No surrender. To the death."

His SS soldiers raised up to the top of the crates and readied their weapons.

A few distant yells were heard beyond the slight hiss of the smoke grenades.

The rumbling of a truck broke the silence.

The red smoke split in the center as one of the German trucks emerged. A driver in a gray coat and flat cap pulled down low drove toward them at less than ten miles per hour.

"Fire!" Wertz yelled.

The SS troops fired wildly at the truck. Two of them stood, exposing their upper bodies.

The windshield shattered and the driver slumped slightly over. The truck veered, crashing into the side of the building.

What the Germans didn't know was that the driver was one of their own, killed early in the skirmish. Whitfield, with the help of a store owner, used rope and sticks to prop the dead man up to look as if he were driving. They used a piece of concrete just heavy enough to press the accelerator to a steady ten miles per hour. A jacket and hat completed the ploy.

The Germans stopped firing.

Within two seconds, they endured a hellish barrage of gunfire.

Jordan, Henri, and Colette shot from the truck's right side. Moody, Laurent, and Phillipe fired from the left, having to climb over the stopped truck.

Henri's dad brought up the rear on Jordan's side.

Five soldiers in front immediately fell.

Whitfield climbed to the top of the cab and shot two more Germans.

A few of the SS troops fired back but were limited as they crouched near crates, overwhelmed and surprised for the second time that day.

One tried to run toward the barricade, firing his MP40 toward the assault team, but they cut him down.

Moody, who had dashed over the hood of the stopped truck, overran everyone and killed three more who had no crates to protect them from the side.

Whitfield eliminated the final threat.

Jordan and Colette caught up to Moody.

Only one German moved. One of those in the front. He sat on the pavement with hands on his head. No weapon at his reach and no threat. He looked up with terror-filled eyes. "Abandon. Ich abandon," he said, mixing his makeshift French with German to say that he surrendered.

Colette raised her Sten to fire.

Jordan pushed it down. "No."

"What about your take-no-prisoners policy?" she protested.

"It'll be good to have one for information."

Moody walked back and forth among the crates as Laurent and Philippe did the same.

"Major Wertz isn't here," Moody said.

Jordan gave him a puzzled look. "What? Where is he?"

Henri's dad stepped up. "That's impossible. He ran down here with them. I'm sure of it."

"Captain? Captain, is that you?" the voice came from inside the garage.

"All clear, Cummings. Come on out," Jordan said.

The garage door rolled up and out walked Cummings, Rud, and a terrified little boy.

Cummings looked anything but happy at his rescue. Blood covered his hands and shirt.

"Where's Jean-Pierre?" Jordan asked.

Cummings shook his head.

Jordan stepped into the garage to see the body lying prone with hands folded over the chest. Goodbye, Jean-Pierre, he thought to himself.

"Any chance you saw a Nazi major run through here?" Jordan said to Cummings.

"No, sir. Last I saw of him he was on the street." He pointed to the corner.

The group of ComDet members sifted through bodies and

confirmed them dead.

"We should make a sweep all the way up the street. We made a big mess. Let's make sure nothing is lingering. Whitfield. Check that kid over there and see if he still has a pulse."

Whitfield nodded. "You got it."

The whole group began to walk away.

Jordan looked at Whitfield, who knelt by the teen's body.

Whitfield spoke. "He's alive. Heck of bump on his head, but still breathing."

Jordan noticed the woman with no apparent wounds. He reached down to lift her up and felt her neck's abnormality. "Bastard," he whispered. "Where the hell is he?" He stood, slammed his fist on the crate, and continued stepping away.

One of the crate's sides began to fall. It banged on the ground.

Wertz emerged, led by his Luger and firing haphazardly. Two shots hit the barricade and the fourth hit Whitfield's left shoulder.

He cried out in pain and fell to the ground.

The rest of the group, nearly half a block away, turned.

Jordan had slung his Thompson. He reached for his pistol.

"No, no," Wertz said. "I've saved my final bullet for you." He pointed his pistol near point-blank range at him.

With blinding speed, Jordan brought his right hand up and slapped the inside of Wertz's wrist. He used his left hand to pull the Luger from Wertz's grasp.

Wertz's mouth dropped.

Jordan turned the gun, said nothing, and fired into Wertz's forehead.

The major dropped to his knees and fell to his back. An end to one piece of Nazi tyranny.

THIRTY-SIX

WHITFIELD HAD NO exit wound. Cummings managed to stop the blood but he'd lost much already. They helped him to his feet as he endured the pain.

A few leading citizens suggested Jordan's group leave. If other Germans arrived, the local citizens could blame the carnage on invading forces. With so much chaos, it might very well be believed. They'd simply say that they did their best to hide as the invading Allies and Germans fought one another. They'd make a quick deconstruction of the barricade a priority. Then they'd move the dead Germans and their trucks away from Rue Vence. Hundreds from nearby streets arrived to help.

"What do you think, Nick? What's our next move?" Moody asked.

"Our mission hasn't changed, but—" Jordan looked up the street. "We had a good run here, but we're almost out of ammo. I don't know that we'd put up much of a fight against a force of any significant size."

"We should go to our friend's flat for a couple of days while things cool down," Colette suggested. She referred to the old man with the pipe who'd hosted them while they planned First Winter Snow. "We can get a doctor for Whitfield."

Moody, Cummings, and an ailing Whitfield looked at Jordan.

He looked them each in the eye. Looked at his Thompson. "Let's go."

Philippe, Henri, and Henri's father Mr. Dray had agreed to

give Jean-Pierre a proper burial and aid the people of Rue Vence.

"We'll deliver our friend for special accommodations," Mr. Dray said, referring to the prisoner.

Colette and Laurent joined the ComDet team for the near-hour-long trek to hide out.

ONCE THE ANESTHESIA knocked Whitfield out, the doctor removed a solid piece of lead from the commando's shoulder and handed it to Jordan.

"Yeah, knowing Whitfield, he'll want to keep this," Jordan said.

The doctor snapped his bag closed. "He'll need lots of rest. Two weeks if possible."

Jordan smiled. "Sure thing, Doc. And thanks. But we're leaving in a day or so."

Six stitches would mend Colette's gash from the bullet that had ricocheted off the pavement.

The exhausted ComDet team rested for three days in the old man's flat. They could have left much sooner, but hoped for a linkup with Allied forces in Caen. Unfortunately, the hope of invasion forces capturing Caen would have to wait for more than a month. They prepared Whitfield for travel, as Jordan wanted his team back in the fight if needed. The long-awaited Normandy invasion merely started the liberation of Europe.

As they had done many times before, they snaked their way out of the city and through the woods via the Resistance network. Laurent had scouted ahead for them and discovered a corridor where they could link up with a British unit. Still dressed as local French, they walked their way out of battle.

"This is where we part," Colette said to Jordan.

"So where will you go now?"

"We're joining another group of Maquis. They're based on the south side of Caen. They can use some help. And I'll keep fighting as long as it takes. For liberty. And vengeance for my family."

Jordan smiled. "Well, they're getting two great fighters. And two great people."

Colette returned the smile.

The awkwardness filled the air as if they should have kissed.

Colette touched Jordan's arm and kissed him on each cheek. "Goodbye, cowboy."

She followed Laurent and disappeared behind a hedgerow.

The four ComDet members made it one mile before drawing their weapons as a small caravan of Germans nearly ran them over. They had less than thirty rounds between them. They managed to duck under a bridge as the caravan passed by.

As they made their next mile, they smelled the salty air. Several branches cracked as they recognized dozens of men walking their way. The friendly sound of British voices met the exhausted crew of ComDet Sixteen.

CAMP DELTA
ALDINE, ENGLAND
June 10, 1944

"I FIND THIS quite incredible, Captain. Almost too incredible." Styles folded his arms and leaned back in his chair.

"Well, maybe we can visit Rue Vence and ask them if you don't believe me, Mr. Styles." Jordan cocked his head, waiting for a response.

"That won't be necessary."

"That's right. It won't be necessary because if that's how

Captain Jordan said it happened, then that's how it happened." Major Tunstall offered Jordan a cigar and he accepted. "Besides, Styles, we did receive the report of radio chatter about a missing company of SS Panzer. Later found and unjustly executed as the Jerry's propaganda put it."

Jordan popped the cigar in his mouth in victory as Tunstall lit it.

"How's your team, Captain?" Tunstall asked.

"Whitfield needs about ten days, and then we'll be good to go. Ready for our next mission."

"Yes, well, we have a mission in mind, and it will take at least three weeks to plan and as many more to drill. In the meantime, you can break in your new team member. I have someone in mind. By the way, I'm very sorry for the loss of Jean-Pierre. He was as fine as they come."

Jordan nodded and Styles looked out of the window.

"So what is our next mission, sir?"

"If you thought jumping into Normandy was dangerous, I'm afraid we'll be pushing your limits even further. You're going into the belly of the beast. Germany. We want you to break someone out of a Stalag. A flyer that was working a very specific type of new technology. Unfortunately, the flak got him and his crew and they had to bail out. We have solid intelligence of where he's held. If the Jerrys find out, or even get a whiff of what he knows, I'm afraid he's in for a good deal of interrogation. And I think you know what interrogation means."

Jordan stood and removed the cigar from his mouth. "Yes, sir, I do. We can handle it."

"I think you ought to tell him the other bit, Major," Styles said.

Tunstall raised a hand. "Yes, of course. This flyer is an old pal of yours from your days at Yale. Ralph Gaines."

ACKNOWLEDGEMENTS

A
S I SOUGHT a thesis topic for my master's in history, I discovered a book by Aaron Bank, *From OSS to Green Berets: The Birth of Special Forces*. I chose to research his story from recently released records at the National Archives. I expanded on his story and offered an outside view of the incredible people that made up the Office of Strategic Services and the Jedburgh program. It's their story that inspired this novel, and I thank them for their service.

I also had inspiration from many fine writers of the espionage/military genre, such as Brad Taylor, the late E. M. Nathanson, Brad Thor, W. E. B. Griffin, and many others. In particular, Vince Flynn, who created the Mitch Rapp character, and whose every novel I devoured. Vince lost his battle to cancer in 2013, and this is my attempt to thank him for his contributions to the craft.

Thanks also to my wife Holly and our five children: Kevin, Brandon, Jordan, Jadyn, and Megan for their support as I pondered and wrote.

Thanks to a few that volunteered to help and offer me insight: Scott Cook on lock-picking; Dennis E. Lee on battlefield wounds; and Minte Krawietz for loaning a prop used on the cover.

Thanks to the Rockwall Christian Writers Group for enduring first drafts and offering critiques.

Thanks to my beta readers: Bernie B. Johnson, whose

mother is OSS veteran Carolyn Edra Hancock; Carter Manierre, son of Jedburgh Team Dodge leader Cyrus Manierre; Judy Beecher, a cousin of Major General William Donovan; Eric M. Bullen; and Karl Young.

Thanks to Loyd Uglow, Ph.D., and Gary McElhany, Ph.D., for direction and guidance on my master's thesis, which shaped the historical background for this novel.

Thanks to my proofreaders, Mary Norsworthy and Debbie Vines.

A special thank you to my editor extraordinaire, Lauren Ruiz of Pure-Text.net. Her coaching, corrections, and suggestions have made this a better novel and me a better writer.

Join the mailing list at darrensapp.com for writing news and release dates of future books. He will not spam you!

www.ingramcontent.com/pod-product-compliance
Lightning Source LLC
Chambersburg PA
CBHW020541020726
47494CB00006B/1868